We read our Bibles, many of us, lived full lives and loved and laughed much, but knew, as we did so, that though for us all, the wise and the foolish, the slave and the free, for empires and anarchies, there is one end, yet would our works live after us, and by their fruits we should be judged in days to come.

A.T. Wilson
April 23, 1940

SOLOMON'S TEMPLE

Musjid-i-Suleiman

&

The Quest for Oil in the Mideast

SAM L. PFIESTER

To Kevin Ikel

From me oil man to Ans Th.

Cover design by Lynn Rohm

Photographs courtesy of British Petroleum

Additional Books by the author:
  The Perfect War
  The Golden Lane, Faja de Oro

To order books email sampfiester@yahoo.com
                    or
Available on Amazon, Kindle, and Nook

ACKNOWLEDGEMENTS

Research of primary sources was carried out at the private BP Archives on the campus of the University of Warwick near Coventry. The closest town to the archives is Kenilworth, located in the Midlands not far from Stratford-on-Avon. At one end of High Street stand the ruins of a 12th century castle, the same castle where in the 16th century Elizabeth I visited her consort, Robert Dudley. At the other end of High Street in World War II a bomb ripped into a hotel, killing 28 people, during Germany's infamous bombing blitz of nearby Coventry.

History in England spans eight hundred years as handily as buildings on the Courthouse Square in Georgetown, Texas span a century. What a pleasantly historical atmosphere to work in, and after a day's work in the archive, what a congenial environment to sip a pint and contemplate events long past!

Poring over old original documents six to seven hours a day might seem to some as drudgery. But for me, the toil of digging through the reports and letters and correspondence and maps was gently rewarded as the thread of a story began to emerge. When the various threads were finally placed into a coherent timeframe, I found myself asking: why hasn't this story already been told in a novel? The characters are nothing less than extraordinary, and the first discovery of oil in the Mideast certainly impacted the world, including our world today.

The BP Archive Manager, Peter Housego, and his able assistants Joanne Burman and Bethan Thomas were most helpful in every way. Conversation among themselves reminded me, as George Bernard Shaw noted, that Americans and the English are two peoples divided by a common language. Although Peter, Joanne, and Bethan politely and efficiently responded to my every request, I could not understand a word they said until their responses slowed to what must have seemed to them a parody of the English language. Perhaps one day they will visit Texas and we can show them that many English-speaking people talk slowly, and convince them that "y'all" is a word the English language needs.

In researching the book I hoped to find at least one female character who impacted the first discovery of oil in the Mideast. None was found. Mrs. Carr was the first European woman to set foot on the oilfield, and that was a decade after the D'Arcy Concession was signed. I also searched for humor in the records, letters, journals, and reports, and again found none. Southwest Persia then, as today, is a tough place to live, and to start an oil empire.

Special thanks to Dr. Stephen Benold for researching the medical supplies ordered by Dr. Young, and for describing the procedure for an appendectomy. Many thanks to my good friend Steve Davis, curator of the Wittliff Collection at Texas State University, who provided support, encouragement, and an ear for listening during lunch breaks, happy hours, and a memorable canoe trip down the San Marcos River. Good conversationalists, and especially good listeners, are difficult to find. And last but far from least, thanks to Rebecca, my bride of forty-two years.

PART 1

Discovery

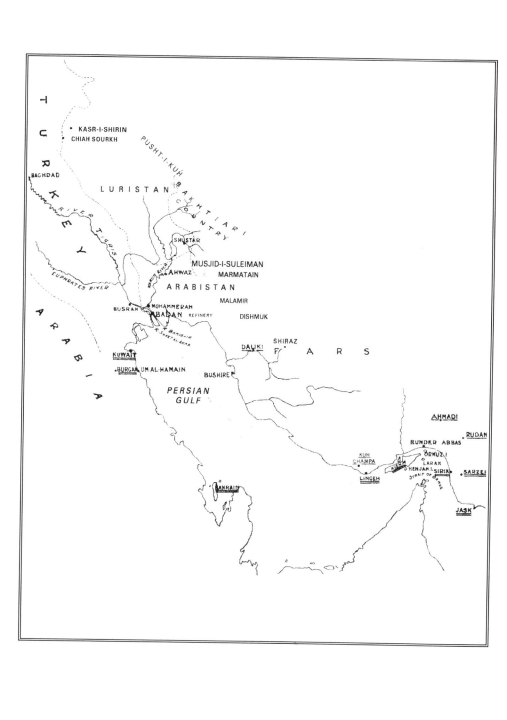

Prologue

I spent my youth as a medical doctor in the oil fields of Persia, arriving there in 1907 when I was twenty-five years old. Many might think it was a youth wasted, so far from Scotland, so removed from family, so disconnected from society and civilization. Who am I to argue? Nevertheless, the years in Persia were lively and fulfilling, and an extraordinary experience which I would neither change nor substitute.

Twenty-six years ago I arrived at Musjid-i-Suleiman, an ancient and desolate site in the foothills of the Bakhtiari Mountains, anxious for adventure and eager to begin work. Through a friend in Glasgow, I had met James Hamilton, a director of the Burmah Oil Company. His company needed a medical doctor on an oil concession acquired by Mr. William D'Arcy in 1901. The remuneration was three hundred pounds per annum plus travel expenses. I had graduated the previous year from Glasgow University as a physician and had already been offered a job with a secure future. However the offer to work for Burmah Oil in Persia was enticing, and the pay was better.

Persia…does the name conjure images? The cradle of civilization, before Christ and Constantinople the empire of Elam, the Parthians, and the Achaemenids, home to Cyrus the Great, Darius the First, and Xerxes. After two days' consideration, I signed on for one year, and stayed for more than twenty-five.

Last month I retired from the Anglo-Persian Oil Company. Although the history of the D'Arcy Concession has been told in part, I determined to put together the full story and tell it in the voice of those of us who lived it.

The story began with a letter I received from Alfred Marriott, dated December 4, 1932. Marriott negotiated the concession on behalf of William Knox D'Arcy in 1901. His letter confirmed that the Concession was not obtained by any "hole and corner" or by "trickery" as now suggested by the Persian government.

A definite sum in cash and shares had been offered to the Persian government in the draft concession, to be paid on the formation of the first company. This was accepted and the Shah acknowledged his word to Sir Arthur Hardinge, our Minister to Persia, to sign the deed of concession.

The Czar received word of the negotiations near their conclusion, and sent a telegram to the Shah making a strong personal appeal not to grant the concession. This seriously frightened the Shah, to whom Russia was a very dominating neighbor, and he told Marriott, much as he regretted it, he felt he could not sign.

Later the same day the Persian Council of Ministry met in closed session. The treasury was more than unusually empty. Marriott was informed the Shah would sign the concession, but that he must pay L10,000 immediately. On his own responsibility, Marriott agreed to pay the L10,000. The Ministers advised the Shah to sign and he did so.

Marriott paid the L10,000 as directed by the Council – half to the Shah and half to the Grand Vizier. How much of it found its way into the public treasury he had no means of ascertaining. The Czar was informed that his telegram was too late to prevent the signing of the Concession.

Mr. Marriott included with his letter to me the journal of his trip to Persia in 1901.*

Dr. Morris Y. Young
London
July, 1933

*Appendix

Chapter One

Dr. Morris Y. Young

The man who greeted me was middle-aged, deeply sun-tanned except for his pale white forehead, which must have been protected from the sun by a hat and gave his face a two-toned appearance. He sported a short mustache. His shirt was sweat-stained. He was seated at a desk covered in papers arranged in neatly stacked piles. He neither rose from his seat nor smiled, but he was not unfriendly.

"I expected you two weeks ago."

"Sir, I was held in quarantine for fifteen days in Mohammerah," I replied.

"I sent word to Glasgow to instruct you not to go ashore in Bombay because of the outbreak of plague. Had you caught the mail packet and left Bombay immediately after your arrival without going ashore, you would have avoided quarantine. Did you not receive the message?"

"No, sir."

"Since it was Glasgow's oversight and not yours, I'll recommend that your salary not commence today when you arrived here at Ahwaz." He glanced at a calendar on his desk. It showed June 9th 1907. "But that it commence the day you arrived in Mohammerah."

"Thank you, sir. When shall I start my duties?"

"Dr. Desai, our present physician, is at Camp Marmatain and is anxious to return to England. I might add, the sooner the better."

"Yes, sir." I knew nothing about the man I was to replace, but thought it circumspect not to inquire about Dr. Desai's medical practices at the present.

Half a dozen natives in the small antechamber were seeking Mr. Reynolds' attention. Consequently, I expected my introduction to be brief. Mr. Reynolds' gaze fixed upon my face. His dark brown eyes seldom blinked.

"I had planned to take you to the camps immediately but two weeks ago seven of my mules were stolen. Our Glasgow overseers have no idea of the trouble and delays caused by the inadequacies of our guards. I repatriated five of the mules; however their packsaddles and tack are still missing. Replacements from Baghdad were supposed to arrive with you on the *Malamir* but did not."

"Yes, sir."

"Do you speak Persian?"

"No, sir."

"Here, study this." Mr. Reynolds picked up a tattered book from his desk and handed it to me. I glanced at the well-worn vellum. It was a Persian-English dictionary by Rosen.

"The sooner you learn the language, the sooner you will be able to attend to your medical duties. You should also learn the dialects. We're drilling in Bakhtiari country. You'll find they are singularly good horsemen who would cut the throat of an enemy with relish. Their chieftains or *khans* are mendacious, greedy, and untrustworthy. Many of the Bakhtiari are nomadic and are adept at stealing, particularly our mules and equipment."

I could only nod.

"Our directors in Glasgow seem to think we're doing business with civilized inhabitants who obey the rule of law. They recently sent their Mr. Parsons to check on our operations. I had asked for a surveyor and received a spy. Are you to report to any of the CSL directors?"

"No, sir. I am to report only to you."

Mr. Reynolds gave out a soft *humpf* as if pleased by my response, and called to the door, "Mr. Elisha!" Returning his unblinking gaze on me, he continued, "Mr. Elisha will show you to your room. Our accommodations here are adequate but not luxurious."

The short, swarthy man in the anteroom entered and deferentially nodded his head.

"Mr. Elisha, please show Dr. Young to his room. And please issue him a revolver. Dr. Young, we will leave for the fields in five days aboard the *Shushan* on its monthly run upriver to Dar-i-Khazineh. From Dar-i-Khazineh we will travel by horseback to the oil camps. In the meantime, make yourself comfortable. There are few amusements for a European in Ahwaz. Mr. Elisha will give you a tour of the village. Only two other Europeans reside here: Mr. Redfern, the representative of Lynch Brothers, and Captain Lorimer, vice consul for the Foreign Office. Both are presently out of town."

"Why do I need a revolver?" I asked.

"The country is lawless. Since the constitutional crisis in Teheran, it's even more so. Only last week a drover aimed his rifle at me, thinking I was about to rob him. At the time I was armed with only a horsetail fly-flick. I ignored his threat, but had I carried a revolver, he would not have been so casual with his weapon. When traveling, keep the pistol loaded and strapped to your waist. It's not so much a matter of avoiding danger as being prepared for it. I've been shot at and you can expect the same. Now if you will excuse me, I must handle the business at hand. Our directors complain that I do not keep them adequately informed, even though when I'm not in the field I mail them two or more reports weekly. I must send another to your Mr. Hamilton in response to complaints by the Canadian drillers about food in the camps. If I can assist you in any way, please let Mr. Elisha know. Can you ride?"

"Yes sir, moderately well."

"Good. You'll be an expert in no time. Welcome to Persia."

I followed Mr. Elisha down a hall to a small room with a cot and a wooden washstand. Mosquito netting hung over the cot. Mr. Elisha placed my bag against a wall and left to procure a weapon. Like Mr. Reynolds' office, the room was Spartan, which was also my impression of Mr. Reynolds.

I opened the window and gazed over the rooftops. My immediate impression was tones of brown: cinnamon brown, chestnut brown, cocoa brown. Nothing was green. Neither trees nor shrubs nor flowers were visible, only baked-mud rooftops. The early morning light cast dark shadows in perfect geometric patterns from their eastern parapets. In the far distance, mountains formed a thin blue wall separating the barren foreground and a cloudless sky. Close to town the broad Karun River swept by, its sediment-loaded beige-colored current moving rapidly for what appeared to be such a low gradient.

The river brought back a mental image of my first welcome to Persia. I had watched a mule being loaded on the *Malamir* at Mohammerah. While walking up the narrow plank from the dock to the ship's deck, it spooked, lunged backwards, fell into the river, and immediately squalled out, thrashing its forefeet frantically in the muddy river water that was soon stained scarlet by its blood. In minutes the mule had been devoured by sharks.

The heat in my room was tangible. I sifted through my medical bag and pulled out a thermometer. The reading was 118 Fahrenheit.

The following day Mr. Elisha guided me through Ahwaz, a wretched collection of simple huts located along the muddy banks of the river on the upstream side of a stair-stepped rapids with perhaps a ten-foot fall, enough to bar boats from proceeding upriver. Above the rapids in the sweep of a bend, the water dashed with a roar through two gateways, the broken relic, Mr. Elisha said, of the dike of Ahwaz, an ancient dam designed to hold back the waters of the Karun for irrigation through a series of ditches to once-fertile fields long returned to desert sand. I was struck by such an engineering feat.

Below the rapids was Nasiri, a newer town whose structures were mainly of stone dug from the ruins of what must have once been a great city. Ancient irrigation canals now filled with sand ran in straight lines to the distant horizon, testaments to civilizations long past.

The Persian flag flew in front of one mud hut. A small cannon next to the flag proclaimed the customs office for the central government. Mr. Elisa explained that foreign commerce had opened in October 1888. A deputy of the Governor-General of Arabistan resided in the hut, and in the adjacent hut resided Mr. Redfern, the agent for Lynch Brothers, which had a concession for shipping goods up and down the Karun on two sternwheelers that dated from the siege of Khartoum.

We visited the bazaar, a warren of booths filled with merchandise, food, and stacks of colorful spices that wafted exotic smells. Arabic women, completely covered except for a peephole, haggled with vendors. Other women whose heads were uncovered mingled in the crowded bazaar as well. The uncovered women, Mr. Elisha explained, were Bakhtiari.

I was particularly interested in salves sold in the bazaar which Mr. Elisha said were medicinal, and determined to learn from the locals about their native cures for sickness. Within the shadowed lanes of the bazaar, the alleyways and shops were cool, but by midmorning the heat became stifling and the people began to retire to their homes. I wondered how drilling operations could be conducted during daytime in the summer months. In this heat, dehydration would soon suck the energy and life from all living species.

I spent five days in Ahwaz. Each day a stream of native vendors and workers passed in and out of Mr. Reynolds's office. From my room I could hear his authoritative voice dealing in foreign tongue with many petioners covering whatever issues demanded his attention. One day I walked to the Vice-Consul's office and met Captain Lorimer's assistant, Ahmed Khan, a most accommodating and efficient Indian who spoke good English. During the oppressive heat of midday I remained in my room and studied Rosen's dictionary, and occasionally asked Mr. Elisha for help with pronunciation.

On the evening before our journey to the camps, Mr. Reynolds asked me to join him for dinner. It was my first opportunity to ask questions about my new assignment. Our meal consisted of unleavened bread and mutton stew spiced with tastes foreign to my experience. The tastes were foreign, but not unpleasant. When we finished the meal, Mr. Reynolds asked if Mr. Hamilton back at the office in Glasgow had mentioned the food at our camps.

"Yes, sir, and he showed me a report about a driller who had died, a Mr. Kerby."

Mr. Reynolds seemed displeased with the mention of Mr. Kerby. "What did the report suggest was the cause of Kerby's death?" he asked.

I paused before answering.

"Malnutrition," I replied.

Mr. Reynolds face flushed in anger. "Yes, I suspected as much. I had every reason to believe their man Parsons wrote the report and made allusions to bad food. Their sympathetic acceptance of statements from irresponsible parties, derogatory of the management of the man running the show, is unwarranted. Kerby's family has hired attorneys to claim damages on the grounds that I failed to furnish suitable food, accommodation, or medical attention."

I didn't know how to respond except to inquire about the camp food. To this, Mr. Reynolds became even more livid.

"Dr. Desai suggested to me, and aroused in the drillers, the belief that their diet has a want of vegetables. He suggested getting vegetables from Dizful by mule, that a journey of a week would not be detrimental to these prophylactic adjuncts to the drillers' diet. I dismissed the suggestion as absurd."

"Are vegetables obtainable in the camps?" I had noted many types of vegetables in the bazaar.

"Potatoes I get from Karachi in cold weather. Tinned vegetables I get from Holland. Onions, eggplant, cucumbers, turnips, watermelons and musk melons are available locally year-round."

"And they complain about vegetables...?"

"The drillers growl endlessly about the food. Yet I have spared no pains to provide good cooks and servants. Ahwaz is the only place where chickens and goats can be bought. Native wheat for bread can be bought locally and local millers will grind the flour. Securing their own food locally requires a little energy and I conclude there is none amongst the drillers."

"And Dr. Desai's recommendations?"

Mr. Reynolds *humpfd* derisively. "The good doctor recommended gooseberry jam for Driller Harris, who claims he cannot eat gooseberries. To be troubled with such trivia! I am responsible for the food and safety of more than five hundred men, not to mention the responsibility for building a thirty-mile road and drilling wells in the most extreme of conditions. Lord Curzon gave very good advice in his speech at the Pilgrim's Dinner on April 6th when he said 'Trust the man on the spot.'"

"It seems to me the directors in Glasgow have no other choice," I remarked.

"I asked Glasgow to be so good as to ship me macaroni, spaghetti, sugar, corn syrup, biscuits, and bottled fruits. They delayed the order for two months, yet react to the complaints among the drillers as if they are not culpable. Did *your* Mr. Hamilton mention my performance?" he asked.

"I met Mr. Hamilton only briefly."

Mr. Reynolds looked at me with an intense stare. "I assumed that you were offered the job because of your close connection with Mr. Hamilton."

"Not at all. I was originally approached and advised to accept this position by a doctor in the same hospital where I served, a man who knew me and was also a friend of Mr. Hamilton. As I was on the eve of accepting a position as House Surgeon to the Glasgow Eye Infirmary, I put it to Mr. Hamilton among other questions 'If I go to Persia, what are my prospects?' His reply, which is perfectly square and straight, was 'at present, none whatever. Only if we succeed and find oil. The risk is entirely yours'. I accepted the conditions and two days later left for Persia."

"Well, well," said Mr. Reynolds. He was clearly pleased I was not Mr. Hamilton's companion.

This offered me the opportunity to ask a question which had been bearing on my mind. "I tell you these circumstances only to prove that 'to rise' was one of my original hopes and for this I took my chance. To that goal, I have a question. Do you think we will strike oil?"

"You ask a question that Glasgow has often asked," he replied. "Mr. D'Arcy hired me in 1901. We have been drilling since 1902 and without measurable success. Mr. D'Arcy is the champion of this entire operation and lost untold thousands of sterling on the first two wells at Chiah Sourk, but maintains faith in our eventual success. Burma Oil bought into the operation in 1904. After three years of expenditures with little to show for it, their impatience grows. As the outcome of their sympathy, have the directors not afforded me the consolation of religion?"

I knew not how to respond to his enigmatic remark, so turned the conversation to the drilling operations, weather, natives, local politics, and geology. In all these subjects, Mr. Reynolds was well informed and articulate.

"We are at present drilling two wells at Marmatain, and building a camp at Maidan-i-Naphtun to house workers and workshops for the Musjid-i-Suleiman wells. We are also constructing a thirty-mile road to ship equipment and supplies from the Karun to the field,"

"When will you know if the wells you are presently drilling will produce oil?" I asked.

"Our rigs may not be capable of reaching the prospective pay at Marmatain. However in December I assured Mr. D'Arcy and our Glasgow directors that I felt certain of success at Musjid-i-Suleiman."

He made this statement with a certainty that only the truly self-confident can muster, at which point he rose and said we must retire, as the *Shushan* left at dawn. Thus ended my first evening with Mr. George Bernard Reynolds, General Manager of CSL, the Consolidated Syndicate Ltd. In contemplating the challenges of drilling a borehole in the outer reaches of a remote, worn, and inhospitable country, he struck me as a man suited for the challenge.

The next morning at daylight we boarded the *Shushan*, a smaller version of the sternwheeler *Maramir*, on its monthly run to the Upper Karun. Our speed was about the pace a man can walk, although we were bucking a current I estimated at six knots. The decks were filled with equipment for the oil fields, and with the clutter on deck of foods and bags and natives crammed close to one another.

Early the second day the river split into two channels. We took the easternmost

Shushan

and smaller channel. I asked Mr. Reynolds if this was a different river.

"It is the juncture of two branches of the Karun. The smaller eastern channel which we'll follow today is the Ab-i-Gargar. The larger channel to the west is the Ab-i-Shatait. Farther to the west you probably saw where a third river, the Ab-i-Diz, joins the Karun."

Earlier I had noted a sliver of green, the only color besides shades of beige I had seen since leaving Ahwaz, and had conjectured the dark green band was oleander plants bordering the banks of another river. We were now approaching colorful foothills, ochre and salmon-colored beds of rock tilted toward distant blue mountains.

"Here we leave Arabic country and move into Bakhtiari lands," Mr. Reynolds explained. "The Sheikh of Mohammerah controls the flat desert and marsh country from here to Mohammerah. The foothills and Zagros Mountains ahead of us are inhabited by the Bakhtiari, who claim to be the original Aryans. It's our lot to deal with both Arab and Bakhtiari."

"And not with the Shah in Teheran?"

"Except for collecting taxes and tribute, the Shah's influence here is hardly felt. In Bakhtiari country, we are left to deal with *khans*, their tribal chieftains, who care for nothing but money."

"Are the *khans* a problem?"

"Our biggest problem is security. We are dependent on the *khans* to provide guards. To a man, their guards are a worthless lot. Our workers are robbed.

Our equipment is stolen. We are disrespected. Just last month one of the *khans*, a man as full of intrigue as a nightingale is pregnant with music, placed his rifle to my forehead and threatened to shoot. I moved his rifle barrel with my forefinger, tapped his chest, and faced him down with a stare. One must not cower at their bravado."

When I signed on for a year, the CSL directors in Glasgow failed to mention the natives. I wondered if relations with the locals could be improved by offering them medical care.

"Could we not provide our own guards?" I asked.

"You ask the obvious. Two years ago Mr. Preece, the British consul in Isfahan, and I negotiated a land agreement with the Bakhtiari *khans*. The company agreed to pay them L2000 per annum in quarterly payments. In return, they were to furnish guards to protect our operations. Their protection is pitiful. We continuously lose equipment. The tribes argue and fight among themselves. Over the *khans'* protestations, I deduct the value of what we're robbed from their quarterly payments, and they howl as if *they* are being robbed."

By the second day I was ready to disembark. Although we were treated deferentially by the native in charge of the sternwheeler, the boat was crowded and our accommodations were minimal. We at last reached Dar-i-Khanizeh, a small village on the eastern bank of the river, significant only because of its terminus as an offloading site for the sternwheeler.

"Are you ready, Dr. Young?"

"Yes, sir."

We mounted our horses for the ride to Baitwand village and on to Camp Marmatain. My horse was small and did not shy when I placed my foot in the stirrup and pulled onto the saddle. The half-light of dawn sheathed the mud huts of Dar-i-Khanizeh in a soft light. Temperatures during the night had cooled but were still well above 100 degrees. Mr. Reynolds explained to me that normally we would travel at night to avoid the worst of the heat, but on this trip he needed the daylight to inspect the progress of the new road construction.

Mr. Reynolds was at the head of six mules and horses, three packed with supplies, and another occupied by Abdullah, the cook. Our path followed the cart road that had been under construction for more than a year. From the banks of the Karun River, its course led at steep angles up the sides of colorful gypsum hills. Gradually we gained altitude, topping out on the steep flank of Talkhaiyat Peak. In places the road crossed gullies and dry washes that, by the look of the jumbled rocks in their center, carried huge volumes of water and debris from floods. The cart path varied from twenty to thirty feet in width and made travel by horse fairly easy. In late afternoon we arrived at Baitwand, where Mr. Reynolds reminded me to keep my pistol on my hip and to watch out for my personal items.

"Baitwand," he said as he pulled his horse next to mine, "is home to families of *sayids*, who claim to be descendants of the Prophet. They are a quarrelsome crowd. Kurds and Turks are better than these savages, the Lurs and Bakhtiari. Even Arabs are better workers than Baitwand villagers."

Baitwand village consisted of a scattering of stone huts alongside the Tenbi River. I could see ahead that the road crossed the river several times. Mr. Reynolds warned over his shoulder not to drink the water. I reached down and sipped the sulfurous-smelling liquid and immediately spit it out. "Do the natives drink this?" I asked.

"Their water comes from springs above the village. Finding enough potable water at Musjid-i-Suleiman is a challenge. We have to boil and filter it for drinking and for use in the boilers. A small tributary of the Tenbi passes through the site of our camp. Its water is so petroliferous we can burn it. I expect to use it to fuel the boilers."

A river of oil, I thought. No wonder he is optimistic about drilling at Musjid-i-Suleiman. We had ridden nearly ten hours through the most desolate wasteland I had ever witnessed, a phantasmagoria of amber and ochre-colored gorges and hills, across boulder-strewn plains thinly covered with white chalky rubble, and now alongside a river that seemed to have originated in the bowels of Hell.

"We should meet Mr. Bradshaw's work party soon," Mr. Reynolds commented, nodding his head upriver where the road disappeared around a bend. "In another month, no later than the end of July, the road to Musjid-i-Suleiman will be completed."

Having ridden over the road, I understood why it had taken more than a year to build. The terrain it crossed was at times steep and rocky, at times it followed dry washes strewn with huge limestone boulders, or followed the gravelly banks of the Tenbi River. When we rounded a bend in the river, an entire section of

Road construction

road construction came into view. An ant bed of activity, hundreds of men, were at work along a mile stretch of road that had left the narrow river valley and was angling over a series of hills to the northeast.

"I see Mr. Bradshaw there." Mr. Reynolds pointed to a rider galloping toward us. "He must have had a scout watching for our arrival."

Bradshaw rode up in a trot on a bay-colored mule. Before the mule came to a complete halt, Bradshaw swung his leg from the saddle, landed on both feet next to Mr. Reynolds and extended a hand in greeting. He was a young man, rail thin and deeply sun-tanned, wearing a pith helmet and sporting a reddish beard. I stepped off my horse, straightened my back slowly and nodded.

From horseback Mr. Reynolds introduced us. "Dr. Young is the replacement for Dr. Desai," he said. "By the looks of it, he's a bit spent from the ride."

I nodded and made no protest.

"Mr. Bradshaw, how is progress? Will you make the mid-July deadline?"

"It's the usual problems, sir. I have written you a report." He handed over a folded paper.

"What is it this time?" Instead of being exasperated by bad news, Mr. Reynolds seemed to expect it.

"Last week one of the men was killed, run over by a cart. Subsequently all the Arabs struck. I had to recruit a new crew."

Mr. Reynolds raised his eyebrows, "And?"

"And the commencement of the rice cultivation begins in a few days and many of the workers will leave us. I'm not making excuses, sir, just explaining circumstances. The road will be manageable by the end of July."

Mr. Reynolds turned to me and spoke, I thought partially with the intent to remind Bradshaw of the urgency at hand.

"Heavy rains will begin by the end of October. After the first rains, the road will be rendered impassable. It's imperative to complete it to Musjid-i-Suleiman in time to move the equipment from Dar-i-Khazineh before the rainy season commences. Otherwise drilling will be delayed by several months."

"Sir, I'm pushing the men as much as I dare," responded Bradshaw. "I extended work hours to eleven hours a day, from dawn to ten in the morning and from four in the afternoon until dark. The heat during midday is unbearable, even for natives."

I silently concurred and started to ask about provisions for drinking water, but decided to hold my questions.

"There is much grumbling, especially from the Baitwand natives about the Lurs I recruited from Dizful," continued Bradshaw. "They quarrel constantly. Harris is in charge of the Lurs. He says we can expect trouble."

"Yes, well you don't eliminate thousands of years of tribal feuds by waving a wand. Keep the groups separated, Mr. Bradshaw. Now, let's inspect your progress."

We spent the next hour moving along the line of road construction. Mr. Reynolds occasionally made comments to Bradshaw about the gradient or about areas still too uneven for a cart to pass. Hundreds of men with shovels and hand tools scraped the hillside, flattening a path for carts. Iron scoops pulled by harnessed mules removed the heaviest rocks. Dust enveloped the entire project like a low-lying fog in the moors. Toward the end of the road construction, Mr. Reynolds pointed ahead to flatter ground surrounded by eroded hills, something of a plateau.

"Maidan-i-Napthun," he said, "which means Plains of Naphtha. It is the name of our camp." I had tied my handkerchief around my mouth, and was too choked by the dust and heat to reply.

"How is work on the camp coming along?" he asked Bradshaw.

"Very well, sir."

Mr. Reynolds spurred his horse to a trot. We had already been in the saddle for more than ten hours and yet he seemed scarcely affected. My knees felt like the cartilage between femur and tibia had been removed and bone on bone was grinding away the remaining tissue.

Camp Maidan-i-Naphtun was laid out like a military cantonment. Bradshaw led us on a tour of the construction, which consisted of the foundation for a steel-frame workshop, a blacksmith shop, a stone mess room with a verandah, and stone housing for Europeans and servants. The camp was located between pad sites for the two boreholes, which were more than a mile apart.

"Here is the dispensary," Mr. Reynolds said, and pointed to a primitive-looking tent.

I was disappointed. How could I maintain standards of cleanliness in a tent? I stepped forward to inspect the structure. It was not even a canvas tent. Instead, it appeared to be made of some sort of animal skin. "What is this made of?" I asked.

"Goat skin," replied Mr. Reynolds. "It's waterproof," he continued, and walked off with Bradshaw.

I examined the seams, which were expertly sewn. Waterproof, perhaps, but not dust proof. Gaps were left between the walls and the packed-ground floor. Inside, the space was dark, too dark for proper medical examinations.

The hospital assistant, a native who spoke only broken English, introduced himself. We reviewed together the medical records and the drugs on hand, which were far from adequate. I began making a list of essential supplies needed for the medical service I hoped to provide.

Finally, after the sun had passed behind high and barren hills to the west, Mr. Reynolds instructed Abdullah to make camp and prepare a meal. He invited Bradshaw to join us. We had brought a young goat which Abdullah had tied atop one of the pack mules. He promptly slaughtered and began to skin it for our meal. I laid my pallet on a flat piece of ground which was still warm from the daytime heat, and stretched out my aching frame.

During dinner Mr. Reynolds asked his employee myriad questions, many having to do with local politics. When Bradshaw mentioned the guards, Mr. Reynolds exhaled with a sigh of disgust,

"The guards!" he exclaimed. "The guards are worse than camp dogs! If trouble breaks out, it will be because the guards fail in their job. I have told Captain Lorimer a dozen times he must demand that the *Ilkhani* furnish competent guards."

It was a theme I would hear for the next year. Indeed, my experience with the guards soon matched that of Mr. Reynolds. I quickly learned to keep the medical supplies under lock and key. Because of their access to camp, the guards were the best of Bakhtiari thieves.

"One more question, Mr. Reynolds." I remembered what I had forgotten to ask. "What does Musjid-i-Suleiman mean?"

"It's the name given to the ruins close to camp," he replied. "It means Solomon's Temple."

Solomon's Temple, I thought. Could the ruins date from the age of Solomon?

The next evening we left for Camp Marmatain, where drilling operations, Mr. Reynolds explained, had been underway for more than a year.

"We will move rapidly," he said casually as he mounted his horse. "We must reach the shade of an outcrop before mid-morning."

Crossing the Tenbi

When he said "We will move rapidly", Mr. Reynolds meant at a fast canter. My horse's gait jarred me with every step. Soon, though, I had re-accustomed myself to the rigors of riding, and fell into the rhythmic cadence that was quickly replaced by the pain of chapped inner thighs, and knees which felt like rusty pistons. Mr. Reynolds halted only once to re-tighten the mule's pack cinch in the waning light. We rode in silence, listening only to the hoof beats of our animals. Our path followed the Tenbi River. In less than a mile we entered a narrow gorge. Tall rock walls enveloped us as if we had ridden into a dark tunnel. I was beginning to enjoy the ride when from a side canyon I heard an eerie guttural 'huff-huff'. Perhaps a hyena, I thought, or maybe a lion.

"Mr. Reynolds." I raised my voice. "Are there lions still in Persia?"

He replied "yes" and continued on without a pause to question why I had brought up the subject. I felt for the revolver on my waist and wondered if it would frighten whatever had made the noise.

We rode all night by the light of a gibbous moon which cast a soft silver luminescence on the surrounding landscape. Shadows were as distinct as shade in daylight. I scanned the area we passed for wild animals. By 5a.m. dawn lit the eastern horizon with a magnificent greeting. When the sun broke the horizon, its deep red-orange orb seemed to challenge our presence, as if to say, "Defy me and you will be scalded and wrought blind." In Scotland we looked forward to sunny days. Here, the sun's presence was a merciless peril.

Not long after first light Mr. Reynolds pointed ahead to a shallow cavern cut into a carmine-colored sandstone bluff. "Good water is near that shelter," he explained. "After the horses and mules drink, take them to the shade of the overhang. We'll rest here until evening."

I gingerly stepped off my horse, removed my boots, and waded knee-deep into the water. It was perfectly clear and surprisingly cool. I saw a few mud huts scattered on the far hillside.

"Band-i-shur," said Mr. Reynolds, without my asking.

After watering the horses and mules, he led the pack train to the shade of the overhang and began removing their loads. I followed suit and threw my saddle against the back wall of our shaded cavern. Fresh and long-dried horse, mule, and camel dung on its floor announced years of previous visitors. Abdullah opened a cotton sack and offered me a piece of unleavened barley bread. Mr. Reynolds tied the animals with a rope from their halters to an iron ring driven into the sandstone wall. Abdullah placed small piles of fodder in front of each animal.

"Better get some sleep, Dr. Young," said Mr. Reynolds. "We'll remain here until dark."

With those words he spread a saddle blanket on the ground, lay down with his head propped against his saddle, shoved his hat low over his eyes, and went to sleep.

Although I was exhausted, I felt curiously alert. The land in some odd way beckoned me. I decided to climb the steep hill above us. The ascent was rough and rocky, but the view from on top was worth my effort. I gazed over the forlorn landscape. To the northeast, distant mountains receded in shades fading in intensity from soft lavender to deep navy. This wasteland held a stark beauty unlike any I had experienced, and imparted a peculiar sense of purity, a kind of ascetic spirituality. In a land so barren and devoid of life, no wonder men looked to the heavens for comfort or comprehension. As I gazed across the desolate waste, I began to understand why three of the world's great religions originated in the desert not far from here.

Chapter Two

Dr. Morris Y. Young

"Dr. Young, it's time to rise. We'll be leaving soon. How are you feeling?"

I had fallen into a deep sleep. Although I was unaccustomed to riding so many hours with so few stops, I awoke refreshed.

"Fine, I'm fine, thank you." I looked at my watch. It showed half-past eight. The sun was already behind the hills in a cloudless sky.

Mr. Reynolds gave a quiet command to Abdullah, who was stirring coals from a small fire fueled with dung. A hot wind gusted through our shallow overhang, blowing dust into our eyes and into the food. While Mr. Reynolds and I hurriedly ate, Abdullah packed the supplies and cinched them on the mules. My horse stood quietly when I threw the saddle over its withers. Good horses, I thought, except for their pace.

Mr. Reynolds was intent to keep us moving forthrightly. He told us he wanted to reach Camp Marmatain by daylight. From our resting place we followed a trail over low foothills, dropped into dry-wash valleys and along narrow ridges. Many of the rock beds were tilted away from the distant mountains, as if when the mountains rose out of the plains, the smaller foothills folded back in salutation. Their banded patterns could be seen repetitively in distant foothills. The ridges seemed to align in a northwest to southeast direction.

Mr. Reynolds must have been guided by the silhouetted landforms. We seldom followed a trail, much of our path being over rocky outcrops. The moon rose and finally the wind died. The country felt wild and untamed. Before moonrise, the stars seemed within reach. I thought it curious why so many carried Arabic names: Aldeberan, Algol, Betelgeuse, Daneb.

Just at daylight we crested a hill and saw below us a small collection of desolate-looking buildings. Not far away a derrick rose from the ground like an oversized, upside-down explanation point.

The camp lay in a narrow valley surrounded by almost vertical gypsum cliffs. To call the place 'godforsaken' would be an understatement. The odd scattering of buildings gave the impression of impermanence. I couldn't help but think of the ruins of Solomon's Temple and thought how, for thousands of years, men had tried to impart order and permanence into a landscape that simply waited patiently until all our efforts and dreams turned to naught.

Pierced into the cliffs high above the valley floor were the mouths of old tunnels. I wondered why the ancients would tunnel so far above the valley floor, and could only conclude that centuries ago when the river levels were higher, the tunnels carried water to fields long fallow.

Reynolds turned in his saddle and said to me. "Camp Marmatain. Your new home."

We rode into camp and were greeted by Bertie, the camp supervisor, who showed us to the mess hall in time for breakfast. Mr. Reynolds nodded to the men and spoke with one. I was introduced to Dr. Desai, who was sitting at a table with a crew of Canadian drillers. He was a small wiry man, permanently hunched over, of Indian descent. The drillers had just finished an eight-hour night shift on the drilling rig. Dr. Desai seemed to scowl when I approached.

After breakfast Dr. Desai led Mr. Reynolds and me to the dispensary, and immediately asked that I sign for all the medicines and medical supplies. The dispensary was in a black tent, which I now recognized as goatskin. A row of cots occupied one wall of the tent. I was pleased that their bedding was clean. Medicines were padlocked in a metal cabinet. After a cursory examination, it was evident I would need a much larger supply. Mr. Reynolds asked that I prepare a list and include it in the monthly health report, which was to be mailed to him the first week of each month. Before he left the dispensary, Mr. Reynolds asked me to join him for a tour of the drilling operations later in the afternoon.

The rest of the morning I discussed with Dr. Desai the condition and treatment of the patients, and the general conditions of drinking water and sanitation. Dr. Desai's answers were curt, and soon I agreed with Mr. Reynolds' assessment that his attitude was poor.

After lunch we rode a half-mile to the rig. I had never before approached a drilling rig. On the way Mr. Reynolds explained that Wellbore No. 1 was drilling below 1300' and had been drilling since September 18th of last year.

I was introduced to the man he had spoken to at breakfast, MacNaughton, who was the head driller, a Scot. He told Mr. Reynolds they had recently encountered a large water flow which he had sealed off by running 10 ¾″ steel casing into the hole.

Over the din of the equipment, Mr. Reynolds explained to me that this was a percussion or cable-tool rig. A long beam rose and fell with a rhythmic motion. A steam boiler and an engine provided the power to move the beam up and down. A half-inch cable ran from a spool up to a pulley system in the top of the derrick, and down into a hole that was cut into a heavy ten-foot square metal plate. The beam moved the cable up and down. An iron bit was attached to the end of the cable at the bottom of the hole.

Bare-handed, some even barefooted, grease-covered natives stood by while MacNaughton with one hand felt the steel cable as it moved up and down, measuring its force when the bit hammered the bottom. As the hole was dug deeper, additional cable was let out to extend its reach. Depending on the penetration rate, the bit was spooled out of the hole and a bailer was run into the hole to bring up the cuttings, which were dumped in a nearby earthen pit. The wooden derrick, Mr. Reynolds explained, was also used for running casing, and would be left in place after the well was completed.

Dressing-a-bit

We toured the machine shop, where the end of a thousand-pound six-foot long iron bit was being heated in a furnace. The temperature inside the machine shop must have been 130 degrees. Natives with sledgehammers pounded out a ridge along the end of the bit, which Mr. Reynolds explained was "dressing" the bit.

"The iron ridge tears into the earth. It's the pounding and twisting of the heavy bit at the bottom of the well that digs the hole."

Except for the steam boiler and engine to raise and lower the beam, the whole process seemed like an archaic way to drill. Yet it was for this grim and hazardous task, I thought, that men in their Glasgow offices spent untold hundreds of thousands of sterling, and why I had been sent to this forsaken outpost.

We rode to Wellbore No. 2, about two miles from camp near the village of Chardine. Before reaching the second rig, Bertie told Mr. Reynolds that he had deducted fifteen days pay from each native working on the rig in consequence of their leaving work without notice. As a result, the head of the village, one Pir Murad, had threatened to rob the camp of our mules and horses. Mr. Reynolds fully supported Bertie's order and called Pir Murad "a truculent old savage" who had caused trouble before.

Mr. Reynolds and Bertie discussed various problems encountered by Wellbore No. 2. From the gist of their conversation, I gathered that the drilling equipment seemed to be working well for a change but the fuel supply for the boilers was running short. The native who was paid to bring fuel, one Mahmood Khan, had been absent for a month while he was off attacking a fort, and had let the fuel dwindle to only a week's supply. Mr. Reynolds immediately called for a meeting with the man left in charge of the supply and soon was in a heated argument over the price of wood in the dialect of their tribe. Over dinner I asked Mr. Reynolds how much longer they expected to be drilling at Marmatain.

"How much longer?" he repeated. "It depends on the geology. For the past ten months we have been drilling through gypsum and salt beds. The target formation is in my estimation a Nummulitic limestone, which should be encountered beneath the gypsum beds. The geologist who chose this site did not determine the thickness of the gypsum beds before we started drilling. I believe it can be accurately measured from the thickness of the section in the outcrop, which is to say, the rocks exposed at the surface. I intend to visit the Asmari Hill and measure the thickness of the gypsum section. If oil is found, it will be below the gypsum."

I was becoming increasingly fascinated by the geology of this land. Like medicine, it seemed that surface clues were present from which a diagnosis could be deduced. "Why was this site chosen?" I asked.

"Have you noticed the contorted bedding in the sandstones and gypsum rocks that we've been passing through since leaving the Karun?"

"Yes," I replied. Many of the beds of rock we had passed were folded and warped. "I can't imagine the forces that caused rocks to bend to such a degree."

"Very observant, Doctor," he replied. "Tectonic forces, which no doubt formed yon Zagros Mountains, are difficult to conceive. Geologists map the surface angles of the rock bedding to find what is called an anticline, which is a section of rock that has been shaped by tectonic forces into an elongated and inverted bowl. Oil is trapped in the anticline by an impermeable layer above the oil-bearing rock, which prevents the hydrocarbons from escaping to the surface. Nevertheless leakage occurs, and is evident as seeps. People have known for millennia that seeps of hydrocarbons are present for hundreds of miles along the foothills of the Zagros. Mr. Boverton Redwood, the company's geologist in London, believes the seeps indicate the presence of buried oil and gas deposits, as do I"

"Are you drilling an anticline here?" I asked.

"Yes, but sometimes geologists fail, in my estimation, to begin at the beginning, to determine which formation is oil-bearing or how deep it might be."

"It seems like a simple question to ask."

"It is not a simple question to answer. Our equipment can drill to two thousand feet or so. We failed to answer the question on the first two wells Mr. D'Arcy drilled at Chiah Sourk, three hundred miles north of here. Perhaps the oil is ten thousand feet or deeper. Who knows? The outcrops give us a clue. My guess is we should move closer to the mountains, which is why I prefer Musjid-i-Suleiman."

"Why closer to the mountains?"

"The hydrocarbon-bearing formation beneath the gypsum beds should be at shallower depths.

"The shallower the better?" I asked.

"If the pay is deeper than our rigs can drill, what's the point of drilling? Our directors and their geologists seem to overlook how deep to drill."

In the brief time that I had known him, Mr. Reynolds had often spoken derisively of the directors in Glasgow. Having now been in Persia and understood an inkling of the monumental task with which he was charged, I was somewhat sympathetic. He turned back to Bertie.

"I received a letter from Captain Lorimer. Our old friend Samsam-es-Sultana has been reinstated as *Ilkhani*, and the Shahab-es-Sultana, on making peace with the Samsam, has been moved to *Ilbegi*. Sarim-ul-Mulk, the man I was putting my money on, is nowhere."

Both men shook their heads in disapproval. "Do you mind my asking what you are speaking about?" I asked.

"Forgive me, Dr. Young. The *Ilkhani* is the appointed chieftain of all the Bakhtiari and the *Ilbegi* is second in command. The two seldom get along. Years ago a split in the Bakhtiari tribes is reflected today in the split in power between the *Ilkhani* and the *Ilbegi*. The Shah or his vizier makes the appointment of both. Politics in Persia have always been a tangle of intrigue and deception. We are left to do business with a succession of mercenary blackguards. The Samsam is the worst of the lot."

"Can he effect our drilling operations?" I asked.

"There is no question of the hostility of the Samsam-es-Sultana toward us. Without his cooperation, we are certain to be robbed, and just as certain, no steps whatever will be taken to bring the thieves to justice. Without the Samsam's cooperation, the people of the country will have a free hand against us and the company's property. Take the case of the seven mules stolen before you arrived, an act *engineered* by His Excellency the Samsam-es-Sultana. Now that the Samsam is in control, we can expect more outrages. I have told Glasgow and the Legation many times that hiring and controlling our own guards is the only reasonable course if we are to conduct business in Persia."

Two days later, a courier arrived from Baitwand with a letter from Bradshaw. Mr. Reynolds read it and handed me the letter, and remarked that the trouble they expected had erupted.

> On Saturday morning, as I was leaving Baitwand, the men of Baitwand, some thirty or so, came and asked for work. As these men had already been employed by me and broken the contract they made, and also were an extremely lazy good-for-

nothing lot, I refused to give them employment. They then went quietly away to the village.

As I reached camp, a *farash* of Harris came galloping up and told me that the Baitwand people had attacked Harris. I immediately sent the head of my Guards and another *sowar* who was with me down to see what the trouble was.

It seems that Rezouk, who has been ill for some time, was leaving with my caravan for this camp. Hardly had they left camp, when they were surrounded by the Baitwand people, who pulled the servants off the mules and thrashed them and then proceeded to stone Rezouk.

Harris came up to see what the trouble was and they started stoning him. He managed to get back to camp for safety. Some of the men tried to get those with guns to fire on the camp but they did not go to this length. The guards who were supposed to be in camp, curiously enough, were all busy – one was in Shushtar, one fetching water, one fetching flour, one lying ill – there being only one man who tried to stop them at all. Kayid Rafi, my head guard, stopped the trouble and brought the *sayids* of Baitwand and the ringleaders up to me. I spoke with them but left the matter temporarily in the hands of the *sayid*.

It is scarcely necessary for me to point out that unless something be done and at once, something very serious is likely to happen up here. From threats they proceeded to blows, and what the next step will be one cannot tell. It is a moral certainty that unless an example is made quickly, not only will there be no chance of the road being finished, but all work will be stopped up here, it being impossible to keep a staff together under existing conditions.

Signed, H.E. Bradshaw, Esq.

"It says the Baitwand villagers *stoned* Harris." I said. "Does he or his men need medical attention?"

"Bradshaw would have asked for your assistance if needed," he replied curtly. I could tell he was fuming.

"Has a European ever been stoned before?" I asked. It seemed a brutal way to show grievance.

"Never!" he replied. "Bradshaw is absolutely correct. The act of stoning a European, even if no serious injury resulted, requires an immediate and forceful response. The Baitwands must be punished. I will demand that Captain Lorimer press Major Cox in Bushire to persuade our Legation in Tehran to remove Samsam as *Ilkhani* and to provide our own Indian guards for security. Stoning Harris is an unacceptable atrocity! This time, the Legation *better* take my advice!"

Chapter Three

Lt. A.T. Wilson

I was at once saddened and at the same time pleased with my orders.

> Lieutenant Arnold Talbot Wilson proceed forthrightly with twenty men of the 18th Bengal Lancers to Mohammerah and thence by land to the Ahwaz Consulate to act as guards for the oil operations of the D'Arcy Concession in Persia.

The added responsibility of command would advance my career. Yet to leave a regiment was like leaving a religious order. My duties in India with the 32nd Sikh Pioneer Regiment had been the most rewarding of my life. Just that morning we had witnessed the inauguration of new Sikh recruits. In full scarlet uniform the regiment had formed three sides of a square. In its center under the drawn swords of Sikh officers, a white-bearded priest gave the oath in Punjabi, which each recruit recited with his hand on the holy book of the Sikhs.

> I swear by the Almighty, on this Sacred Book, that I will serve the King-Emperor with life and limb, in heat and cold, by sea and by land, with obedient heart and loyal tongue.

Following the recitation of the oath, the priest uttered the Sikh war cry and salutation. From the ranks came the same answering cry, charged with deep emotion. The order was then given to open ranks to receive recruits. The line of men opened until a space was left into which gap stepped a recruit, next to his father or uncle or brother or cousin. Finally all of us, British officers and the entire Sikh regiment, formed a line and paraded past the colonel.

Who could not be moved by such ritual, by such display of loyalty to the King of England from foreign natives of our far-reaching empire? Indeed, who could willingly leave a coterie of friends and fellow soldiers who had maintained *Pax*

Britannia for a century and had fought with honor in so many campaigns, only to be shipped off for guard duty in the remote sands of Persia?

During my two-year assignment to the Indian army I had learned a good working knowledge of Hindustani, Punjabi, Pushtu, and Persian. Perhaps it was because of the latter, my familiarity with Persian, that landed me the new assignment.

I had picked up Persian earlier in the year when my close friend, Lt. Cruickshank, and I took leave and traveled the length of Persia, from Bandar Abbas to Shiraz and thence to Isfahan and Teheran. We traveled without resources, living on lentils and rice, dates and unleavened bread. We took neither cots nor tables and pitched a tent only when rain seemed likely, a precaution to avoid the attention of potential thieves. Water we drew from ancient domed cisterns, places where caravans of camels and donkeys camped, leaving the water covered with green scum and often soiled by the rotting bodies of rock pigeons which had fallen into the cistern from nests in the roof. Living so closely to the local economy encouraged and refined my conversational Persian.

Cruickshank was an amateur ornithologist. I excelled with the plane table. On our journey we examined ruins of ancient civilizations. Most impressive were two great stone bridges more than a thousand years old across the Shur River, each of forty arches, dating from the Sassanians, who ruled from 224AD to 651AD. Persian architecture I found astonishingly beautiful, especially the palace at Isfahan.

As I traveled through the country, I could see that Persia was in the midst of a constitutional crisis. The new Shah was forced to allow the creation of the *majlis* or parliament, agreeing to share power with legislators. Persia had for millennia been ruled by leaders whose armed might loosely held the differing factions together, or more accurately, kept them apart.

Cruikshank and I parted ways at Shiraz, and I proceeded on through Persia to Baku and Russia, a place of disorder, dirt, lice, and great schemes, and on to Germany, a place of order and cleanliness, and finally to England for three months leave. It was a journey that whetted my interest in Persia. Little did I realize how influential the journey would be for my future assignment.

I left India and boarded the *S.S. Kola* with my Sikh lancers and headed up the Persian Gulf, a journey that took five days. On board I met a well-known French archeologist, Jacques de Morgan, head of the French Scientific Museum at Susa, where he was excavating the Palace of Darius and the tomb of Daniel.

Twenty years previously Messr de Morgan had conducted the original geological work across the foothills of the Zagros. He said it was largely his work that had inspired other geologists to examine the many oil springs, resulting in the D'Arcy Concession, whose operations I was now ordered to protect.

The ship dropped us at Mohammerah, the home of Sinbad the Sailor and the land of Abraham from Ur of Chaldees. King Darius and Xerxes had their palaces only a hundred miles north. We had arrived at the oldest historical centre on earth, where the first civilizations flourished and my revered teachers and prophets from the Old Testament had once walked.

Mohammerah was thirty miles upstream from the Persian Gulf on the Karun River, the only navigable river in Persia. In 1856 the British navy had bombarded the town and sent ships upriver to Ahwaz, the same route Alexander covered in 320 B.C to conquer the Acheamenians. I was the guest for a few days of the Consul, Mr. William McDouall, a gentle-voiced man who had married a Persian woman. His wife and the younger children lived "behind the screen" as was the Persian custom. He knew a great deal of local history, was a scholar of Arabic and Persian, and was one of three Europeans in the little town, the others being a Belgian Director of Customs and a European assistant surgeon on quarantine duty.

The view from the Consulate down the Shatt-al-Arab, the combined flow of the Tigris and Euphrates, and up the Karun is a sight to treasure. Date-palm groves lined both rivers and the lands in between. Just below the Consulate the turbid reddish stream of the Karun mingled with the clearer waters of the main river.

Mr. McDouall introduced me to Haji Rais ul Tujar, the chief merchant and agent of the Sheikh of Mohammerah, who controlled the lands from Mohammerah to the Zagros foothills, an area known as Arabistan. He looked with suspicion upon activities that might enhance the power of the central government and diminish his own. Mr. McDouall and I explained that we were only passing through Arabistan on our way to Luristan, the mountainous country beyond his jurisdiction, the land of the Bakhtiari. After some haggling, we arranged to put our horses and kit on one of the Sheikh's steamers for the trip upriver to Ahwaz.

The following morning at sunrise, I and my twenty Sikh cavalrymen left for Ahwaz onboard a sternwheeler up the broad and muddy river. We disembarked the following morning thirty miles downstream from Ahwaz, whence we proceeded over a flat and dry desert to a town even less inviting than Mohammerah.

Before entering Ahwaz, I drew our horsemen in parade formation, the horses two-by-two and the men in full regalia, and rode through town, a mere collection of mean huts. By the look of the stares, my band of proud Sikh horsemen made an impression on the locals.

In the distance I saw the Zagros Mountains. I knew that I was looking at the ancient wellsprings of the world's oil industry. Ur of the Chaldees, whence Moses started his journey westward, is known locally as Mughir-Umm-Qir or the Mother of Pitch. Noah's ark, like local craft, was "pitched within and without" and the tower of Babel, the Gate of God, was built with "slime", i.e. bitumen, for mortar. Herodotus mentions the practice and also the town of Hit whence all the bitumen used in Mesopotamia still comes. Layard constantly refers to its use in his Nineveh and Babylon and there is a tradition here that the burning fiery furnace in to which Shadrach, Meshach, and Abednego were cast was at Kirkuk where there is a lot of natural gas always alight, and Plutarch probably mentions this place in his Life of Alexander.

At the consulate in Ahwaz I met Vice-Consul Captain D.L.R. Lorimer of the Indian Political Department, to whom I was to serve as Consular Assistant. He was dressed casually in the official blouse of the foreign office, but his collar was open and his sleeves were rolled up. His air was friendly and welcoming. I instantly took a liking to my new chief. He stood and extended a hand.

"Welcome to Ahwaz, Lieutenant," he said upon my arrival, "I've been expecting you."

"It's good to be here, sir," I said. "Like God said to Isaiah, *behold I do a new thing and will even make a way in the wilderness, and rivers in the desert*," I replied, and shook his hand.

Captain Lorimer loved languages and books and maps, and was interested in the native people and everything around him. He told me he had been in this remote post for four years. He stayed in touch with the outside world through *The Times* daily edition, which he received six weeks after publication, and through Reuter's telegrams. Listening to Captain Lorimer made me feel that my prospects were shaping up. Then he handed me a telegram. Lt. J.G.L. Ranking was being sent to assist me. Unfortunately he was my senior by a few months and would therefore be in command of the guards.

"Have heart, Lieutenant," said Captain Lorimer. "Heat and disease have a way of winnowing those whose constitutions are less fit for duty in Persia. By the look of you, you will make out nicely."

I was twenty-three and in good physical condition. "Yes, sir," I replied. "I was looking forward to commanding the guards. My only chance for advancement is through command but perhaps I will find another route."

I knew there was no scope for both Lieutenant Ranking and me, so the junior must seek his fortune elsewhere.

Chapter Four

Dr. Morris Y. Young

I spent my first months in Persia settling into the new assignment. I interviewed each of the drillers and blacksmiths separately in order to determine their individual medical needs and to ask for suggestions to improve conditions in camp. Most had signed on for a three-year contract and were anxious for their contracts to expire. I found the Canadian drillers to be amiable but to a man complained about the food. The Polish blacksmiths were dour. The Armenians and servants from various backgrounds spoke pidgin English and were uncomplaining about the work or the food. In the evenings, I read from Rosen's book on Persian, it being obvious that the only meaningful way to interact with the people was to speak their own language.

I carefully prepared a long list of required medical supplies. Every attention was paid to price, quality, and quantity. The list was long and included aloes, rhubarb bismuth, caffeine citrate, calomel, cascara sagrada, cathartic compound, Dover powder, Easton syrup, elaterin, eyonymin, gentian, menthol, pepsin quinine bisulphate, ergotine, atropine sulphate, cocaine hydrochlor, physostignine, Fehling's test, argyrols and other medicines.

I began caring for natives as well as workers. The response from the local population was immediate and overwhelming. Every morning by first light, peasants from the surrounding villages gathered outside the dispensary. Some traveled long distances, often several days journey, to our camp and took up temporary residence in the neighboring villages for a period of treatment.

Most of the medical cases involved cysts and boils, skin and eye irritations, and gastronomical problems. Treating camp workers and natives consumed long hours, from dawn until past sunset except for a four-hour hiatus during the heat of midday.

Female patients were few. Nor were there many children. This I was told is due to the Eastern custom, and must not be mistaken for the idea that they are any healthier than the men. As disease knows no sentiment, it compels them to come when they can hold out no longer. They are mostly neglected cases, difficult to treat, and I regret to say, with but little chance of recovery.

The females were unveiled and in youth were comely but by middle age are worn and shriveled. Their costume was a shapeless dress with little or no underclothing. They lead a hard life, tending and milking the flocks, churning the milk, making butter, and running household chores which, for the nomads, meant pitching and striking the tents. The men sow and reap the crops, primarily rice irrigated from the river, cut wood, and endeavor to rob and fight each other whenever the chance occurs.

The heat I found bearable, but only just. I kept a daily record of the temperatures. During July, the maximum reached in the shade was 124F degrees, the minimum 106F degrees, and the mean daily 113F degrees.

In August, the maximum temperature was 118F and the minimum 100.5F. Hot winds prevailed throughout the month. Under such conditions, working in a goatskin tent was challenging, but we managed by rolling up or down the sides of the tent for ventilation and light, and to block the blowing sand.

Before the weather cooled, issues with both wells shut down drilling operations. Mr. Reynolds returned to Camp Marmatain to oversee correcting the problems. When I asked him what had gone wrong, he told me nine-inch casing had been set to 1,530 feet on Wellbore No. 1. Upon drilling a few more feet, an eight-foot bed of salt had been penetrated, which damaged the drilling cable and clogged the boiler. The center of the fire-box tubeplate on the boiler could not be detached. Wellbore No. 2 had been halted due to a damaged casing shoe.

"What caused such a thing?" I asked. His answer was indecipherable to me, something about the shoulder of the eccentric bit. He told me the casing had become too near the tool and the top joint of the casing had parted.

"The casing dog stem should have been welded above the right-hand thread box. Probably due to the parting of the casing and its subsequent fall a few feet, the bottom length was bent. I see that while drilling with poles, it takes a blacksmith all his time to weld up the broken poles, they all breaking at the same place, the original weld joining the pin to the bar. The welds were bad in all cases."

I was constantly amazed at Mr. Reynolds' understanding of wellbores. His explanations made me realize how drilling was an odd business. Most problems occurred at the bottom of the hole. Since you could not *see* the problem, it took deductive reasoning and an understanding of the mechanics of downhole equipment to figure out how to *fix* the problem.

He advised running 7.5-inch casing to 1,457 feet in the No. 2 and indicated that due to the requirement for ever-smaller casing, he did not expect they could drill but a few more hundred feet. I asked him if had measured the outcrop to determine how much deeper to drill.

"Due to the Harris incident I was unable to visit the Asmari Hill. Just as soon as I have time, I intend to."

Mr. Reynolds went on to say the road from the Karun to Musjid-i-Suleiman had been delayed because no agreement with one of the *sayids* of Baitwand could be reached to use his old and out-of-use millrace. After the stoning incident, he had ordered Harris to carry a revolver.

"As he has been treated somewhat roughly, Harris is not inclined to quarrel with the laborers. I fear that, if a row to occur, he may fire his revolver and so bloodshed will ensue. It will be difficult to know where it will stop."

To all of these issues, whether mechanical with the wellbore or political with the locals, Mr. Reynolds held court like an Oriental adjudicator empowered to right all problems. His handling of such a wide range of issues, often in a foreign tongue, was impressive. He also kept the workers under tight command. The story of one of the Canadian drillers who ran afoul of Mr. Reynolds had already become legend around the camps. After being hired by the company and making the long sea journey, the man disembarked from his ship in Mohammerah. There, he drank too much and got into a fight with a native. The next day Reynolds demanded he sign a contract testifying what had happened and obligating him never to drink while in the employ of the Company. The man refused to sign and Reynolds fired him on the spot, without concern for how he might replace him or how the man might pay for his passage back to England.

By September the days were somewhat cooler. Maximum temperature in the shade dropped to 110F with an average of 102.5F. The season was gradually changing. Cooling temperatures and the state of the river water brought on by the rice cultivation were the main causes of sickness. I took the greatest care with the camp's drinking water, most being boiled before use. Further, as the best prophylactic, I issued doses of quinine daily. A week's supply was given to each person, to be renewed when finished.

In mid-September, Mr. Reynolds showed up again at Camp Marmatain, accompanied by Bradshaw. He told us the road to Camp Maidan-i-Napthun had finally opened on the 23rd of August, and that supplies were being hauled weekly to prepare for drilling the two wells at Musjid-i-Suleiman.

"Due to the excessive heat, we are having great difficulty with the mules. When crossing the Tenbi, they drink the salty and sulfurous water and in turn, become listless and lie down with their loads."

"Who could have predicted such a problem?" I asked.

"Yes, well," he replied, "operations in Persia are rife with problems. I tackle them one at a time. I have instructed the muleteers to water the animals from tanks before crossing the river."

He went on to say that he was convinced further drilling on the two wellbores at Marmatain was wasting time and money.

"If examination of the two holes show what I expect, what we have met in the No. 1 wellbore we shall in all probability meet the same in No. 2. It would be expedient to stop one of the two holes, in which case Drillers Knapp, Currie, and Woolsey could be shifted to Musjid-i-Suleiman."

The No. 1 was drilling at 1,805 feet and the No. 2 was at 1,560 feet and was having difficulty keeping the hole straight owing to steeply inclined strata.

"It may never reach the Nummulitic limestone," explained Mr. Reynolds. "Steeply inclined beds are not horizontal to their original deposition. Think about drilling a layered cake. Tilt the cake on edge and instead of drilling through the layers, you would drill down a single layer. With this news, I am convinced reaching the limestone is not a possibility."

"I must examine the outcrop," he continued. "Dr. Young, I would like you to accompany me to Asmari. On the way I want you to examine Pir Murad, a truculent old village chief who opposes our every effort."

We left camp late in the late afternoon, arriving at Pir Murad's village in time to see the old chief, who was obviously quite sick. He seemed very suspicious of me at first, but eventually allowed me to examine him. I carefully pulled back his sleeve and saw a gaping, red hole in his arm. Apparently an old bullet wound had become infected. I spent an hour re-opening and cleansing the wound, and removing pieces of the bullet. While I poked and prodded, then cut and probed, he sat stoic as a statute, never showing the least pain. I left ointments for him to dress the wound every three days. Mr. Reynolds spoke his dialect, and relayed my instructions.

The trip to Asmari Hills required nearly a week. The heat had abated somewhat so we were able to ride in early morning and late afternoon. I was beginning to see the countryside beyond its own starkness, not as threatening so much as imposing. Certainly it was a landscape foreign to Scotland. The vast blue dome of the Persian sky, in contrast to the grey cloud-covered skies of home, held forth the promise of punishment, but also of atonement.

Asmari Mountain

I was astounded at Asmari. The limestone mountain rose like the arch of a giant leviathan's back, an elongated dome emerging from the alluvial valley sands next to the Tenbi River. We set up camp on the banks of the river and Mr. Reynolds quickly set about measuring distances between the hills and a sandstone cliff across the broad river valley.

While Mr. Reynolds and the surveying crew were busy measuring distances, I spent time at the village. Upon discovery that I was a medical doctor, the village turned out en mass and began showing me their individual needs. Although I quickly depleted my medical supplies, it reinforced the fact that free medical care was the key to friendlier relations with the natives. I made a point to ask about women and children, and was brought to the tents of some of those most in need. Gastric problems were rampant. Rice plots along the river were now inundated to soften the ground prior to planting. Drinking water was fetched from the rice fields, which was contaminated by infectious bacteria derived from the human and animal waste used to fertilize the fields. How, I wondered, could we provide safer drinking water for the people?

On our last evening in camp, Mr. Reynolds presented his drawing to me.

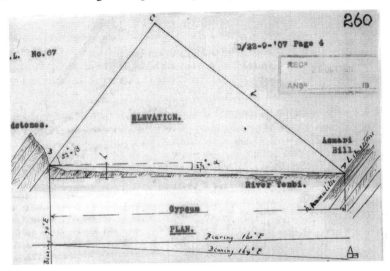

"Referring to the sketch," he pointed to his map, the point A is situated on the surface of the Nummulitic limestone of the Asmari on the left bank of the Tenbi at an *imamzada*,ar burial site of a religious man named 'Sultan Ibrahim'. The point B is situated on a band about nine inches thick of broken shells cemented together, found near the top of the gypsum beds, an unmistakable stratum and one found at this horizon all over these parts. It is overlaid with the usual sandstones dipping conformably to the limestone and gypsum beds. He showed us his calculations:

Difference of Barometer readings at B & A = h = 252'

Dip of Gypsum beds 52 degrees = B

Bearing of strike 70 degrees

Inclination below horizontal plane of A from B = 2 ½ degrees

Bearing of Imamzada from B = 164 degrees East

Thickness of Gypsum beds = b = AB Sin = h Sin /Sin

"Hence b = 252 x .8141/.0436 equals 4,705 feet," he concluded. "This, though, is in the plane four degrees off the square to the strike line, but as the angle is so small it need not be considered, and the thickness of the beds of gypsum may be taken to be 1,500 yards."

I may not have followed his geometry but I understood its implications. If his calculations were accurate, the two wells could never reach the limestone.

"Drilling further at Marmatain is hopeless," he concluded. "Further troubles with the Kuhgula tribe and Bakhtiari prevent us going to Bulferis and measuring the outcrop there. The only other confirmation of the thickness of gypsum would be at a ford on the Karun called Bird-i-Kumchi where the rocks are cut through by the river. Without climbing the face of the cliff, I can tell you the gypsum there is comparable in thickness."

"Will not the gypsum be the same thickness at Musjid-i-Suleiman?" I asked.

"I think not," he replied. "The limestone is on the surface here in the Asmari Hill. The beds dip to the northwest in the direction of Musjid-i-Suleiman, where I expect the depth to the Nummulitic limestone will be less than two thousand feet."

"When you convey your conclusion to the directors in Glasgow, will they agree with your measurements?" I asked.

"They have already instructed me not to abandon the wells at Marmatain until one of Boverton Redwood's geologists can assess the situation."

"Is Boverton Redwood familiar enough with the wellbore?" I asked.

"Mr. D'Arcy entrusted him with evaluating the prospects for finding oil when we acquired the Concession in 1901. Six years ago he sent a Mr. Burls to examine the region. Burls recommended drilling at Chiah Sourk, and a few years later another of Redwood's colleague chose the sites at Marmatain."

"Were the wells at Chiah Sourk dry holes?" I asked.

"We found a small quantity of oil," he replied. "I could not shut off the flow from one of the wells, so left it under the supervision of an old Kurd chieftain, Karim Kahn, who owned the seep near where we drilled. His family has sold bitumen from the seep for three hundred years. He maintains our rig and plant and in return sells the crude oil from our well for his own benefit."

Karim Kahn

To our surprise, on the way back Bertie, the camp supervisor, met us when we were still nearly two hours from camp. As soon as he saw our caravan, he kicked his horse into a gallop. We could tell something was amiss.

When Bertie reached us he explained that Pir Murad, the old warrior whose wound I had cleaned, had intimidated the entire camp.

"What do you mean by *intimidated?*" asked Mr. Reynolds.

"Yesterday afternoon he rode up to the rig at Marmatain and abused our Kurd laborers. He threatened to shoot them all if they did not stop working, saying it was his land. The Europeans were also abused. Pir Murad went right up to Knapp, shook his fist in his face and threatened to kill him."

"Give the old savage medical care and he repays with this!" Mr. Reynolds was furious.

"All the men have quit work," continued Bertie. "The drillers are threatening to leave as well."

"My god!" swore Mr. Reynolds, this time louder. "What about the guards? Where were the guards? Captain Lorimer promised me the Indian guards should arrive any day!"

"They have not yet arrived. Mahmoud Khan says he is unable to deal with Pir Murad, he not being his *ryot.*"

"Bertie, return to camp immediately and inform the drillers I will meet them as soon as we arrive. Tell your Kurd workers to assemble in front of the Marmatain plant. I refuse to be intimidated by a miscreant who thinks he is the Shah of Persia."

He ordered the caravan to pick up the pace and upon our arrival in camp some two hours later, Mr. Reynolds rode directly to the assembled natives. Without dismounting, he spoke sternly in Kurdish that they would not be leaving, that they were required to return to work, and that he would forthrightly deal with Pir Murad. Following that admonishment he rode to the mess hall where the drillers were waiting, and told them under no circumstances would they quit work, that he would personally handle Murad, and that they were to go back to work immediately. When driller Knapp protested, Mr. Reynolds stared at him for a few long seconds and in a softer voice repeated, "You shall return to work immediately. I will deal with our friend Mr. Murad," whence he took four guards with him and rode off to Pir Murad's camp.

At dinner, after he returned, I inquired how the interview played out. He said he told Murad he would be held responsible for his actions and speculated that

Samsam-es-Sultan was behind the incident. Captain Lorimer, who had been in Isfahan for several months, had informed him that the Samsam's party of sixty to seventy followers had robbed and stripped to the skin several European travelers on the Teheran to Isfahan Road, and were harassing Europeans at every opportunity, and was responsible for Pir Murad's actions.

"As soon as I return to Ahwaz, I will write the directors of the *trivial* difficulties we have in dealing with a gentleman of His Excellency Samsam's peculiar habits," said Mr. Reynolds. "Now, please pass me the beans, Dr. Young."

I left Camp Marmatain in caravan with Mr. Reynolds, the drillers, and MacNaughton. We were moving equipment to Musjid-i-Suleiman to assemble the rig, draw-works and other machinery for the two wells. We dropped MacNaughton and the drillers at Camp Maidan-i-Napthun and Mr. Reynolds and I rode to Dar-i-Khazineh to catch the *Shushan* on its return to Ahwaz.

We missed the *Shushan* by a day and were left to ride horseback the sixty miles to Ahwaz. Five miles before reaching the Karun, Mr. Reynolds' horse stumbled to its knees, wrenching Reynolds' inner left thigh, and causing him considerable pain. In spite of his pain, we continued to ride and in two days reached Ahwaz.

While I was in Ahwaz administering to Mr. Reynolds, a terrible crime occurred. One of the local Arabs, assisted by his son and nephew, murdered a man, cut him up, put the pieces into a sack, and threw it into the river. A water carrier who was filling his water skin discovered the sack and reported the matter to the Sheikh of Mohammerah. The three men were arrested and called before the town to be publicly thrashed. I witnessed their punishment, an event biblical in its brutal justice.

They started with the oldest – a man who I would say was about fifty years of age. They licked him with sticks and whips until his whole body was raw flesh from his toes to the crown of his head. The other two received the same treatment. They confessed nothing until the mob started sticking red-hot irons into them. When they told the whole story, it tallied in details with the story told by one of their wives.

After the thrashing, one of the men was able to get up and walk to the prison but the other two were unconscious. The next morning they received another thrashing and branding. The old man never flinched, so they cut his ear off and started thrashing him again, whence he cried for God to give them the strength to hit him harder. In the afternoon he was again beaten but by then his son and nephew were both unconscious. They laid on him for another two hours before they stopped. He died about half an hour afterward. They threw his body out into the street. The younger men survived.

I was astounded that the law of these lands valued vengeance over mercy. And that a man being beaten to death by his own villagers could ask God to give them strength to beat him harder.

Before I returned to Camp Marmatain, Mr. Reynolds showed me a telegram from the CSL directors. Due to the lack of confidentiality, all telegrams were encoded, this one having been decoded by Mr. Reynolds, who kept the codebook locked, he having the only key.

"Do not abandon wells. Shut down temporarily." The telegram further stated that the company would send an expert to confirm Reynolds' opinion that the gypsum beds were 1,500 yards thick.

"Another expert," Mr. Reynolds said, with some exasperation. "In '01 Boverton Redwood sends a Mr. Burls, who recommends drilling at Chiah Sourk, it being an ancient seep used for millennia as a source of bitumen and near the main road from Baghdad to Teheran. Hundreds of thousands of sterling and two years later, Mr. Redwood sends out another expert, a Mr. Dalton, to confirm that we should suspend drilling. When our Scot landlords assumed control of operations in '05, yet another of Mr. Redwood's experts chose sites at Marmatain, disregarding the distance to markets if we make a discovery, or how deep we should drill. And now, hundreds of thousands of pounds and two years later, Mr. Redwood is sending yet another expert, Mr. Cunningham Craig, to tell us what is already clear – that we haven't drilled deep enough and the hole conditions make further drilling futile."

I asked Mr. Reynolds if drilling operations in Persia have always been so troublesome as those we are encountering.

"Troublesome?" he said. "You call this troublesome! In April '05 I and my two servants and a guide were fired on, some fifteen shots. That, sir, was troublesome. What do you find so troublesome about the present operation?"

I had not been in Persia long enough to fully understand all the issues, but it seemed every day new and nearly insurmountable circumstances arose.

Choosing the right location to drill was critical, but it seemed every expert had a different opinion of where and how deep to drill. Moving a rig and all the material to such remote locations was a logistical nightmare and a vastly expensive task. Hiring foreign drillers and providing them servants, meals, living accommodations, and medical care would have been challenging in Scotland. And all of this before drilling even began. Once drilling commenced, hole conditions and cave-in's, steeply inclined beds, inadequate fuel supplies for boilers that salt up because of contaminated water, and no telling what additional mechanical problems arose. Add to that the problems inherent in feeding and working nearly a thousand mules and hundreds of men who came from different tribes, whose cultures are based on conflict, whose justice is meted with punishment from the Old Testament, and whose leaders are truculent and rapacious. The result was relations with natives at rifle point or at the threat of work stoppage. And all of this had transpired in my first ninety days in Persia. I couldn't imagine what other challenges Mr. Reynolds had faced in the past six years.

"Perhaps I meant 'challenges', sir," I replied.

"Dr. Young," he continued, "of course we have challenges. Which is precisely why I lack patience with our Scottish directors. Not a single one, not even Mr. D'Arcy, has set foot in Persia. No one in Glasgow can grasp the challenges. Yet they second guess my every recommendation, complain that I do not keep them informed and dispatch geological experts to pass judgment on the obscure while overlooking the obvious."

I was sympathetic, and noted without expressing it to Mr. Reynolds yet another challenge -- keeping the trust of the directors, who were betting fortunes on our success.

"MacNaughton will remain at Musjid-i-Suleiman to assist Bradshaw," he continued. "You are to return to Camp Marmatain to assist Bertie. I do not wish to leave him there by himself. If trouble erupts with the Lurs, I rather fear for him. Bereft of McNaughton, the Canadian drillers I find somewhat chicken-hearted."

"Do you want me to tell Bertie to stop drilling?" I asked. "The directors instructed you to stop temporarily."

"Not at all," he responded curtly. "To stop, even temporarily, at the present time would lead the Lurs to think we had stopped in deference to them, and nothing that we could say would lead them to think otherwise.

Chapter Five

Lt. A.T. Wilson

Mr. George Reynolds, a man in his fifties and fit as a younger man, rose and shook my hand. When he moved from behind the desk, he limped slightly.

"I have looked forward to this day," he said with evident satisfaction. "Our dependency on local guards has been an ill-conceived disaster. Your Indian guards will not replace the native guards, but will enforce the security that they have failed to provide. May I introduce you to Mr. Cunningham Craig, a man sent here by the Company to examine the geology."

After the introductions, Captain Lorimer asked Reynolds about his limp.

"Two month ago my mule stumbled. I wrenched my upper thigh," explained Reynolds. "Dr. Young ordered me not to attempt to ride for at least a fortnight. While laid up with the sprain, a most malignant insect bit my feet and ankles. I'm only now fully recovered."

"In spite of his injury, Mr. Reynolds accompanied me on a tour of the field," inserted Craig, "and was most cordial in guiding me for the past month. Without his help, my field work would have been seriously hindered."

"Mr. Craig, did your field work reveal any insights into the oil prospects?" asked Captain Lorimer. "We hear that drilling at Camp Marmatain is shutting down."

"Yes, Captain, I will recommend that operations at Marmatain be suspended."

"Mr. Craig and I have had many discussions about the geology," said Reynolds. "He agrees with me that hole conditions at Marmatain preclude us from reaching the objective horizon, so we will temporarily abandon the project and move operations to Musjid-i-Suleiman."

"Do you expect different results there?" I asked. I knew nothing of drilling, but was curious if one location was to be abandoned, why would the next would be better.

"I have always believed the location at Musjid-i-Suleiman superior."

"What is the objective horizon?" asked Captain Lorimer.

"You've touched another point of contention, or I should say, of disagreement," replied Reynolds. "I think the limestone, like that of the Asmari Hills, to be the oil-bearing horizon."

"I differ with Mr. Reynolds," said Craig. "If the only oil-bearing strata to be met are those beds of limestone exposed at the surface at Asmari, the production of oil can never be great, and cannot be expected to repay the cost of drilling because the limestone is too impermeable and will not allow oil to freely flow through the rock. However, cavernous limestones or porous sandstones *above* the Asmari could have potential."

"What is *your* opinion of the chances of success at Musjid-i-Suleiman, Mr. Craig?" asked Captain Lorimer.

"Mr. Craig does not like the location for our No. 1 well at Musjid-i-Suleiman," answered Reynolds, "which I personally chose, having received no geological direction other than my own."

"But which will add valuable geologic information," added Craig. "I mapped the exposed bedding over more than two square miles at Musjid-i-Suleiman and found the geology to be extremely complicated. The company sorely needs a topographic survey of the entire area."

"You need surveying, do you say?" I asked. "If so, may I offer my services? I have extensive surveying experience." If I was not to be in charge of the Guard, perhaps I could best use my time surveying. Reynolds was enthusiastic at my suggestion.

"Excellent idea, Lieutenant," he said. "Yes, indeed. I have needed topography since moving operations to Luristan, and have repeatedly asked the Company to send a surveyor. Captain, would I have your permission for Lieutenant Wilson to map the topography, beginning with Musjid-i-Suleiman?"

"I suspect the Intelligence Branch would like surveys over this part of Persia," replied Captain Lorimer. "Most of the country beyond Shushtar is labeled 'unknown lands' on our maps. It can possibly be arranged. Can you give me an estimate, Mr. Craig, of how much longer you will be drilling in the Musjid-i-Suleiman area?"

"I have not yet put my research into a coherent picture," responded Craig. "When I return to England, I am to write a report of my findings, which will be confidential, but I can tell you that the gentle folding and flat structures so favorable to the production of oil in other areas are entirely absent in this district. It does not necessarily follow that the district is to be condemned on that account. The numerous sharp flexures may be regarded as parts of one large complicated anticline."

"I wasn't asking for proprietary information," replied Captain Lorimer, "but now that the consulate has provided guards for your operation, we would like some estimation of how long you think they will be needed."

"The first well at Musjid-i-Suleiman should give us much needed information. I predict we will find an unconformity within the Tertiary and thus the first well will be no more than a few hundred feet in depth. Nevertheless I expect a certain quantity of oil is likely to be obtained. Well No. 2 will be a much more important test of the area. The unconformity will probably be far out of reach in this locality, and although the limestones are certainly thinning, oil-bearing beds, either calcareous or sandy, above the Asmari limestone may be expected. Unless a very thick mass of gypsum is encountered in Well No. 2, I would suggest its being carried to a depth of at least 1,500 feet, which might require close to a year."

"Captain Lorimer," said Reynolds, "although I am confident our drilling at Musjid-i-Suleiman will be successful, only the drill bit can determine how long it will take. You can expect that your guards will be here for several months, and if we find oil in commercial quantities as I expect, for several years."

Several months I would look forward to. The thought of several years in this backwater wilderness was another matter. Advancement to higher ranks could not be accomplished as assistant commander to a small Indian guard at the fringe of the empire.

"Mr. Reynolds, will my guards be billeted at both camps?" I asked.

"At the present time your guards will be separated into two groups, ten at each camp. Their primary responsibility is to ensure the native guards perform their duties. Guards of the guards, you might call them. Soon after the first of the year, we will temporarily abandon operations at Marmatain, at which time we will leave a small group to look after the shop and materials left behind. The remaining guards will be shifted to Musjid-i-Suleiman. The Bakhtiari, who are experts at thievery and would not know the truth if it slapped them in the face, have settled near our camps in their winter pastures."

I knew from my travels through Persia the past spring that the Bakhtiari were nomadic. I had assumed they duplicated the pastoral existence of the books of Genesis or Job, but knew nothing of their habits or culture.

"You will be glad to know of your friend, Pir Murad," said Captain Lorimer to Reynolds.

"My friend who threatened to shoot all the Kurd laborers if they did not stop work?"

"Major Cox informs me that Pir Murad is now a prisoner at Ram Hormuz of Naib-ul-Hukumas, who gave him a good beating, fined him 50 *tomans*, and now has him chained in prison so that others should learn a lesson."

"Good news, Captain, which explains the report from Mr. Bertie that the sons of Pir Murad stole two mules in revenge for their father's arrest and fine. Bertie reported that the drillers at Marmatain were awakened by a dozen shots, possibly a put-up by the guards after the mules had already been stolen. But the old reprobate deserves his due. If only justice were swift with the Harris affair. Any news from His Excellency the Samsam?"

"Under written orders from the Samsam, the two ring leaders were caught, returned to camp, tied to one of your jims, and flogged," answered Captain Lorimer.

"Very good," said Reynolds satisfactorily. "However, it would have had far better effect if the Baitwand villagers had been punished immediately after Harris was stoned. The *khans* have failed to show the respect due to us."

"I have recommended to Major Cox," continued Captain Lorimer, "that the L500 quarterly payment to the *khans* for guards be stopped. What are your thoughts?"

Reynolds' brow furrowed. "As soon as the payment is stopped, we shall lose our property for certain, and loss of life is dependent simply on the attitude which may be adopted by our men. If they control themselves under what will doubtless be great provocation, their dignity and not their skin will be hurt. If, on the other hand, they resist or strike a Lur, it is certain both dignity and body will suffer."

"Would your men strike a native?" asked Captain Lorimer.

"I am of the opinion if a blow had been struck by Knapp when threatened by Pir Murad, a fight would have ensued and the Canadians would have left. The *khans*, having failed to show us the respect due to us, expressed to us at Kima last spring that they could not control their tribesmen. How could the tribesmen respect us when they hear that their chiefs do not? It is absurd to expect."

"So long as punishment is meted to those who stand in the way of our rights," said Captain Lorimer, "you will be able to continue drilling under the

Concession. I only hope you find oil soon. It has been nearly seven years with little to show for all the effort."

Reynolds gave a *humpf* and stood up, indicating it was time for us to leave. "Captain, you sound like my directors," he said. "Now if you will excuse us, Mr. Craig and I have work to be done before Mr. Craig leaves tomorrow on the *Malamir*. Lieutenant Wilson, it is a pleasure to have you and your guards join us."

Reynolds impressed me as direct, authoritative, and confident, the kind of man who well-represented the Empire. I was hopeful his offer to conduct survey work for his company would be acceptable to my superiors. After we left his office, I asked Captain Lorimer if he agreed with Reynolds' timetable.

"He knows more about drilling in Persia than any man alive," replied the Captain. "Without him, the whole oil scheme would collapse. If Reynolds says 'for several months', you can bank on it. Your assignment to Persia is subject to the success of the oil venture."

I did not express my sentiments that a dry hole would not disappoint me. In the meantime, the conversation with Reynolds brought up several questions.

"Captain Lorimer, can you tell me more about the Persians? They seem a mixed lot."

"Persians are of four races – Turks, Arabs, Kurds, and Persians proper. Their soil is not rich, the climate is harsh, the distances great. Persians proper are inclined to be antagonistic to all non-Persian minorities, except for the Turkish-speaking element which predominates in northern Persia. They dislike Arabs. They dislike Kurds as such and because they are Sunnis. They dislike the Assyrians of Urmi because they are Christians, the Parsees because they are not Moslems. Nor do they like the Bakhtiari, the Baluchis, or the Lurs of Pusht-i-Kuh because they are to some extent independent of the central government. There should be some unifying force, but it is not on the horizon."

"And what of the tribes?" I asked. "Reynolds refers to the Lurs and to the Bakhtiari. Are they the same? He must believe they are all liars and thieves."

"Reynolds has strong feelings about most subjects. He is an excellent manager for the company's business, but at times, and I mean this without being overly critical, his opinions reflect his prejudices. As to your question, the Bakhtiari are a subdivision of the Lurs. They are divided into groups, such as the Kuh-i-Galu or Khugula, and into tribes, as many as two hundred different tribes, such as the Qashabi, Sarhandi, and Mamasensi. They are a fierce and independent people. They withstood the Achaemenids, the Medis, Alexander the Great, and Antiochus, but were subdued by the Arabs. Much like the Bedouin of Arabia, tribal and clan feeling is very strong. Obedience and loyalty are observed within a patriarchal form of government, which means deference to chieftains, their *khans.*"

"Does the central government control the Bakhtiari?" I asked.

"Teheran exacts taxes from them, and demands a contribution in the manner of one out of ten young men serve the military. But the tribes are all semi-independent and very sensitive of restraint, and always prone to rebellion."

"Do you respect them?"

"Respect them?" repeated Captain Lorimer. "They are hospitable, simple-minded, and innocent of the debaucheries of city Persians. They are also fierce, ignorant, and mendacious. They glory in plunder and are adroit thieves."

"They sound intriguing," I concluded. "Where did they originate? I've heard of Turks and Kurds and Arabs, but not of Lurs."

"Who they are and from where they came is as yet unsolved. Rawlinson, who passed through their country sixty years ago, says that their language descended from Farsi and is related to the tongue of the ancient Sassanians. Suffice it to say that they are Aryan and have lived for centuries in the Zagros Mountains."

"Are they Muslim?" I asked.

"Most profess to be Shiah Muslim and respect the Prophet, but they have their own holy men who practice rites more ancient than Islam."

"I would very much like to conduct surveys in their territory," I said. "*So the Lord scattered men abroad from thence upon the face of all the earth.* The tribes of the Zagros sound like an interesting lot."

"The tribes are in constant conflict with each, and most are hostile to foreigners," said Captain Lorimer. "The oil company has mollified some of their bickering in the area of drilling. Or I should say has *allayed* some of their disputes, by providing cash jobs as a divergence from killing and stealing from one another. For millennium, though, the tribes have fought each other. I was wounded a couple of years ago when I approached the Mirs territory in Pusht-i-Kuh."

"You were wounded? What happened?"

"The Mirs claim an area in the Pusht exclusively their own, and attempt to exact a tax for crossing their territory. I refused to be intimidated by such territorial claims. When riding through a mountain pass in the Pusht, I was shot, luckily in the arm, by an assailant."

"Has the Pusht been surveyed?"

"Never." The Captain smiled. "Perhaps it's a job you could tackle, Lieutenant."

I could tell by his smile that Captain Lorimer thought I would be foolish to attempt such an endeavor. But the more I heard about the Bakhtiari, the more I wanted to learn, and the more I learned, the safer might be survey work.

"Now it's my turn to ask a few questions," the Captain continued. "You have only recently returned from England, correct?"

"Yes, sir," I replied. "I was home this past summer."

"What's the talk? Articles in *The Times* speak of the German naval build-up."

"It's true. The Kaiser may be Queen Victoria's oldest grandson and the King's nephew, but he's no friend of England. While I was home, Germany resumed work on their all-big-gun battleship. A year ago the Kaiser promised not to. He and the Bakhtiari have some common traits, don't you think?"

"Have you heard about the Kaiser's interview with *The Daily Telegraph?*" asked Captain Lorimer, and he pointed to a newspaper on his desk. "It is outrageous."

"Captain, I've been traveling for the past month. What article in *The Daily Telegraph?*"

Captain Lorimer picked up the newspaper. "In the Kaiser's own words, 'You English are mad, mad as March hares.' And he goes on to say 'What of the German Navy? Against whom but England is it being steadily built up?' Quote. Unquote."

"He's been rattling sabers since he became Emperor," I responded. "The article makes it sound like England and Germany are at war."

"Probably the Entente triggered his paranoia."

"Entente? I'm sorry, Captain, but I'm not familiar with the Entente." Even while in Ambala I had kept informed of political activities at home, thinking if a career in the army failed to advance my ambitions, perhaps my best hope for distinction would in politics. But during my travels from India to Persia, I heard little of current news.

"We recently signed the Anglo-Russian Entente, which divides Persia into three spheres: Russia in the north, Britain in the south, and a neutral zone in the center. We in Ahwaz are in the central zone."

"The neutral zone? Why should this region be neutral? We are drilling wells in the neutral zone."

"It's neutral in the sense that neither Russia nor England has exclusive political and commercial concessions in central Persia as we do within our own zones. However the fact that we are already here with established consulates and the CSL is drilling for oil in the foothills favors British interests, but leaves commercial concessions open to others who might apply."

I asked who in the world would want commercial concessions in this remote region.

"The Germans have obtained a concession from the Ottoman Sultan to build the Turkish sections of the Berlin-to-Baghdad railway."

"How does that affect us in Ahwaz?" As a political officer, Captain Lorimer looked at the world differently than my narrow view as a junior military officer.

"The Kaiser's rapid build-up of the German navy is a direct threat to our naval superiority," replied the Captain. "He is building a railroad through continental Europe to the Mideast, which potentially opens a hostile approach to India through the Persian Gulf. And now in an interview with a reporter in *The Daily Telegraph*, he is fuming that Germany's rights can only be guaranteed by military strength and command of the seas…against Britain."

"For five hundred years we were at war with France. For the past hundred years we fought wars and made treaties to stop Russia's expansion toward India. Now we're signing agreements with France and Russia to check Germany. Do you find it odd?"

"Not so odd, Lieutenant. Germany is pushing for hegemony on the continent. And they're challenging our superiority at sea. Call it nationalism. Call it militarism. Call it paranoia. Call it what you like, but it is a real threat to England and to India and to our presence here in Ahwaz."

"A threat to us here? How in the world?" I couldn't imagine a more remote outpost. How could events in the wider world affect this far-flung hovel of mud huts? The only impact of our presence in Ahwaz was to stifle my military career.

"Have you considered if CSL discovers oil?"

Chapter Six

Dr. Morris Y. Young

Shortly after the first of the year, I moved the dispensary to Camp Maidan-i-Napthun, near the Musjid-i-Suleiman operation. If drilling there did not meet with success, my tour in Persia would last less than the year I had signed on for.

In January another European joined our camp, Lieutenant A.T. Wilson, who was in charge of the Indian Guards brought to supplement the security of our two camps. Wilson was an energetic man, full of curiosity and quotes from the Old Testament, and enthusiastic about the native cultures. He constantly asked questions and soon began dressing like the natives in knee-length felt robes. He also wore a round felt hat, and grew a beard. I asked him why he wanted to dress like the Bakhtiari.

"Because their dress is warmer than ours," he replied casually. "You should try it."

"Yes, well my dress demands a certain level of cleanliness. Your felt robe has never been washed, has it?"

"That's why it repels the rain," he replied with a smile. "I am hoping the Intelligence Branch allows me to survey the Bakhtiari country. Nearly this entire area is marked on our maps as unexplored. Less than a year ago a friend and I traveled on the other side of the Zagros. Living like the natives allows for a certain freedom, do you think?"

I'm sure he was right. I had heard of travelers like Wilson, other Brits who undertook any discomfort to experience the native cultures, eat their foods, dress in their garments. He followed a long line of explorers, from Burton to Curzon. Most of them carried a retinue of servants and equipment enough to make living in the countryside comfortable. Wilson was different. The inconveniences of living like a native did not bother him, even if it meant spending days with little to eat in driving rain.

When I closed the dispensary at Camp Marmatain, I took every possible care and attention to pack and transport the medicines and supplies. By the spring of 1908 the dispensary in Camp Maidan-i-Naphtun near the Musjid-i-Suleiman wells was in full operation.

During the move, I continued to care for native patients. Word of our medical practice continued to spread and, for the first time, the company's presence was appreciated rather than resented. In January 778 patients were administered to, of which nearly half were surgical cases and the others were medical cases. The number of women and children who sought medical attention increased, but did not reach fifteen percent of the total.

Amongst the tribesmen who camped in the countryside, infectious diseases were not uncommon. I treated patients with measles, smallpox and typhoid fever. I tried as much as possible to quarantine the sick from the healthy. Explaining the germ theory to the Bakhtiari natives met with limited success. Quarantine, or keeping the infirm from exposing everyone else, was the only prevention at hand.

I performed minor operations, using cocaine solution as a local anesthesia, but soon determined that operating on serious cases would have to be handled at the dispensary as well.

The No. 1 Musjid-i-Suleiman commenced, or as Mr. Reynolds says, spudded on January 23rd, 1908. Reynolds was present to oversee the procedure. While at our camp, he checked out the new dispensary. We had rolled down the sides for warmth, but for light I had made roll-up felt windows. Mr. Reynolds expressed pleasure with the dispensary and with my medical practices, and was especially pleased with the response from the natives.

After he complimented my medical practice, I thought it opportune to bring up a matter of some sensitivity in camp. Rumors had spread that he turned over a company clerk to the local governor, and that the clerk would be executed for moral indiscretions. I found it difficult to believe, and broached the subject to get at the truth and curb the rumor.

"I heard about Phillips," I said. "Is it true?"

"True? What are you talking about, Doctor? I fired him and turned him over to the Deputy Governor."

"They say he fell in love with a native Persian woman, one of the upper class."

"He was caught in Ram Hormuz under suspicious circumstances in a garden with a woman. I doubt if she was of the upper class."

"It sounds innocent enough to me."

"After Phillips' rampages, the Governor claimed not a single virgin remained in Ram Hormuz. Given that he was an employee of the Company and charged with such offenses by the governor of the province, I was left with no option but to discharge him."

"Will he be executed?" I asked.

"Of course not. The Governor took his money and shipped him out of the country. It's enough, Dr. Young, to put up with the complaints of the drillers and machinists when their tinned spaghetti is not served hot. I have no tolerance for drinking or cavorting with the locals."

I worried about my own chances for meeting a suitable mate in this remote assignment. "I am frankly surprised more incidents of this nature are so rare."

"They will not occur on my watch," replied Reynolds. "The unmarried men can find a mate when they return to England or Canada or Poland or wherever they call home."

For certain, Musjid-i-Suleiman was no place to meet women.

Camp Maidan-i-Napthun

"Have you started the drilling yet?" I asked. The drillers had explained to me the problems in spudding the well. The hole had to be exactly vertical, and often the sediments close to the surface would cave in.

"Doctor," replied Mr. Reynolds. "I have done this enough times to know where *not* to locate a well. Because I was not consulted in choosing the site for the first well at Marmatain, it was located close to a gulley. We had great difficulty in drilling the first hundred feet due to boulders caving in the hole.

The No. 1 wellbore here, in spite of Mr. Craig's reservations, is well-suited not just for the geology, but also for the drilling conditions."

"Did you receive the geologic report from Mr. Craig?" I asked. "I remember he said the No. 1 will not have to be drilled very deep."

"No, I have not. I have repeatedly asked for the geological reports, but the directors prefer to keep them to themselves. They did, however, concur where to locate the second well."

"When will you spud the second well?" I asked.

"By early March."

"If the Musjid-i-Suleiman wells are not successful I fear the Company will shut down operations."

"Doctor Young, only time and effort will determine whether the No. 1 and the No. 2 produce oil. Until then, we must all pull our weight and not worry with distant futures. I appreciate your work and your high level of professionalism. We must simply do our best and leave the discovery of oil to a higher order, to our own expertise, and to perseverance. I hope we can convince the directors to persevere."

By the end of March the nomadic Bakhtiari began to leave the area, taking their flocks over the snow-capped mountains to greener pastures. It was a great exodus, one which had transpired every spring for millennia. Shouting men pushing their sheep, goats, and cattle toward the mountains, braying donkeys piled high with bundles, women carrying babies in wooden cradles on their backs, a helter-skelter migration to the mountains.

Mr. Reynolds returned to Camp Maidan-i-Napthun to oversee the No. 2 well, which spudded on March 25th. Dormitories for the workers and the galley and mess hall were by then completed and in full operation. Most of the tools and equipment from Camp Marmatain had been moved to the new workshop. The health of the Europeans was in good condition, partially because I required that water be boiled for all workers.

I was interested in geology and in my mind likened how geologists predict the subsurface by mapping the surface to my diagnosis of disease with only the outer symptoms to offer hints at their cause. When he arrived at camp, I quizzed Mr. Reynolds about the strata.

"The No. 1 is drilling below seven hundred feet, well below the unconformity that Mr. Craig predicted. We encountered a slight sign of oil at a few feet in depth, but since then nothing." He said this with a slight satisfaction. I asked him if the lack of oil signs concerned the directors.

"Of course, but too much is underway for them to simply pull the plug now. The No. 1 has been drilling exceedingly well, much faster than the wells at Marmatain. At this rate, we could reach two thousand feet by mid-summer."

"And if we do not encounter oil by mid-summer, what are the prospects for continuing the operation?" I asked. The question had been on all of our minds. The term of the Canadian drillers' contracts was fast approaching. Mine would be up in June. "Some of the men are making plans to return home."

"Yes, well so am I, Doctor," he replied. "My contract expires this month. I have told the Company I would extend for six months, so long as they would permit me to arrive in London no later than July 31st with a first-class ticket on the P&O."

"Does this mean you think our chances of discovering oil have dimmed?"

"Not at all," he replied. "So long as the two wells are free of major drilling difficulties, by the end of July we should reach the limestone that I believe will be productive. However if we are not through the gypsum by the time the wells reach two thousand feet, I would guess the directors will shut down operations entirely."

"So much money has been spent," I sighed, "with so little to show."

"It's the nature of the business, Dr. Young. This is not a game for the faint of heart or the short of funds. I have predicted we will discover oil here at Musjid-i-Suleiman. I have told the directors as much on several occasions. The question in my mind is whether it will be commercial."

"What do you mean by 'commercial'?" I asked.

"The No. 2 well at Chiah Sourk flows 150 loads a day, an amount equal to about one hundred barrels. A goodly amount, you might say. Yet it's much too small, you see, to warrant the infrastructure necessary to develop an oil field. It's not finding oil that matters, but finding it in *commercial quantities*. Can you imagine the cost to build a pipeline from here to the coast? Not to mention the cost of a refinery."

I had not given consideration to the quantity of oil that might be found. If 100 barrels a day were not commercial, what would be considered enough? To this question, Reynolds made no reply.

Chapter Seven

Lt. A.T. Wilson

My first day at Camp Maidan-i-Napthun, I met Dr. Morris Young, the company's doctor. He had arrived in Persia only a few months before me, and had recently moved his dispensary from Camp Marmatain into a large black tent constructed of sewn and stretched goatskins. Outside the dispensary, natives sat patiently in the lee of the cold wind on the sunny side of the tent waiting their turn for examination. Most Persians I had seen were healthy enough specimens. By the look of this lot, however, they sorely needed Western medicine -- bloody wounds wrapped in filthy patches, appendages covered in sores and rashes, faces broken out in boils, intestinal issues that smelled badly. I wondered what they had done for ailments before Dr. Young arrived, and knew the answer. They cured themselves or died.

Dr. Young was an intense man, not much older than myself. Already he knew enough Persian phrases to manage basic communication with his patients. He constantly asked his assistant for a word or a translation. At dinner that first evening, I asked him how he liked his assignment. I was surprised at his enthusiasm. Bringing medical services to the natives and preventive medicine to the camp workers was a task he seemed to revel in. His primary concern was how to purify the drinking water. Water from the nearby stream was nearly pure naphtha, unfit for man or beast, or for that matter, unfit for the boilers that were running the two rigs.

"I've set up a distillery to purify stream water. We bring it by goatskin bag from two miles away, a terrible inconvenience, but quite necessary."

I agreed. Near the villages, I never drank un-boiled water. "I can't imagine what the natives used for medicine before you arrived."

"It's one of my projects, to learn from them what plants and dosages are used for different treatments. It could help my practice."

The Canadian drillers believed Dr. Young was something of a genius. Even the suspicious tribesmen who relied on ancient shaman and concoctions of brews from desert plants overcame their distrust and fears of medical operations if performed by Dr. Young. Homer said it best. *A good physician, skilled our wounds to heal, is more than armies to the public weal.*

I determined to soak myself in the life and lore of this place – in its geology, natural history, botany, zoology, dialects, ethnology, and archaeology. Because my duties at camp required only a small portion of my time, I spent the spring of 1908 surveying the country, starting with Camp Maidan-i-Napthun, which was on a flat plain or *maidan* in the center of the company's Musjid-iSuleiman drilling operations, and slowly extended my triangulations outwards. As I moved farther north into the mountains, the effort required climbing and descending four or five thousand feet every day. I grew a beard, partly to save trouble when traveling, partly because most Persian tribesmen grew beards. When traveling in tribal territory I often dressed as a Persian, and adopted Persian habits of eating and drinking. It made life much easier and cheaper.

We set out by way of Raghaiwa for Marmatain. Near Ram Hormuz, a few miles south of Marmatain, we passed mounds and ruins our native guide called Qal'eh-I'Khatun. I was fascinated by them, and determined to find out more about the imprint of past civilizations whose remnants dotted the Persian landscape.

On our route we flushed blackleg partridges and smaller quail. At a distance I spotted a wolf, or perhaps it was a leopard, and a cinnamon bear. In the far distance I saw the blue escarpments of limestone and beyond them snow-capped mountains. The weather on our march to Marmatain was uncomfortable. It rained on us for hours. Wet clothes do not trouble me if in the evenings I can dry them while wrapped in wet blankets next to a campfire. But the storm was so violent and the rain so heavy that we had no campfire to keep us warm and dry our clothes. However *heaviness may endure for a night but joy cometh in the morning.*

Camp Marmatain I found to be isolated, desolate, and uninviting. The place smelled of rotten eggs. I was happy the drilling was halted there and moved to Musjid-i-Suleiman.

The closest town of any size to Musjid-i-Suleiman is Shushtar, a flea-bitten, fly-infested picturesque mass of ruins which I visited often, and was intrigued with the ancient diversion dam that split the river. Rock pedestals spanned the rushing waters, one time used for a gristmill. It was yet another magnificent engineering feat of civilizations long disappeared.

Shushtar diversion dam

The ruins at Musjid-i-Suleiman intrigued me as well. Dr. Young knew nothing of their origin but he understood them to be an ancient fire temple. I searched the Song of Solomon for any hint of their origin. Although it was one of my favorite chapters – I read the Bible nightly – I found no mention of such a temple in the land of Elam.

At the ruins I met an ancient holy man bent over a small flame, which must have been sourced by a seep of gases. He chanted words in a language I did not understand. I asked in Persian what he was doing. He neither replied nor looked at me.

I spent a week in the Karun gorges, camping at Bardiqamchi where the Karun runs in a defile with perpendicular cliffs rising a thousand feet on each side. Twenty years ago a massive rock stood in midstream, which set up a great whirlpool that drowned cattle, men, and women every year. However the *Ilkhani* had it blasted to smaller pieces with dynamite, and it was now a ferry crossing.

Rafts made of inflated goatskins tied together carried women and children

Gufa boat

across the half-mile wide river, its water frigid and swollen by snowmelt. Mules and horses swam across, held with head ropes by men on unstable inflated floats. Others paddled *gufa* boats waterproofed with bitumen. A few men swam unaided. I swam across to show that an Englishman was as good as they in the water, which was very cold.

The ferry crossing was at the mouth of a great gorge from which gushed the river's mighty flow. I determined to float the gorge, which no Persian had tried. They advised against it, saying my men and I would be drowned.

I had observed natives crossing a swift torrent while holding onto two inflated goatskins. When the Bakhtiari moved their sheep and cattle across a river, it took a balancing skill to stay on top the bladders, but with a little practice, we felt confident of our chances.

The passage through the gorge was tremendous. Floating past the thousand-foot high limestone cliffs carved no doubt by the erosive power of the river, I experienced a feeling of insignificance, that I and my compatriots are just a speck in the great march of time, and at the same time a feeling of the beauty and awesomeness of God's earth. We saw great fish swimming in clear pools fed by huge springs issuing from the limestone. We passed the remnants of three great bridges, probably dating from Sassanian times. Twelve hours after launching, we reached the ferry crossing at the mouth of the gorge. In celebration, we bought and killed a goat and ate a square meal.

I live so simply that I enjoy a full stomach of meat and rice as much as any of my men and think about it and look forward to it as a landmark in life.

Since Lt. Ranking was in charge of the guards, my oversight of their activities takes only a half an hour or so a day, or at most a few hours a week. The rest of the time I spend working at Persian, either reading or writing, or talking the local dialect, or in surveying and compiling detailed reports for military purposes.

The Bakhtiari tribesmen excited intense interest in me. I envy them their hardy ways, which I try to copy. My only shelter is a tent. Like them, I wear a cotton shirt, loose cotton trousers and a loose felt coat without sleeves, even in the coldest weather and even at night, though it often froze during the winter months.

Bakhtiari shoes are of cotton, the tops woven with great artistry, the thin soles made of folds of old cotton cloth tightly packed and threaded from end to end with strips of rawhide. For scrambling over rocks, shoes of the Bakhtiari were far superior to European boots.

The Bakhtiari are happy, as I was, on one good meal at night and a fairly good meal of dates and bread at midday. Our staple diet was very thin flakes of barley bread or thicker cakes of bread made from acorn flour, ground on a flat stone with a well-rounded smooth boulder and soaked from some days in running water.

We seldom drank fresh milk. Buttermilk was universal, as were curds and butter, sometimes spread fresh on bread but more often clarified and used with rice. As in David's day, when available I lapped water from streams with my right hand. Only townsmen put their noses into the water.

Rice was much in demand. The best sort was red rice roughly husked by pounding it in a wooden mortar. Lentils were a luxury as was meat, which is either boiled when the animal is old and tough, or grilled over a wood fire. I lived on this fare and nothing else, for I could not afford to carry tinned provisions, and would not even if I could. I had never been fitter and could climb all day with nothing but a few ounces of dates and a couple of flaps of bread washed down with buttermilk from some hospitable nomad.

In April the nomads began to leave for the highlands in search of grass. By May I had surveyed all the ground within reach, from Dizful to Ram Hormuz and from the Karun to Ahwaz. Temperatures by then were 110F in my tent. Following local custom, I had deep caves dug into the hillside and spent midday in the cave reading a great deal. I was gradually collecting a library of books dealing with this part of the world, and with Persia in general. At the same time, I busied myself in completing the manuscript of my first big Intelligence

Report.

I did not want to become a Persian expert in a backwater. My ambitions lay in India, not here, though I loved the life. My only fear was lest my present activities might tie me for ten years to this line of work. Apart from anything else, Persia is no place for a married man, even if he is content to remain childless, which is far from my ideas. I am at present with Horace in his youth, *puellis idoneus*, and am not immune to feminine charms.

I was much alive to the beauties of the country. From a hillside camp facing north looking across the Karun, I could gaze at the silver thread of river a thousand feet below and only about half a mile distant to the opposite side, so steep are the slopes. In spring the countryside around me was green except where patches of white revealed the underlying gypsum. To the south and east rose hills of sandstone of as many shades of red as the sandstones of the Devon coast, steeply inclined and so rocky that no grass could grow on them. Just across the Karun a scarp of conglomerate fifteen hundred feet high and almost vertical dominates the gorge. Beyond it a tangle of gypsum hills with overlying sandstone. In the distance the great limestone mass of the Zagros Mountains rose in successions of roughly parallel ranges increasing in height to the north, running NNW. The snow-clad peaks were a hundred miles distant but perfectly clear. It was the sort of view one might see in Switzerland.

The sweetest of music waked me before dawn, the sound of the kids and lambs calling and the dams answering. Each tent has its own flock, and each flock its own shepherd, usually one or two boys. Every sheep and goat was as familiar to them as their own family, even when the flocks mingled. Each flock was milked by the wives and daughters.

Dawn came slowly in the shadows overlooking the Karun. Clear-cut outlines of bare hills of literally every color revealed themselves against an upper background of grey, changing in succession to delicate shades of blue, green, and finally pink. Then the golden disk of the sun rose over the shoulder of the hill and the camp began to stir as the hoarfrost vanished from the surface of my little tent and meager pile of baggage. The hills and plains were carpeted with flowers. In the valleys great beds of wild narcissus grew in profusion. My men would bend low in their stirrups to smell the heady fragrance as they rode slowly through the fields of flowers.

I could remember no time when my mind and eyes and ears enjoyed such a feast of beautiful and interesting sights. As Henry Newbolt wrote, *Oh mother earth, by the great sun above thee, I love thee, O I love thee.*

Spring in the desert is a season of renewal, when God's mercy and grace are revealed in the splendor of nature. *For behold, the winter is past; the rain is over and gone. The flowers appear on earth; the time of the singing of birds is come and the voice of the turtledove is heard in our land. Song of Solomon 2:11-12.* By May, however, the season for renewal quickly faded and the land returned to a season of dormancy and menace.

Shortly after the tribes left for their summer pastures, the holy man I had seen on my first visit to Musjid-i-Suleiman again appeared at the ancient ruins. When I approached him, he scarcely acknowledged my presence, but when I greeted him with, "Allah Akbar", he mumbled a reply which I did not understand. His long white beard extended nearly to his waist. His head was bare, unlike Bakhtiari men, who wore round felt hats. He squatted next to a flame that emanated from a crack in the limestone floor of the ruins. He must have lit the flame himself, else I would surely have noticed it before.

I enquired about his worship, and he answered in Persian with a question, *"This I ask thee, O Lord, answer me truly. Who among those to whom I speak is righteous and who is wicked?"*

I wasn't sure how to reply, but quoted Proverbs. *For the Lord gives wisdom; from His mouth comes knowledge and understanding. He layeth up sound wisdom for the righteous.*

The old man gazed at me for some time, then disregarding my presence, turned his attention back to the flame and began chanting in a dialect I did not recognize. The next time I met Captain Lorimer, I intended to ask him what he knew of the man and his religion.

The ruins at Musjid-i-Sulemian

Chapter Eight

Dr. Morris Y. Young

On the evening of April 8th, a native was brought into camp with what I diagnosed as acute appendicitis. His color was pale, and when I palpated his right abdomen under his ribcage below and to the right of his umbilicus, he moaned from the severe pain. If my diagnosis was correct, within a few days the appendix would rupture and he would die. I figured there was little to lose, so I determined to operate. My training had been a physician with a specialty in eyes, and not as a surgeon, however I had taken anatomy courses and observed operations. Lieutenant Wilson was in camp and I asked him to assist me in the procedure. He readily agreed.

"Wash thoroughly, scrub down with isopropyl alcohol, put on these clothes and gloves," I told him and handed him a clean cotton robe, mask, and hat. "Cover your face and beard. My assistant will drip the chloroform and keep the sweat from my eyes. You will hand me the instruments as I instruct."

"Doctor, I have often wondered how your profession performs an operation. What a lively opportunity!"

Lively opportunity for you, I thought, but not for the chap under the scalpel. Aside from minor sutures, I had never opened a human, nor witnessed an appendectomy.

"Yes, well Lieutenant, if you'll just do as I say, this should be over in an hour."

The temperature was already well above 100F. I had rolled up the side of the tent for better light, and was thankful the wind was not blowing dust as it so often did. The patient was laid out on a wooden table. I had shaved his abdomen and placed a sheet over his body. He looked about wildly, but remained put. Already a large audience of natives gathered near the opening to observe the procedure.

"The main risk," I explained to Wilson, "is to give him too much chloroform. Too much will kill him." I could only imagine the bad publicity this would receive, given the audience. "If he vomits, he'll aspirate, which can cause pneumonia, but it's a risk we must take."

"Just tell me what to do, Doctor."

I had considered a spinal tap with tropacocaine hydrochloride, but wasn't certain where the cauda equina nerves exited the spinal cord. I wished for ether, but it was too volatile to ship. Chloroform was the only choice for anesthesia, and I had secured a quantity with the last shipment of medicines.

"Follow my instructions. I will keep them simple. Scrub up, and we'll be ready to start in twenty minutes."

I fitted the face screen over the patient's face and told my assistant to tell him he would soon be asleep and everything would be fine. I had spoken at length to my assistant about the procedure, explaining the quantity of chloroform to drip onto the mask, but I administered the initial dose. Within two minutes the patient was asleep. I did not want him to be too soundly asleep in fear that he might not wake up, but enough asleep to relax his muscles. To insure that he was unconscious, I gave him a good pinch. When he didn't move, I motioned to Wilson.

"Lieutenant, scalpel please."

I asked my native assistant to take the bottle of chloroform, drip only when I told him to, and then only three drops. I knew from anatomy courses to cut one layer at a time. Gingerly I made a five-inch midline incision from a point just below the umbilicus to the pubic bone, cutting the skin only slightly. With the incision outlined, I told Wilson to be prepared with the hemostat. When I cut into the next layer, a thin layer of fat, as I sliced through each blood vessel I instructed Wilson to clamp the vein with his hemostat.

"Keep the vessel clamped, and point the curve of the hemostat toward me. Now hold it just so until I tie off the blood vessel."

I was practiced at tying sutures, and quickly roped the silk thread behind the hemostat, wrapped a knot, and tied off the end of the vessel. Just before sweat dripped from my brow, my assistant wiped my forehead. One down, I thought.

Slowly I continued to cut through skin and fat, tying each vessel, and wiping the excess blood from the incision. Simple enough, I thought, and continued to cut, clamp, and tie…cut, clamp, and tie. Beneath the fat, the fascia opened easily and without bleeding, exposing two abdominal muscles. I knew from caring for wounds that cutting into the muscle to get to the abdominal cavity would be a bloody mess. By probing with my hands, I was able to spread the two abdominal muscles apart. Good, I thought, good. I looked up at Wilson. He nodded.

Below the muscles was the peritoneum, the lining of the abdominal cavity. Grasping the peritoneum with a hemostat, I opened it a few millimeters, and looked into the abdominal cavity. With a quick slice, I exposed the patient's intestines. The smell of rotted meat filled the air. I knew the appendix was right at the end of the large intestine, so I lifted the whole mass of guts and started pulling on the small intestine hand over hand, as if I was pulling in a rope. When I felt where it expanded into the large intestine, I lifted the mass of entrails so I could see, and there it was, an enlarged appendix, discolored and swollen larger than my middle finger. I was relieved my diagnosis was correct.

"Is the ugly-looking worm his appendix?" asked Wilson.

I nodded and held still while my assistant wiped my forehead. Thank goodness it wasn't July. The patient moved slightly and I told my assistant to apply three more drops of chloroform.

"Ok Lieutenant, take the clamp while I hold the appendix where you can see it, and clamp it off close to the cecum."

"The cecum?"

"The big intestine, right where it attaches. Leave room for a stub."

Wilson did exactly as I asked and I quickly snipped off the appendix, dropped it into a pan on the floor, and tied the stump with silk thread. I dipped the hemostat in phenol and pressed the end of the stub to sterilize the cut, then pushed the cecum back into the right lower quadrant of the abdominal cavity and looked up. Wilson stared at me and nodded but didn't understand my relief.

"Hold each layer together like this," I told him. "You hold. I'll stitch."

Together we put the layers back together one at a time. I sewed them with a whipstitch using a surgical needle and silk thread. In what seemed like ten minutes, but was in actuality more than an hour, we were finished.

"Good job," I said. "Thank you, Wilson." I thanked my assistant, too, and told him to thoroughly clean the patient's abdomen with alcohol and to lower the tent wall. I noticed the group of natives was even larger, and were murmuring among themselves in excited tones.

When we had removed our robes and masks and were cleaning up, Wilson asked me if I had noticed the natives' reaction when I snipped off the appendix. I had been concentrating too much on the operation to pay attention to my audience.

"Did you see the boy steal the appendix from the pan?" he asked.

"What are you talking about?"

"While we were stitching up the patient, a young boy crawled beneath our feet, snatched the severed appendix from the pan, and ran with it back to the patient's family. They crowded around while he showed them his prize. I can't imagine what they were thinking, but if the man lives, you'll replace the Prophet."

Little did Wilson know how anxious I had been, but the case had been straightforward and, thankfully, I had encountered no complications.

"Yes, well he should live. I don't know about replacing the Prophet."

Four days later the patient walked out of the dispensary, climbed onto his horse and rode back to his village.

Wilson and I had become good friends. I found him to be curious about many subjects. Even though I was no conversationalist, we often talked late into the night. His father, who had been headmaster at Clifton, had influenced him substantially. He told me he was a faithful and practicing Christian, but could not accept the virgin birth or the miracles of Jesus except as allegory.

Wilson was right about one thing. Following the successful appendectomy, more and more villagers came to the dispensary. Word of the appendectomy must have spread because a few local sheiks and one or two *khans* began depending on our services as well. It started when I was returning from Ahwaz onboard the *Shushan*. The Governor of Dizful was a passenger and was ill and called for my medical advice. I administered to his needs and afterwards enjoyed a pleasant conversation with him. He was exceedingly friendly, and notwithstanding his failure to give Captain Lorimer a safe conduct through his country, he promised to allow Lt. Wilson to survey wherever he chose.

On that same voyage, the notorious Sheikh Farrhan was aboard and sent word for me. To judge from the great ovation he received all along the Karun – thousands of natives crowding about the banks of the river and cheering him -- I could only conclude he exercised some influence over the populace. As the slave of today may in this country be the master of tomorrow, I of course spoke with him. He was very amicable, and asked me to administer to his sick child, to which I agreed.

When the *Shushan* reached Dar-i-Khazineh, the Sheikh and his retinue asked me to accompany them downstream across the river, where the boy was in camp. Close to the riverbank floated a large, strange-looking barge. A hundred or more skins, each the inflated body of a goat, were tied together for flotation and upon them were thrown a covering of richly-embroidered rugs. On one end of the barge a canopy of red silk held by four posts served as an open-sided enclosure. The Sheikh ordered his men to carry him, his family, and me on their backs to the barge, where we disembarked and sat on silk pillows under the canopy. The Sheikh informed me that the raft had been built overnight. It looked and felt more substantial than an overnight project, but I believed him.

At a signal, the boatmen pushed off and the swift current carried us rapidly back down the river. As it was late in the day, the flowing river's torrent was tinted gold by the setting sun. We disembarked on the back of the Sheikh's men and proceeded to an encampment of tents.

The Sheikh's servants covered us with attention. One brought a silver bowl and another a silver pitcher. From these they poured water over our hands for washing. A sumptuous meal was laid out. No women were present. I did not know if this meant there were none in camp or if they were out of sight.

The next morning I looked after the Sheikh's young son. Like so many here, he was suffering from gastro-intestinal complications. I dosed him with belladonna and urotropine, and left a quantity of pepsin. Within an hour he felt better. The Sheikh was pleased and ordered his men carry me back across the river and to provide a horse for my journey back to Camp Maidan-i-Napthun.

Chapter Nine

Lt. A.T. Wilson

Toward the end of April, Reynolds told me the directors had advised him that their funds were nearly exhausted and that they could not see their way to raising further capital for work under the Concession. Since Captain Lorimer was away and as I had no cipher, I wrote hastily to Major Cox in Burshire to tell him what appeared to me to be a short-sighted decision, one which might involve the cancellation of the D'Arcy Concession. The search for oil would quite certainly be continued, but by the Germans or by one of Rockefeller's companies. In neither case would any difficulty be found in raising capital. After all, the Concession covered more than three-fourths of Persia. I was amazed that the directors of the Consolidated Syndicate Limited should risk the complete loss of a concession covering all oil deposits over the greater part of Persia without consulting the Foreign Office of India.

I discussed the whole situation long and earnestly with Reynolds. He was a self-trained geologist. My own father was a geologist. The smattering of understanding I had acquired from him convinced me that Reynolds' confidence was justified and that his courage would be rewarded. In the bitterness of his soul he said many hard things of the faint-hearted and peevish men in Glasgow who were ready to abandon an enterprise which might mean so much to Britain and Persia.

"I recommended they continue drilling until we reach the limestone," he told me. "The directors agreed to consult with Mr. Redwood. Faint-hearted or foolhardy, neither has a place in this business. If they hadn't the courage to see the project through, they should never have taken the risk."

"Mr. Reynolds, I wrote Major Cox in Bushire a letter expressing dismay at your directors' intentions to stop drilling."

He expressed his thanks but dismissed it as futile.

In mid-May, I returned to Musjid-i-Suleiman from a week of surveying and found Reynolds in the mess hall alone, smoking his pipe. He was in something of a contemplative mood, which was unusual for him.

"Lieutenant Wilson, good to see you," he said. "How are your surveys coming along? The temperature is warming up a bit, isn't it?"

"Yes, sir," I replied, and repeated that I had sent a letter to the head political officer in the Persian Gulf for the Indian Foreign Office, in hopes that he might influence any decision by the CSL directors to stop drilling.

"I appreciate your efforts, Lieutenant," Reynolds replied. "I have asked our directors for written confirmation to halt."

"How deep are the wells now?" I asked.

"We ran 8" casing to 924 feet in the No. 1 on May 6th. The unconformity anticipated by Mr. Craig has not been met. Three days ago while drilling in shale the bit became unscrewed from the sinker and was left in the hole. It is now lying over to one side at the bottom and will be difficult to fish out. As the strata we are drilling is soft, we are trying to move the bit upright to latch hold if it. To this end I have sent to Marmatain to bring over a special tool."

I couldn't imagine latching onto a thousand-pound bit at the bottom of a thousand-foot deep hole, and asked how great were the odds for success.

"Difficult to calculate," he replied. "A great irony, isn't it? Just as the hole starts giving off a strong smell of gas, of petroleum gas, our directors talk of abandoning our efforts, and now this."

In April he had fumed at his directors' short-sightedness, at their lack of tenacity and unwillingness to leave the comforts of Glasgow to visit the site where so much of their shareholders' money had been spent. Now he seemed oddly resigned.

I could only imagine what he felt. For seven years Reynolds had faced every political, logistical, managerial, and mechanical challenge imaginable, only to be told to shut down drilling before reaching the limestones. I told him the directors of CSL were Scotsmen of the hard-headed, short-sighted sort who would not hesitate to sell the concession to Russia if they saw a profit.

"A great irony," he repeated.

Reynolds said he would remain at Camp Maidan-i-Napthun for another week to try to recover the lost bit. He announced to the drillers and the other Europeans in camp that operations might soon be concluded. The drillers were excited at the news. Most of them did not look forward to another summer in

Persia.

I asked the doctor what he intended to do if drilling stopped.

"What to do?" he said. "You have a place in the Army of India. I can only return to Glasgow and take up a medical career. The past year here has sped by, has it not? It seems I've only been here a short time. I took a risk and was hoping to make a contribution."

The doctor was not the literary sort, but I could not help but quote Omar:

> *The worldly hope men set their hearts upon*
> *Turns ashes – or it prospers, and anon,*
> *Like snow upon the desert's dusty face,*
> *Lighting a little hour or two – is gone.*

After the special fishing tool arrived from Marmatain, Reynolds and the drillers made a half-dozen attempts to latch onto the bit. On the third day their efforts finally met with success. Reynolds' mood immediately improved. After drilling resumed, he sometimes bent his ear over the hole, listening, he said, for sounds of bubbling. The following day we could all smell gas, and in the sunlight could see it rising from the hole. We seemed so close to success. How could the directors arbitrarily stop operations without examining the site and making a pragmatic assessment?

The No. 2 well was drilling without problems below 700 feet. The No. 1 had already surpassed 1000 feet. Reynolds told me that a comparison of the two holes led him to believe that there was little difference in the deeper strata passed through by both wells, which he deemed a good sign. However the No. 2 had given off no sign of oil or gas and on the 24th it struck a very hard bed of salt. Then it happened, almost unexpectedly.

On May 26th, 1908, I was sleeping outside my tent close by the No. 1. At 4 a.m. I was awakened by shouting and a roaring noise. I ran to the well and beheld a spectacle I will never forget. Oil gushed fifty feet or more above the top of the derrick to a height of more than a hundred feet. The black liquid quickly covered the drillers and all of the equipment. The accompanying gas nearly suffocated the workers. It was a great event. We had struck oil in the No. 1 Musjid-i-Suleiman at 1,180 feet.

Discovery Well

PART 11

Development

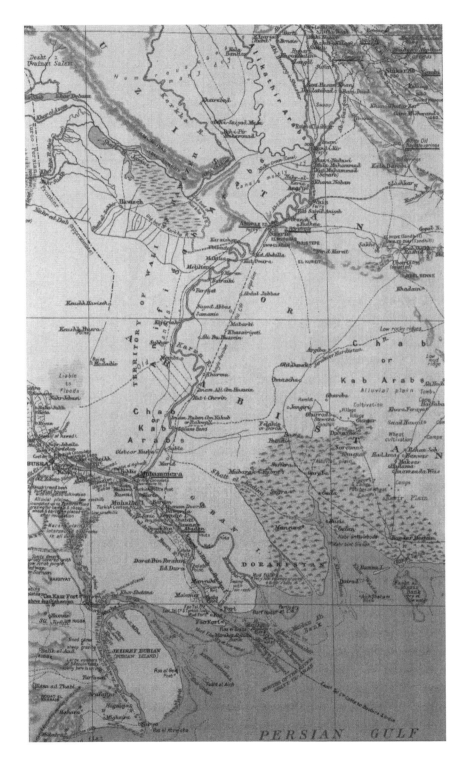

Chapter Ten

Lt. A.T. Wilson

Reynolds immediately took command. His first concern was to save as much of the oil as possible. He ordered workers to dig a ditch to divert the oil from the wellbore. Other workers were put to work digging a great pit about two hundred yards away. At the same time he and a team of drillers attempted to cap the well, which was no easy task. Finally they managed to fit a wellhead over the flow and by first light the oil had been diverted into the ditch and from there into the pit.

At my first opportunity I saddled my horse, rode to Shushtar, and telegraphed the news to Captain Lorimer in Ahwaz: "See Psalm 104 verse 15 third sentence and Psalm 114 verse 8 second sentence". As I had no codebook, I figured quotes from the Christian Bible would sufficiently encrypt the message. The first verse says *"that he may bring out of the earth oil to make him a cheerful countenance".* The second reads *'the flint stone into a springing well.'*

Upon my return to camp later in the afternoon, I was still elated at our success, and approached Mr. Reynolds to congratulate him. His clothing was oil-stained; his hat ruined by the oil. Upon my announcement that I had informed Captain Lorimer by telegraph, his countenance clouded.

"Lieutenant, we have not even measured the amount of flow. Is the well commercial? Have we found only a small pool? Will it stop flowing by sunset? It's too soon to report to your superiors."

"Yes sir," was all I could manage, even though I knew my superiors expected me to report the development immediately. It was of course too early to know whether the discovery was commercial. But even the possibility of such an outcome, after all the years of trial and effort, called for a telegraph to the Foreign Office, if not for a celebration.

"Your telegram forces me to telegraph my superiors before I have all the information," he said and wheeled back to direct the workers.

That evening I wrote my father and mother a letter, as I did almost daily.

It is a great event: it remains to be seen whether the output will justify a pipeline to the coast, without which the field cannot be developed. It will provide all our ships east of Suez with fuel: it will strengthen British influence in these parts. It will make us less dependent on foreign-owned oil fields; it will be some reward to those who have ventured such great sums as have been spent. I hope it will mean some financial reward to the engineers who have persevered so long, in spite of their wretched top-hatted directors in Glasgow, in this inhospitable climate. The only disadvantage is personal to myself – it will prolong my stay here!

The test was performed from 6 p.m. on the 27th until 6 p.m. on the 28th into 400-gallon tanks. The flow was taken off the wellhead from a two-inch tube. After the test the valve was closed and during the night, the gas forced the oil up to the surface from the back of the 10" casing. The gas appeared to have an enormous pressure. The flow was measured at 297 barrels per day.

Reynolds was not happy with the amount. He telegraphed his directors but said nothing, he told me, of the commercial aspects. We all understood that the flow was too little to justify the huge sums necessary to develop the field.

Reynolds was more encouraged a few days later on May 31st, when the No. 2 was at 915 feet. Reynolds told Dr. Young and me at dinner that hole conditions seemed to indicate the proximity of oil.

"I found the cuttings to show unmistakable evidence of oil being near by their smell, and the slight evolution of gas on emptying the pump. I anticipate we shall strike oil at about the same level it was struck at No. 1."

He told us he had telegraphed his directors and asked whether to continue drilling. If No. 2 proved to be productive, we were without tanks to contain it. He also asked for permission to move the machinery and rig from the No. 1 borehole to the No. 3 location.

"When will we know if the No. 1 is a great discovery or just another Chiah Sourkh?" asked Dr. Young.

"It depends on future development," replied Reynolds. "Since the No. 2 is more than a mile from No. 1, if it produces oil, even at the rate of the No. 1, and if it produces from the same horizon, we may have made a significant discovery. How significant can only be determined by drilling more wells. At this stage, it is mere speculation."

Reynolds was not one for hyperbole. My excitement from witnessing the great flow of oil shooting over the No. 1 derrick had changed to somber reservations about the No. 2 and the prospects for having discovered a large field.

Gas was struck at No. 2 borehole late in the evening on June 5th. I had just returned from Shushtar. Reynolds was still in camp. He had been here since mid-May, longer than at any other time, and was still waiting for instructions from Glasgow whether to move the rig from No. 1 to the No. 3 location, and whether to continue drilling the No. 2 into the oil zone. The next morning oil was found at the top of the No. 2 hole and the smell of gas was even stronger. Reynolds directed the drillers to run 9 inch casing to 1,010 feet, and to move it up and down every other day to keep it free, pending instructions from Glasgow. He ordered me to return to Shushtar to send an encoded telegram to the directors, and if that failed, to telegraph Busrah in care of the British Consul.

The following day oil started flowing out the top of No. 2's casing. Reynolds immediately ordered the drillers to screw a wellhead onto the casing. While securing the wellhead, oil suddenly shot some thirty feet above the derrick. Thankfully the flow quickly died. As soon as it ceased, Reynolds ordered the workers to tighten the wellhead to the casing so that the flow could be controlled.

At dinner he told Dr. Young and me that the No. 2 made him think we had found a sizeable oil field, possibly a significant one if additional wells had better flow rates. He also mentioned his contract was drawing to a close, and he would be returning to England by August 1st.

"I am not certain yet if I shall return to Persia," he told us. "My contract expires at the end of July. Whether I return will depend on what the Company offers me to extend. I will request time off during the summer months."

I glanced at the thermometer. It registered 118F degrees inside the dining tent. Dr. Young and I both commiserated with his comment.

"A noteworthy letter arrived from Glasgow," he said, and removed a folded envelope from his shirt pocket and handed it to me.

14 May 1908

G.B. Reynolds, Esq.,
    c/o Messrs. Lynch Brothers
    Ahwaz

Dear Sir:

With reference to your queries in a number of your recent letters re closing up if operations are unsuccessful and employees come home, we would like if possible to put the two wells at Musjid-i-Suleiman down to 1,500/1,600 feet and if no oil is found at this depth, to abandon operations, close down, and bring as much of the plant as is possible down to Mohammerah. You will therefore arrange your men to fit in with this proposition. If you specially want home by the 1st of September – the expiry of your additional six months – and you think that Mr. Bradshaw is capable of taking charge until the close of operations and the removal of the plant etc, to Mohammerah kindly allow him to do so, but if you do not consider him capable of seeing everything closed down we would ask you to arrange to remain yourself until the close. We are willing to pay Mr. Bradshaw the additional wages he asks for the time you require him without making any further fresh agreement.

In the case of Dr. Young, you should engage him for a further year and give him notice four months before you close down.

With reference to mechanics, smiths, etc. you will require to make the best arrangement you can. Elisha will, of course, remain until the close.

With regard to packing of the plant, you will arrange same to stand a voyage to Burma. Is it possible to charter a small vessel to carry it direct there?

As we wish to take Mr. D'Arcy with us in this matter and have not had an opportunity of consulting him, we attach three temporary symbols. You might wire us an approximate date on which you expect to have the two wells down to 1,500/1,600 feet. We know you cannot give this information accurately but you can perhaps give us an idea.

"What do you think of it, Lt. Wilson?" His expression could be described as wry, but he did not smile.

"I think it was good that you convinced them to continue drilling," I said, and handed the letter to Dr. Young. "Otherwise they would have abandoned the whole endeavor only a few feet from discovering the first significant oil field in Persia."

At this comment, Reynolds smiled. I was reminded how seldom he looked happy.

"Let's hope it is significant," he said. "I doubt if I convinced them to continue," he replied. "Dr. Young," he looked at the doctor, "if you are willing, your contract has been extended for another year."

Had I not discussed the matter with him in April, when the directors originally recommended halting operations, I might believe that the decision to continue drilling was the directors alone. The only written evidence was the letter he showed to Dr. Young and me. Perhaps they would have reached the decision to continue drilling without Reynolds' encouragement. But I think not.

By July the temperature reached 125F degrees in my tent every day. A hot wind blew continuously from the northwest, the *shamal* of Mesopotamia. My men, hardy Punjabi, found it hard to endure. Their mounts found it even harder.

By sending a spare horse ahead, I could travel from Camp Maidan-i-Napthun to Ahwaz, covering nearly a hundred miles in a day. Dr. Young said that I was a standing contradiction of all medical laws. After three months, I was as fit as ever, though thin. I ate what the country provided but ate very little so did not overwork my stomach. I found the survey work to be rewarding, albeit strenuous.

I left camp at 4 p.m. on July 7th 1908: 124F and rode or walked for six hours. Ate some dates and bread and slept under the stars till 4 a.m. Then four hours journeying – a long halt under the scanty shade of a small tree till 4 p.m., then forward again to the foot of the Mungasht Mountains with a week's dry barley bread, thin as paper, some dates, lentils, curry powder and a live goat. On July 8th I spent the heat of the day in a cave, sending my mount and two mules eight miles for water. Then a stiff climb up the rocky slopes, sparsely wooded with a kind of oak. It was a joy to be among trees again. My guide spoke glowingly of a spring half way up the hill – sweet as sugar, clear as crystal, abundant as a river. When we reached it we found it almost dry, choked with the droppings of ibex and bear. We cleaned it out and got a bucket full in the course of half an hour.

The guide was an uncouth son of the hills – the accuracy of what he said must be judged by the probable state of his own feelings and his estimate of our own, like a journalist.

The next day brought me to the Malamir plain, famous for Sassanian bas-reliefs. The track which I followed was well-graded and walled and in places, well-paved. It is certainly Sassanian dating from 500 A.D. or so, or perhaps even older. I shot a mountain sheep on the way down. We ate it that night, another feast, so we gave the goat to our guide in lieu of cash. On paper I made a profit, and he was well content.

I spent a day crossing the Malamir plain, following a track described by Layard. From this point the map showed a blank, "unexplored", so I moved slowly, surveying all the way.

Next day down the Karun, which here rises when floods are heavy as much as fifty feet, I saw the pillars of a bridge standing stark in the stream, fully exposed to the tremendous force of the water but looking as if they had been erected a few years ago. How the builders – it is certain that the bridge dates either from Sassanian or early Muslim times – were able to erect these solid masonry pillars in the midst of a swift stream, with such strong cement that it has bound stone to stone perfectly and made the whole pillar a single monolith, is something worthy of close investigation.

I spent another ten days surveying the region. Twice I swam the river, and placed my survey instruments inside an inflated skin. I love this life, and although I missed my regiment in India, I felt my surveys were accomplishing a meaningful service which might one day be useful to England.

Reynolds left for London on August 1ˢᵗ. He placed Bradshaw in charge of work at the camp, and said he would return if given an acceptable contract. On the 8ᵗʰ of September, I wrote my parents:

> Reynolds will not get fame, money or credit for all the work
> he has done here. He is a great man, who inspires real respect
> in Englishmen and Canadians and real affection in Persians

and Arabs. He is not easy to deal with and his correspondence
with his directors is sarcastic and bitter.

On second thought, the *khans* disliked him because he did not cave in to
their demands for more money. The drillers respected him, but did not like
him because he was not sympathetic to many of their complaints. The workers
were afraid of him.

The No. 3 well spudded on the 28th of July and on the 4th of September, at
280 feet, it blew out, flowing at a rate of more than 3,000 barrels of oil per
day. Bradshaw had just completed two large pits; one held 300,000 gallons and
the other 500,000 gallons. Within a week both pits overflowed. The oil was
allowed to run into the Tenbi. A week later the flow had slowed and by the 25th
of September it had halted altogether. Only 10,000 barrels were wasted.

I regularly interrupted my surveying to report to Captain Lorimer in
Ahwaz. I found his assistant, Ahmed Khan, to be most helpful in answering
my questions about the local customs and dialects of different tribes whose
territory I passed through.

The Times daily edition was always available on Captain Lorimer's table.
Though it was six weeks old, it was still news to me. I particularly enjoyed
The Times Literary Supplement, and thus stayed reasonably informed of the
outside world. For local news I also relied on the Captain's observations. Events
in Teheran, he informed me, were dicey.

"Shah Muhammad Ali is continuously overruling the parliament. The
change from more than two thousands years of dictatorship to a shared power
with politicians is not an easy transition."

"I can't imagine it is," I said. "Why would the Shah want to share power?"

"He doesn't want to. Mr. Preece, our consul in Isfahan, told me that ever since
the Shah succeeded to the throne, his reign has led to greater discontent and
corruption. He is addicted to greed and duplicity, and among other vices, he is
a drunkard. He has endeavored by all means in his power, not even shrinking
from the most repelling atrocities, to extinguish the popular movement to
liberty."

"Can the constitutional movement survive here in Persia?" I asked.

"The East is not meant for parliaments," Captain Lorimer replied.
"Parliaments are the modern road for ambitious men to gain power and wealth,
but will never take root in this soil."

"It took England a few hundred years for Parliament to implement its authority to govern. Perhaps Persians expect too much to quickly."

"Since we signed the Entente with Russia last year, I might add without input from Persia, any chances of Persian autonomy are dead. The idea of a reformed Persian state was never what we and Russia intended."

"What *was* intended?" I asked.

"I suppose the intent was to ease the animus between Britain and Russia. Germany is our common threat."

"Because of its naval build-up?"

"Admiral Fisher believes that Kaiser Wilhelm's naval build-up is a direct challenge to our supremacy at sea. He says a threat to the British Navy is a threat to the empire."

I knew of Admiral John Fisher. Behind his back he is called Jacky Fisher. He is the First Sea Lord, and many people believe he is the greatest admiral since Nelson.

"But have we not been building ships, too?"

"With Mr. Asquith now at the helm, the Liberals are pushing for social reform. Lloyd George and Churchill want Russia to build more ships and ask Germany to slow the tempo of battleship construction so that our own Naval Estimates can be reduced in order that social programs can be afforded."

"Will Germany agree?" I asked.

"It's doubtful. Admiral Fisher predicts if their battleship construction continues, we will fight a war with Germany."

"Really…fight a war with Germany? Do you believe Admiral Fisher is correct?

"He makes a point. Why should a continental power like Germany try to match our naval strength unless to challenge us at sea?"

"Depending on Russia to build more ships seems a risky way to insure our own safety. Is that why have we made agreements with France and Russia?"

"I question whether such agreements are advisable. For years we adopted Lord Salisbury's doctrine of 'splendid isolation' and avoided entanglements with continental nations. Under our new leadership, Britain's foreign policy is tied with other countries'. Events in Bosnia may presage the future," replied Captain Lorimer.

"What events in Bosnia?" I had not read the newspapers in the last month.

"Emperor Joseph proclaimed annexation of Bosnia and Herzegovina. Germany supported Austria. Russia sided with the Serbs. We have an entente with Russia. War seemed imminent until Russia backed down."

"I swear," I said, "if I'm stuck in Persia when war breaks out, I shall resign my commission if they don't send me to the front."

"Lieutenant," Captain Lorimer advised, "you should be patient. In spite of Admiral Fisher's predictions, Britain has maintained peace and open seaways throughout the world for the past one hundred years. I see no reason why diplomacy cannot continue to bridge our differences. After all, the European monarchies only need to call a cousin or a niece or nephew to resolve any crisis. It's all in the family."

"All in the family, maybe, but so help me, if we become entangled in a war, or even a good skirmish, I want to be at the front."

Captain Lorimer laughed. "It's easy to speak like a warrior."

"I don't mean to imply that I dislike my duties here. I love the surveying, and the wildness of the country and its tribes."

"As do I. And the poetry. Have you read Hafiz?"

"Who is Hafiz?"

"A Persian poet from the 14th century who lived more than two hundred years after Omar Khayyam."

"I love the *Rubaiyat*," I replied, and began to quote:

> "Wake! For the Sun, who scatter'd into flight
> The Stars before him from the Field of Night,
> Drives Night along with them from Heav'n, and strikes
> The Sultan's Turret with a Shaft of Light."

"If you love the *Rubaiyat*, you will love Hafiz as well," he replied. "Gertrude Bell translated his works."

Little did I suspect then that Gertrude Bell, whom I had never heard of, would work for me -- at first in friendship, and later as adversaries -- in organizing the civil government of Mesopotamia. Captain Lorimer answered Omar with a quote from Hafiz.

> "Oh cup-bearer, set my glass afire,
> With the light of wine! Oh minstrel, sing:
> The world fulfilleth my heart's desire!"

"Hafiz sounds like Omar!" I said. "*Set my glass afire with the light of wine.* Visual, isn't it? Your verse reminds me of something I'd like to ask you about the native religions here. Do you know of an ancient holy person who worships at the ruins of Musjid-i-Suleiman? I found him there twice chanting over flames, but he would not engage in conversation with me."

"I have not seen him, but I'd wager he is a Zoroastrian, a religion here long before Christianity. Their temples were built over seeps of natural gas. Can you imagine living in the Bronze Age when the world was lit only be wood fire and suddenly finding a source of warmth and light that burned for eternity?"

"The eternal flame...what a powerful symbol. Do people still claim to be Zoroastrians?"

"Oh yes, especially along the foothills where seepages of natural gas occur. Fire temples still exist at Hush Kourie and Nasr-i-Shirin. In this country, the Prophet is a newcomer. Have you read *Also Sprach Zarathustra* by Nietzsche?"

"The German philosopher? I've heard of him," I said. Captain Lorimer's breadth of knowledge, which he called his "residual pool", continuously amazed me.

"Nietzsche's *Zarathrustra* echoes the ministry of Jesus in the New Testament. Zoroastrian stories have parallels in the Old Testament. I'll lend you my copy. After you read it, let's discuss the parallels and the differences."

He took a book from a shelf and handed it to me. The pages were heavily notated. "Was Zoroaster a man or a religion?" I asked.

"Like Christ, he was a man whose message became a religion. His was the first monotheistic religion and eventually was adopted by the Achaemenians. About 550 B.C. Darius, the son of Cyrus, linked the legitimacy of his descent with *Ahura Mazda*, Zoroastrianism's supreme being. Central to Zoroaster is the cosmic struggle between good and evil. *But of the tree of the knowledge of good and evil, thou shalt not eat; for in the day that thou eatest thereof thou shalt surely die.*"

"Zoroaster sounds like Genesis!" I was astounded at the similarity.

"Exactly. Many of the Old Testament's roots are found in Zoroastrian beliefs. Rawlinson believed Cyrus was 'God's anointed' in Isaiah and in Ezra and Nehemiah."

"Isaiah and Ezra of the Old Testament?" I was again surprised.

"It was Cyrus who freed the Jews from Babylonian captivity so they could return to Jerusalem and rebuild Solomon's Temple. His son Xerxes married Esther and lived at Susa. Here we walk in their footsteps."

I asked if there was a connection between Solomon's Temple in Jerusalem and the ruins near the oil discovery, and quoted 1 Kings 5:3 *The Lord promised my father David, "Your son, whom I will make King after you, will build a temple for me.*

"It's a possibility that the ruins at Musjid-i-Suleiman date from Solomon's times," he answered. "I asked the archeologist de Morgan to examine them. He told me those at the oil camp follow the same Phoenician design described in the Book of Kings as Solomon's Temple in Jerusalem, but he is too consumed with Susa for a close examination."

I couldn't help but wonder if the name didn't convey its connection to King Solomon. "With the discovery of oil," I said, "perhaps the ruins should be re-named Solomon's Mine."

During the long hot summer days when I was not surveying, I spent hours on the rig, sometimes helping the Canadian drillers. They lived in small domed stone houses not far from my tent. They were independent men, good-hearted but rough. Only the head driller, MacNaughton, had much technical knowledge. The drillers constantly complained about their food, eschewing fresh food in favor of "canned" provisions. They lived uncomfortably, and found no satisfaction in the orderly presentation of food in which every Persian takes pride. Their conversation was filled with small grievances.

Last week I hosted a dinner for them in my tent, borrowing their tables and cutlery. I served a soup made from the bones of an old cow that my cavalrymen had killed and eaten. This was followed by chicken stuffed with raisins, pistachio nuts and almonds, boiled first and then grilled with a sauce made of walnuts and green chilies, garnished with rice and egg plant. Then came figs, apricots, cherries and stewed plums, three kinds of melon, cucumber, lettuce, and a cream cheese made in my kitchen from milk. The freshly ground coffee was pure mocha; otherwise, everything was grown locally.

Following the meal I served rum made by taking a big watermelon, extracting the seeds and filling it with brown sugar. After a month of hanging in the kitchen, it held a pint or so of good, pure, strong liquor.

My guests took their fill of every course and began to complain of their own food.

"Only fellows like you can afford to live so well," said one to me.

My pay was infinitely smaller than theirs. I replied that *their* cook had prepared the dinner, and that all they had eaten and drunk was bought in the nearest bazaar and was the "dirty native food" they despised. I hoped that the meal would wean them from the mule loads of tinned provisions they consumed every month.

In August I commissioned a larger tent, one with four doors, two of which were closed all the time to keep out the burning wind. From the other doors I could keep watch of my men and the horses. I kept the horses from wandering toward the river to a ravine which was so full of gas that foxes, jackals, porcupines, jerboas, and even birds were often found dead in.

Every evening at sunset I climbed the three-hundred foot gypsum hill behind my tent for the view and the fresh air. Below I observed the newly built road, over which often passed droves of mules or donkeys bringing wood or straw, and carts or jims, which are like English timber wains, bringing machinery and pipes, each pulled by from eight to twelve mules. More than nine hundred mules were employed in keeping the camp supplied with provisions and equipment for drilling.

The local laborers were well paid, but had to pay the head of his gang, and the head had to pay his village, who in turn paid the *khans*. It was their form of taxation, and was not so harsh as to discourage enterprise but enough to benefit the entire tribal group. It was much cheaper than our Indian system and required no officials, no pensions, and no paper.

The nomads with their sheep and goats were in the mountains until cold weather drove them back to the foothills. Apart from those who worked the oil fields, those Bakhtiari who were not herders lived in the villages and produced the food. These tribesmen lived in reed huts, and waited patiently for the first rains to plow. Now and then a party of local Bakhtiari tribesmen rode by, looking like assassins, decked out with Martini-Henry rifles, cartridge belts, and knives.

My survey work was done on my own responsibility and mostly at my own expense. Hence I did not travel with tents, tables, beds, chairs, and camp baths. The Foreign Department did not give me orders, which could have been misinterpreted, but left me free to go where I cared. If all went well, I was praised. If anything went wrong, they could blame me. It was really a good system, so long as I reported to gentlemen like Captain Lorimer or Major Cox, whom I had never met but who would act as a buffer if necessary.

In October, when the weather had finally cooled, I rode to Camp Marmatain and from there, planned a two-day journey to Dishmuk, a place hitherto unvisited by any European. The region was unmapped and rather inaccessible, and was the center of the Kuhgula country which lay between Behbehan and Isfahan. I took a good supply of purgatives, quinine, and some telescopes as gifts. I rode my best horse for the sake of prestige and appearance. In Persia a man was known by his mount and his accouterments.

The Kuhgula were notorious robbers. Their aeries were so inaccessible that no Persian governor had any success controlling them. I thought if I could get in touch with them, I might be able to secure the safety of the Lynch road from Ahwaz to Isfahan.

I camped at the foot of the great limestone mountains which run from near Behbehan to Malamir. I was not welcomed. Guides were promised but did not arrive. They were frightened both of the Kuhgula and of oil development. I could sympathize. European penetration did not always help an oriental country to a happier life. These people preferred to bear the ancients ills they know rather than to risk new and unknown trials.

I carried no food and could buy only buttermilk, very dry bread, and dates. Finally I procured the services of a guide. Two hours after we started up the long valley leading to Dishmuk, he refused to go farther, saying he would be killed by the fierce Telbis, who would take me prisoner and hold me for ransom. My servants also took fright, so I sent them all back and went on alone, with my best horse, a fine stallion of very good breed, my best rifle, and some presents.

An hour later shots were fired over my head. I shouted friendly words, but more shots followed. I could not see the riflemen but I judged from their shooting that they were not out to kill. So I dismounted, took cover, loaded and fired a few rounds, and shouted more friendly protests.

Presently a wild man appeared, unarmed and clearly frightened. I said I was alone, on a visit to Ali Murad Khan, Telbi of Dishmuk. He ran back, returned in a few moments with four armed men to whom I repeated the tale. They announced they were Ali Murad's men and would escort me to him, which they did with rough courtesy.

They were the wildest lot in speech and appearance that I had yet encountered, and spoke an almost unintelligible dialect with a lot of Pehlevi or old Persian words. One of them had a homemade sling and killed a partridge with a stone at thirty yards to show his skill. They were thin, tough, wiry, barefoot, wore spare homespun clothes, and leapt from rock to rock like goats. They would make good infantry if not put into boots and drilled too much.

Another hour brought us to the top of the pass from whence I looked down on Dishmuk, a collection of reed huts in the center of a plain nestled around a white fort built upon a limestone hillock. Limestone mountains sparsely wooded with oak rose up three or four thousand feet on every side.

The entire village turned out to see who I was. At the foot of the paved track which led steeply up to the fort, a son of Ali Murad met me. He was a very handsome youth of twenty or so, magnificently built, with fine delicate features. He greeted me in the local dialect with courtesy, as if he was accustomed to receiving strangers, and escorted me to the door of the fort, where I dismounted and entered. Here the Khan himself met me. He was a man of fifty, handsome as his son, a dignified figure dressed in the manner of Persians almost a century ago.

Ali Murad praised me for leaving my former escort of craven dogs and coming alone. I need fear nothing, he said. The Telbi knew how to treat honored guests.

Before entering the room I removed my Persian travelling shoes. A new pair was brought for my wear in the fort. Tea was served, and coffee. Then came talk and innumerable questions. Dinner was served. Being an infidel, I was given a separate dish of mutton and rice.

After ceremonially washing with an ewer and basin that must have been three hundred years old, I ate in the Persian fashion with my hands. Finally the chaplain arrived to read the Quran and say prayers, in which we all joined. That night I slept on very comfortable bedding along with half a dozen men, including two unmarried sons, in the great dining room.

Before dawn I was awakened by the call to prayer. While they said their prayers, I read the small Apocrypha, which I always carry unless I have a Prayer Book. I kissed it before replacing it in its case. This was the Persian custom with the Quran. The Khan saw me do it and voiced his approval.

Later that morning the Khan mounted me on one of his mares and we set out hunting. He wanted to see what I could do with my rifle. We rode as far up a ravine as we could and then began climbing. Luckily I was nearly as fit as they were and could keep up with the third son, the one who had met me at the village.

When we had climbed some two thousand feet, a barefooted scout let us know by a sign that game was in sight. I crept breathlessly up a tilted surface of limestone, and below me saw ibex. I fired at one about two hundred yards away. I dropped it -- it was a lucky shot, but missed another.

With shouts of joy, the scouts dashed down to cut its throat before it died. The boy with me was as delighted as if he had shot it himself, repeating to me "you have honored our house. You have brought good luck."

I dared not take notes or make observations in public lest I should arouse suspicion, but in the afternoon I was able to take a number of bearings from the fort. That afternoon the Khan asked me to tea in his public room, where I could be seen by his henchmen. My rifle, a cavalry .303 with Vernier sights, was inspected by expert eyes and approved by everyone present. So also were binoculars and saddle. I began to talk of returning. Ali Murad Khan would not hear of my returning after so short a stay.

After much talk he turned his attention to my stallion. Might he put it to one of the mares? I readily agreed. Perhaps to two or three? This would mean a longer stay but he would guarantee that the time would be pleasantly spent. I should have a private room and every comfort. He was as good as his word.

I spent four more days with him, shooting every day and listening every evening to a blind storyteller, a well-known and popular figure in these remote parts. He had been in Isfahan three weeks ago and had a very good idea of the truth behind the newspapers.

He related to the Khan the events in Teheran and the character of the leading figures, their family history and political records. He spoke of grain prices and harvest forecasts. He discussed the governors of cities and provinces and told of a few marriages.

After thus reporting current events, he turned to romance and to classical Persian poetry, sometimes altering well-known stanzas of Sadi and Hafiz to topical adaptations. He sang an old Lur or Kuhgula song, bringing in the names of famous tribal leaders of bygone days. He had an unfailing memory and a voice like a bell.

One night he recited the story of Sohrab and Rustam in its original form as told by Firdusi. It moved me almost to tears. Speaking nearly in the dark as we sat around the small charcoal fire, he relied entirely on modulations of his voice to give dramatic effect to the successive speeches of the boy Sohrab and his old father Rustam. The blind storyteller held us spellbound for nearly two hours. Then tea was served and water pipes passed around. He took a little food and then started on a fresh tale.

When the chaplain came in and was received by the Khan, the old man asked if it was his pleasure that the company should hear some religious verse. The chaplain readily agreed, and after first calling for water for ceremonial ablutions, intoned in a high voice the call to prayer, for he was a *muezzin*. Everyone stood and followed him in his genuflections and prostrations.

I stood awkwardly by the door, looking over the moonlit valley and stark hills beyond. When prayers ended we took our seats again and the blind man began his psalms, followed by a prose narrative of the sad fate of the patron saint of Persia, the martyred Huzain, which reduced many of his audience to genuine tears. It was a great oratorical performance. He ended on a more joyful note and we all retired to bed.

On another night, the Khan summoned a local *darwish* to tell us amusing stories in a dialect I found hard to follow. He had a merry face, a club of immense size as his stage property, and a wonderful capacity for mimicry and gestures. This performance was outdoors in a courtyard where half the village had assembled. I have never heard Persians laugh loudly or unrestrainedly before. They were as merry as British soldiers at a sing-song.

At last I induced the Khan to let me go. I left my rifle as a present, and the telescopes for his sons, and some money for the blind storyteller. The Khan was cordial to me to the last and provided me with an escort until almost in sight of "the black-hearted offspring of dogs on the other side of the Mungasht", by whom he described my Bakhtiari friends.

It was a great experience, but I decided not to record it adequately in my official diary lest I be told not to do it again. I had no business, strictly speaking, to go beyond Bakhtiari territory. Yet the results promised well. There might be oil in his Kuhgula territory, and my trip began the task of getting people accustomed to the sight of a European and making them realize we are not so very different from them. At present, many Persians, like the Kuhgulas, use bullets as visiting cards. But this phase will pass.

I continued my surveying in November, covering Arabic lands to the Hindian River, eighty miles east of Ahwaz, accompanied by my servant, Mirza Daud, who is reliable, wholly honest, and cheerful. A network of ancient canals now filled with desert sand attested to what had once been fields of sugar cane, and likely wheat, barley, rice, sugar, cotton, opium, and indigo. The reports and surveys I sent to the Intelligence Branch were received with enthusiasm, and encouraged me, without specific instructions, to continue surveying wherever our maps showed "unexplored". I determined to learn some Arabic in order to extend my surveys into lands controlled by the sheikhs.

When in Ahwaz, I reported to Captain Lorimer, and always enjoyed his company. His knowledge of the local geography, customs, and tribes I found invaluable for my work. I also looked forward to catching up with events at home by reading his copies of *The Times*. I read that Kaiser Wilhelm declared that the average German disliked the English. His saber-rattling might check the utopian schemes of Anglo-German friendship so promoted by peace propagandists. Why should anybody like us? The only moral course for a nation's rulers is far-sighted self-interest.

In late November I returned to Camp Maidan-i-Napthun after the absence of a month. I required fresh clothes, not having changed my dress during the weeks of my travels. I looked forward to being among my books and papers. My servants and men were exhausted, though they rode more and walked far less than I, and they never climb.

I inquired of Dr. Young how was camp under Bradshaw's supervision.

"Not as cohesive as when Reynolds is in charge," he replied. "The men complain more, perhaps because they have a more sympathetic audience."

Reynolds' authority acted as a glue that bound European and native alike. He listened to complaints, but they had better have legitimacy else the complainer would be castigated for whining.

"Do you think he will return?" I asked.

"He told me he would if the directors agree to his absence during the summer."

All Europeans were sympathetic to such a request.

"The enterprise works without him," I said, "but not nearly as efficiently. I don't see that the directors have an option. How are your patients? Any more operations?"

"The number of patients continues to grow. I have requested that the company build a more permanent dispensary. We have outgrown the tent."

"You should include an observers' room," I suggested. "Watching you perform medical procedures does far more for British goodwill than the Legation."

"Yes, well perhaps so, Lieutenant. At least until a patient dies."

"I hear of your medical miracles far afield. Were it not for you, the Legation could be pressed to explain what good our enterprise is to the people." Persia is not a country whose leaders worry about the people," he replied, and I agreed.

While my men rested before our next surveying expedition, I determined to explore Shushtar, where the Karun splits into two branches. I stayed in a ruined saint's tomb, an *imamsadeh*. Since it had no door, we entered by a hole in the roof, through which a cold east wind blew.

Above Shushtar for a distance of seventy-five miles as the crow flies, the Karun runs through the noblest mountain scenery, falling some nine thousand feet in elevation, where it is often compressed into narrow gorges with perpendicular walls rising from one to three thousand feet. About three miles north of Shushtar, the Karun emerges from a pink sandstone ridge and then widens into an alluvial plain. About six hundred yards above town is a diversion canal, today known as the Ab-i-Gargar. a work of great antiquity which Rawlinson, whose book I have read with great interest, described as one of the most intricate objects he had ever witnessed. Today water gushes through the gorge hewn from the rock upon which the town sits. At one time, the entire volume of the Karun was diverted through the canal, leaving the riverbed dry.

The diversion canal, which today is navigable to Dar-i-Khazineh, where the oil company offloads its supplies, was built in order to divert the river while the Bridge of Valerian was constructed. In 260 AD the Roman Emperor Valerian, in attempting to relieve Edessa, was taken prisoner by King Shapur, and held prisoner for seven years, according to the epic poet Firdusi, in the castle at Shushtar. The poet says the Persian king used the Emperor's time in captivity

Valerian's Bridge

to learn from him the techniques of bridge building.

The colossal endeavor to bridge the mighty Karun stood as testament to the ingenuity of the ancients. This great work of ancient engineering had forty-one arches and a span of more than five hundred seventy yards. A gap in the center of the bridge was swept away by a flood in 1885. Today primitive rafts of inflated goatskins hauled passengers and goods across the strong current channeled through the gap. Several passengers are drowned every spring.

I watched a caravan of camels from Dizful drop off a load of reeds enclosed in locally woven sacks, which were then loaded onto rafts and ferried across the gap. Curses and prayers of passengers could be heard over the shouts of the ferrymen.

Many of the population of Shushtar are *sayids*, or descendants of the Prophet, who wear large green turbans and are an indolent lot. When Messrs. Lynch's agents first arrived here in the late 1880's, the *sayids* treated them as unclean infidels and refused even to procure them drinking water. Today they readily accept the oil company's money but are poor workers.

Every house in Shushtar has a *bad-gir*, a tall chimney to catch the breeze in summer and bring it down to the *sardab*, a deep cellar in the soft rock in which the inhabitants spend most of the heat of the day. The narrow streets were shady. I could not help but compare the splendor and discipline of the ancients whose engineering feats of sixteen hundred years ago the present occupants lived by, but whose indifference and indolence stood in stark contrast to their ancestors.

From Shushtar I travelled west to Dizful, where I was a guest of our consul. My verandah overlooked the Diz River, which foamed with red water from the recent rains. Downstream I saw another broken bridge of great antiquity, much like Valerian's Bridge in Shushtar. Beyond the river to the west lay the great mountains of the Pusht-i-Kuh, unmapped and almost unknown. Even the lower ranges are snow-capped. Behind them rose tier after tier of limestone ranges, roughly parallel and separated by deep valleys. Tribal feuds made traffic through the mountains impassible.

In 1904 on a caravan route long since abandoned, Captain Lorimer was attacked, robbed, and injured after a visit to a Lur chieftain in the Pusht-i-Kuh. For centuries, it seemed to me, tribes of the Luristan had fought each other in a cycle of revenge that had never been broken. I decided to visit the Pusht-i-Kuh as soon as an opportunity arose, to survey lands yet unexplored and to witness this ancient tribal culture.

My first call was to a highly esteemed religious dignitary, Khan Mujtahid. He did not shake my hand, for I was to him *nejis* or unclean, but he treated me with gracious hospitality. I asked him if he knew of the ruins in Musjid-i-Suleiman and he nodded his head solemnly.

"An ancient fire temple," he said. "Built by worshipers of Zoroaster centuries before the Prophet showed us the Divine Reality."

I asked more questions and he answered by referring me to an elder who lived close by our oil camp. I wondered if it was the ancient holy man I had seen at the ruins. When I left his house, the son of a Persian chieftain was waiting for me. His father had sent him to extend an invitation for lunch the following day.

Lunch was in the Persian manner. We sat cross-legged on our heels and ate with our right hands. I found it just as clean as our way. Who knows who washes the spoons and forks? We ate one of their great delicacies, sheep's eye.

When offered the chance to accompany Shiekh Haidar and his son to visit Shush, the ancient city of Susa, I jumped at the offer. I had met Jacques de Morgan, who was in charge of its excavation, on the ship from Bombay, and was anxious to discuss his archeological endeavors at the citadel of Daniel.

On the way to Shush, near a grove of willow trees, I saw a lion. My companion wanted to shoot it, but I dissuaded him. There are so few left and they feed only on wild pig. On our journey to Shush, my men were in high spirits and sang Persian love songs, comparing the little valleys through which we rode to the cleft between the rounded breasts of their loved ones, the fresh springs to their lady's eyes, a hollow in the open plains to her navel.

The great mound at Susa overlooked the palace of Artaxerxes. Monsieur de Morgan had built a very fine castle in the French medieval style on the mound. We proceeded to the castle, where I renewed my acquaintance with the renowned archeologist.

Susa, de Morgan told me, was one of the oldest cities in the world, dating before 4000 BC. It had been the political center of Elam, and had been destroyed around 650 BC. The city was rebuilt by Darius the Great around 500 BC and was his favorite residence. Herodotus of Halicarnassus wrote about the Achaemenid Empire and its kings. But Susa's greatest fame was found in the Book of Esther.

As I youth I had studied the Book of Esther. To stand on the same ground as Xerxes, Esther, and the prophet Daniel, to contemplate that events described in the Bible, the holiest of books, took place where I now stood awakened in me a deeper appreciation of this worn and weary country where so many of the pivotal events of early Western and Mideastern civilization began.

I slept in an Arab camp as the guest of Sheikh Haidar and his son. In the evenings, after our investigations of the ruins, we talked of horses and rifles, of shotguns and the breeds of sheep and goats, buffaloes, camels and cattle. The Sheikh spoke of the social and marital customs of the Persians, Arabs, and Turks. His descriptions made me understand the blood of centuries past still coursed through the veins of its peoples.

I decided to return from Susa to Ahwaz in one day, so ordered spare horses, and left Dizful in full moonlight at 4 a.m. By midday I was at the ferry at Shushtar, where I mounted a fresh horse on the opposite side of the river and rode another thirty miles to Band-i-Qir in five hours. Again I mounted a fresh horse, and rode into Ahwaz at 10 p.m. thoroughly tired and cold. Over one hundred miles in one day was not bad. The Persians and Arabs looked upon my ride with merit.

The last days of 1908 I spent at Camp Maidan-i-Napthun and dined often with Dr. Young, who described his healthcare with an enthusiasm I can only describe as holy. His hospital has been an immense success with the natives. Dr. Young has become proficient in the local dialects and is respected by local peasants and *khans* alike. He was not interested in European politics or home affairs. His interests lay in local happenings, where no trouble was too great for him to render assistance. I wished there were more like him. He had the power of growth, which the engineer and drillers here seem to lack.

I found waiting a letter from Major Cox, asking if I wished to remain in the oil fields or would prefer to return to India. I replied that I wished to return to India, but that I was at his command. By the time he received my reply, he had heard the news of the success of the well. He responded to inform me that, with the encouraging developments at Musjid-i-Suleiman, my duty remained in Persia.

Thus ended my first year in Persia. It had been strenuous, but I was happy. I calculated I had covered three thousand miles on foot and on horseback, and had mapped roughly the same number of square miles in territory previously noted on our maps as unexplored, much of it where no Englishmen had set foot.

Chapter Eleven

Dr. Morris Y. Young

Reynolds returned from England in mid-December 1908. When he took over from Bradshaw, complaints and disagreements among the men disappeared, or at least openly. Perhaps it was because he did not tolerate discord. Or perhaps he provided a single provenance to resent.

As my contract with the CSL would expire in June -- I had already extended for one year under the same terms as I was hired -- I asked Reynolds for advice and for his evaluation of the future prospects. He believes we have found a significant oil field but only additional drilling will justify spending the massive sums to build a pipeline and refine it for marketing.

"Do not count, Doctor Young, on the generosity of the CSL directors. I told them the terms I would accept to extend for five years, terms which were reasonable considering the mammoth task before us. When I met your Mr. Hamilton in London, he informed me that I had opened my mouth considerably wider than he bargained for."

"What did he consider unreasonable?" I asked.

"Leave each alternate year of my engagement during the summer months. In India, the entire government retires to Simla for the summer. Is it asking too much, was my mouth too wide open, to ask for what has been given to government workers of India for more than a century?"

"Did they renew your contract?" I asked tentatively.

"Yes, but only after the intervention of Mr. D'Arcy. I have been appointed General Field Manager for a period of five years and will receive a total of twelve months leave to be taken in two or more installments 'as may best suit the Company.'"

"Is that unreasonable?"

"What does 'as may best suit the Company' mean? They further said it has not been decided how the Company will be managed – whether by agents or by an office staff in Mohammerah, or directed from the U.K. They tell me I could be placed under the authority of an agent."

I could well understand Mr. Reynolds' bitterness. He was not the sort of man to report to an agent.

"Mr. D'Arcy informed me the Company appropriated L30,000 in January to cover the drilling at Musjid-i-Suleiman. By the end of March, those funds were spent. Glasgow agreed to continue drilling and to spend an additional L20,000 if Mr. D'Arcy would put up half."

"Did Mr. D'Arcy put up the L10,000?" I asked.

"The directors are tight-fisted Scotsmen who do not understand the nature of risk. After seven years of toil and untold expense, just as we saw the potential for a significant field, they wanted to stop drilling. Now, after the success at Musjid-i-Suleiman, they tell me my mouth is open too wide."

I could only empathize with him. "So Mr. D'Arcy put up an additional L10,000."

"Mr. D'Arcy simply refused to answer their request. They continued to fund the operation, and the rest is history. Here you are, Doctor. I have written a recommendation for you."

After my conversation with Reynolds, I was left again with uncertainty. Would the Company find the huge sums necessary to build a pipeline and refinery? No one was sure they could pull off such a feat. Beyond that, we all sensed that the project carried implications more momentous than the challenges of raising vast sums of capital or of making profits for shareholders. Our discovery of oil had extended the reach and dominion of Empire.

Meanwhile, I had to deal with the hard-headed Scots to negotiate my contract. In requesting a five-year extension, I determined to ask for L400 the first year, rising L25 each year to a maximum of L500 for the last of the five years. I also asked that I be granted two months leave each year, including the first two years, the object of the leave being to escape the hot weather, that this leave be granted only during the hot weather, and the first installment of it be at the beginning of summer in 1910.

I also recommended that the Company provide a small condensing plant for drinking water at camp. Including the Indian Guards, our camp employed 178 men. At two gallons per man per day, the requisite plant would not cost a great deal, and would certainly protect us from a cholera epidemic.

The next morning at breakfast Reynolds' mood was worse. He threw a telegram on my desk. Mr. C. Willans had been appointed his assistant.

"Do you know Mr. Willans?" I asked.

"I met him in London. He has no oilfield experience and cannot speak the languages."

"Why would the directors assign you an assistant without your recommendation?"

"They have never shown my opinion the consideration that I have a right to expect. I also requested the use of one of Lt. Wilson's surveyors for topographic work here at Musjid-i-Suleiman. I can expect the directors will shuck my recommendation for a surveyor and send out a plumber."

I did not wish to chuckle, because his point was valid. Surely the directors had a sound reason to send out an unseasoned and unknowledgeable man to assist Reynolds.

"I must return to Ahwaz today but will return at the end of the month with Mr. Macrorie, yet another geologist."

I knew what was coming next.

"His will make the fourth geologic report from four different geologists. I feel certain Mr. Macrorie will disagree with the previous three."

The task of keeping nearly two hundred employees and hundreds of natives in good repair filled my days and that of my assistants. Accidents were common, as when one of the workers at Camp Marmatain was kicked by a mule, causing a wound in his cheek which penetrated the roof of the mouth and extended to below the eye. By the time he presented himself the wound had already become septic. Locals told me their women heated the oil shale and applied it to such wounds. I thought such a treatment might at least prevent infection, so heated the shale and extracted a black sticky substance. The distilled tar I found to be very good with skin infections. The worker responded well, and within a week was back at work.

Work on the rigs involved manually handling the equipment. Many workers suffered from abscesses, boils and ulcers about the palms of their hands and fingers. The iron material that they handled during the summer months becomes so frightfully hot that no human hand could touch it. The men provided themselves with pieces of cloth, usually imperfect material which they picked up anywhere in camp, to cover their hands. I recommended the company furnish them gloves. The result was an immediate reduction in hand and finger sores.

I was pleased when the season for plague ended with the advent of cooler weather. During late summer Bagdad, Basra, and Mohammerah had suffered from outbreaks. More than sixty deaths had occurred, which impacted our operations as many of our native staff were from those places.

If climatic change can be measured by disease, then autumn can be defined as the time of fevers. Many workers and especially the natives came down with enteric fever. Isolation, imperfect as it was, worked reasonably well in camp. Isolation became more difficult in native villages. A case of enteric occurred at a native encampment in our neighborhood. I promised to attend on the condition that the patient's tent be removed some distance from the others. My request was refused. After warning the elders of the danger to themselves and their families, I left their encampment. Returning the next afternoon, the patient's tent was still in the same place but all the others had disappeared. Since Mahomed would not leave the hill, the hill left Mahomed.

In late January 1909 wellbore No. 4 was drilling below 1,000'. Reynolds sent word that he would be in camp to oversee the final stages. No doubt the directors were anxious. After the spectacular blowout and quick depletion of the No. 3, one more failure could end expectations that Musjid-i-Suleiman was a significant oilfield.

Since 1906 Reynolds had employed many Kurd workers, Sunnis from Kermanshah, a city near the first boreholes at Chiah Sourkh. He believed they were better workers than the Lurs, who were Shi'as. To prevent conflicts, Reynolds kept them separated at work.

January was the Mohammedan holy month, when Shi'as demonstrate grief for the murder of the Prophet's grandson. To honor the martyred Husain, the Shi'a workers assembled one night and, with torches in hand, began a march to the ruins at Musjid-i-Suleiman.

I was in the dispensary when I heard a shot, and immediately ran to see what happened. By the time I arrived at the scene, Shi'as and Kurds were at each other's throats. I pushed through the angry crowd and saw a man holding a revolver and another lying on the ground, profusely bleeding from a wound in the face. He was still alive. I took the revolver, and placed the man who had fired the shot behind me. Pointing to the wounded man, I told two men to pick him up and follow me.

When we started to the dispensary, the head of the Lurs guards stepped in front of me and demanded the man who had fired the shot be turned over to him. I was in fear of such an event. He was a Kurd and a Sunni. The Lurs, a Shi'a, wanted him for revenge and extortion.

The Lur gave an order for his men to take the Kurd. Lieutenant Wilson arrived just in time. He was dressed in a black robe like a Bakhtiari, and with his long black beard, looked like one.

"Move your men back!" he shouted to the guard and stepped in front of me. "Move back!" he shouted again, and took the revolver from my hand.

The Lur guard refused to budge.

"I said *now*!" Wilson barked.

Wilson pointed the revolver in his face, and meant business. The Lur backed away, yelling to Wilson that God demanded justice, that a cur-dog Kurd had killed his brother Lur.

"Doctor, get to the dispensary! Hurry! I'll follow."

Wilson stood between me and the Lurs, some thirty to forty men. While my assistants carried the wounded Lur, Wilson held tightly to the man who fired the shot and, facing the angry crowd, followed me to the dispensary.

While I examined the victim, Wilson stood guard. The bullet had ripped through the victim's upper nose and lodged behind his left eye. Hemorrhaging was severe. The man who shot him, a Kurd named Kadoori, said he intended to shoot at a torch in the nighttime procession. Instead of hitting the torch, the bullet struck Ali Papi, a Lur.

After cleansing the wound with boiled sterile water and dilute pyrogallic acid, I applied *morrhua* to stop the bleeding, packed the wound cavity with clean gauze, and administered a dose of strychnine to increase the victim's blood pressure. I could do nothing else until he either died or stabilized. I washed up and asked Wilson what should we do with Kadoori.

"Keep him here tonight, Doctor," he replied. "Two of my sepoys will stand guard to ensure his safety. We must protect him from the Shi'as."

"Had you not arrived, the Lurs would have taken him."

"Yes. A blood feud right in camp."

"Heaven knows how that would end," I said.

"As the Kurds are well-armed," he said, "the Lurs would have suffered."

"And drilling would have halted, perhaps for months," I added. "I will tell the Lurs that Reynolds will resolve the incident, and that we will do everything possible to save the man's life."

About noon the next day, Reynolds arrived at camp, accompanied by a geologist, Mr. Macrorie. Reynolds immediately took charge, gathering depositions of the principals in the presence of the head of the Lurs guards. Evidence showed that the whole affair was an accident.

By the time Reynolds arrived, the *Ilbegi*, Sidar Mutasham, the second most powerful *khan* among the Bakhtiari, had sent a message delivered by two horsemen, demanding that Kadoori be turned over to them. Reynolds refused, and sent a diplomatic note to the *Ilbegi* explaining that the Kurd was not his subject. Reynolds then convened a court of justice, listened to the plaintiffs, after which he explained that it was an accident, and levied a fine on Kadoori, payable to Ali Papi.

As the bullet wound healed, scar tissue blocked the wounded man's left maxillary sinus from draining through his nostril. And, because the original wound was contaminated, the non-draining sinus became infected, and began to abscess. In order to restore drainage, I carefully extracted one of his incisors, and shoved a pick through the now-empty socket and into the sinus cavity. Otherwise, infection would spread within the tissues surrounding the sinus cavity and he would have died of infection. In three weeks, the man was dismissed from my care.

The No. 4 wellbore turned out to be a good well. Before he left camp, Reynolds said he was now confident we had discovered a large field. How large could only be conjectured, he said, but I could expect to stay in Persia if the directors met my request to extend my contract. When he returned to camp two weeks later, he handed me a telegram. It read "Accept Doctor Young's terms but cannot grant more than eight months leave."

"I pointed out," Reynolds explained, "that the Company would have difficulty in finding a medical man to take charge here who is keener on his profession than you, or who would realize more than the possibilities of his position in assisting his employers interests and acting loyally by them."

Needless to say I was disappointed. I took the telegram, placed it in my pocket for later consideration, and reflected how easy for a director in Glasgow to dismiss a request for leave in July and August each year without the least idea what living through a summer in southwest Persia meant.

Chapter Twelve

Lt. A.T. Wilson

I spent January 1909 in Ahwaz as assistant to Captain Lorimer, who had been on tour for six months. His able Indian assistant, Ahmed Khan, understood Persian and did an excellent job of running his office while he is away. Nevertheless there were many reports to be filed and maps to be updated, so Captain Lorimer asked for my assistance. We criticized and corrected each other's reports and maps, and devoted much of our thought to the future development of the oilfields. From information placed at our disposal by Reynolds, it seemed probable that the field was commercial. Reynolds recommended that land for a refinery be purchased on Abadan Island. I was asked to evaluate such a site, and in February sent a recommendation to the CSL on the relative merits of two sites, one on the island and one across the Karun.

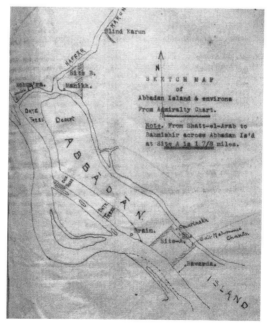

For political and commercial reasons, I thought it desirable that the refinery should be near Mohummerah, which is where our consulate, the post, and the telegraph services were already established. The pipeline should be located to avoid crossing the Karmin Marsh and the Jarrahi marshes, which flood during the spring run-off and during the autumn rainy season. Whether my recommendation carried weight or not, the refinery was located on Abadan Island.

Reynolds suggested that we enlist Major Cox to purchase the land on Abadan Island for the Foreign Department from the Sheikh, believing that a direct approach by representatives of the Company would be ruinous. Major Cox responded that he would manage the negotiations but that the Sheikh would certainly unmask the subterfuge and would resent such a maneuver. Major Cox believed if the Sheikh could prove the land did not belong to the Persian government, he could sell it directly to the Company at a reasonable price. Such a sale would entrench the British interests within his territory. The Sheikh feared the central government more than our own commercial interests.

I returned to Camp Maidan-i-Napthun in late January, the month of *Muharram*, which corresponded with our Lent and ended in the celebration of the death of the martyred Husain, patron saint of Persia and all Shi'as. While there, a Kurd, who was a Sunni, accidentally shot a Persian Shi'a just outside my tent. I prevented the man from being turned over to the Shi'as, and accompanied him and the wounded man with Dr. Young to the dispensary. The local Bakhtiari guards demanded the surrender of the Sunni. I refused on the ground that they had no jurisdiction over Persians who were not Lurs.

It was the first open clash between my Indian Guard and the local guards. Some of our best men were Sunnis from Tabriz. The Company also hired at least a hundred Sunni Kurds. The *khan's* men were Shi'as and blustered and threatened to apprehend the Sunni who fired the pistol. I told them I would shoot if they tried.

In the next few days the Shia's declared that Sunnis were being protected by me and that no Shia was safe. Fortunately when the injured man recovered, he was the first to insist that the incident was an accident.

While surveying a fortnight later, I was attacked by natives who rolled boulders from the sides of a steep ravine onto my location, and fired shots at me, I think with an intent to kill. I took cover and shouted that I intended to return fire and would shoot to kill them, at which they fled.

To my regret, Captain Lorimer took leave later in the spring. He was balm to my soul. We had so much in common. He was in love and intended to ask a young lady to marry.

After he left, I became the de facto advisor to Reynolds. He was a gentleman, well-read, authoritative, knowledgeable about all facets of drilling and the local tribes, fluent in Persian, Arabic, and many local dialects, but he had no assistant to handle local matters. I was thus enlisted to help arrange land acquisition, rent buildings, and handle various issues caused by the shipment of more equipment to the oilfields and surveying the route of a pipeline to its terminus.

Reynolds was fifty-seven years old, and often at ends with his own directors in Glasgow. He worked with the Persian government under the terms of the Concession but depended on the provincial administration of Arabs and Bakhtiari within their territories. His work depended on our Foreign Department, as well as the support of the British and Indian guards. His was not an easy tight rope to walk.

Persia was at low water politically. Even though it was fairly united racially, compact geographically, and politically homogenous, the growing constitutional crisis in Teheran divided the country. The monarchists wanted to retain the central power of the Shah. The constitutionalists, many of them Bakhtiari chieftains, wanted to cede power to Parliament. The men we dealt with, whether the Sheikh of Mohammerah or the Bakhtiari *khans*, could not obey both. Reynolds worried that the terms of the concession would be altered if a government hostile to its operations gained power.

When rain came it was like Psalm 83. *The hills rejoice; the folds are full of sheep; and the fields stand so thick with corn that men laugh and sing.* By March the wheat and barley fields sown in the autumn sprouted and turned an intense green. The countryside blossomed with wildflowers. Miniatures of daisies and marigolds, narcissus, tulips and crocuses budded, blossomed and went to seed in three weeks. Garlic and anemones in great clouds colored the desert and lit up the ravines. Scores of flowering shrubs were *born to blush unseen and waste their sweetness on the desert air.*

One day in April I rode a hundred twenty miles, from Mohammerah to Shustar, in thirty hours on three horses sent in advance. This left me with eight hours for eating and sleeping. My object was to see the Governor-General in Shustar in order to secure his assent for the oil company to begin sending loads of pipe to the oil fields. The fact that I rode almost non-stop to him was a compliment and produced the desired effect. After receiving his written consent, and after a good dinner, I returned the next day to Ahwaz, a trip of sixty-four miles.

As more activity arose from the oil fields, more diplomacy was required to handle delicate negotiations between the oil company and the locals. Unfortunately Captain Lorimer's head clerk, Ahmed Khan, who had been in Ahwaz since 1904, was returning to his native India for re-assignment. When I told this to Reynolds, he brought up an interesting question: would Ahmed Khan stay on to be liaison with the native guards? The company had assigned Charles Willans as Reynolds' official assistant, but he did not speak the languages and was too green to help with the myriad hats required to keep progress in building a refinery, laying a pipeline, and developing an oil field.

One day Reynolds posed a question to me. "Mr. Elisha will be leaving our services soon. How would I go about receiving approval for hiring Ahmed Khan in his place?"

"You would have to go through the Foreign Department of the Government of India in Simla," I suggested.

"Would they agree?"

"My recommendation would be that the Foreign Department *lend* you his services. In that way you would not have to negotiate his terms, but would simply have to repay the government's cost."

"I could throw in a free house and free meals and wages for two servants," Reynolds clearly had given the proposition some thought.

"Subject to Captain Lorimer's approval, I think the Foreign Department would agree," I replied. "Will your directors?"

Reynolds gave out a *humpf*. "Their latest reprimand is for my using a stamp bearing the words 'Manager, Concessions Syndicate'. I found it in Bradshaw's drawer and assumed the directors had permitted him to use it. When I used it on correspondence to them, they believed I was usurping authority. It's my responsibility to handle every problem, but not within my authority to stamp a letter with 'Manager, Concessions Syndicate' or to hire my own assistant. We'll see what they say about hiring Ahmed Khan."

He received recommendations for Ahmed Kahn from more than twenty people in the Foreign Department and in the military who had worked with him. All recommendations were highly complimentary and strongly favorable. To Reynolds' satisfaction, the CSL agreed to hire Ahmed Khan as the company's liaison with the natives.

Chapter Thirteen

Dr. Morris Y. Young

By 1909 my policy for providing medical care to the natives began to reap rewards beyond the healthcare of laborers and nomads. The biggest breakthrough with the local chieftains occurred in response to a request by the *Ilbegi* and second most powerful Bakhtiari, Sirdar Mutasham, Shahab-e-Sultana to attend to his son, who had suddenly taken ill. I immediately left for Malamir across the mountains where most of the Bakhtiari *khans* lived because of its temperate climate.

Sirdar was a small man with a large personality. He dressed like the other Bakhtiari *khans* in a black coat, white sash, full skirt-like trousers, and a round felt hat. Although he had lived much of his life in the open, his house was spacious and attended by many servants. My room was on the second-story with a view of the mountains.

I had heard of Persian hospitality. The evening meal that first night might have been described in *Arabian Nights*. We were seated on cushions in a room lit by candles in tall brass holders. The candlelight danced on the ceiling and walls, creating lively patterns on the colorful geometric décor. From a side door a servant with a huge platter of food on his head kicked off his slippers and entered the dining area bare-footed, a sign of respect. Others followed, a half dozen. All stood before us with huge brass platters on their heads, platters piled with food. Another servant, with an elaborate gesture, spread a white cloth on the rug before us, where the trays were placed.

Enough food was served for a multitude -- nuts floating in the juice of dates, enormous loaves of native bread placed on fresh greens, great bowls of rice seasoned with mint, crushed walnuts and raisins, dishes heaped with roasted mutton, and to add perfume to the scene, silver vases filled with attar of roses. After the meal the Sirdar welcomed me in the florid phrases of hospitality that are common among the *khans* when hosting strangers. He informed me that word of my medical miracles had spread among the Bakhtiari, and was pleased that I should honor them with my presence.

I stayed as the Sirdar's guest for several days, during which time I administered medicines to the boy. When I first arrived, the child was nauseated and had a severe case of dysentery. I administrated *calumbae* to stop the vomiting, which had an immediate and favorable effect. For dysentery I administered calomel and *plumbi acetas*, or lead acetate, knowing that large doses can be toxic. After a few days, the boy was much better, and was up and about on the day of my departure.

Dr. Morris Young with Sirdar and sons

While at the Sirdar's, my endeavors were directed towards an improvement in our relations with the *khans*. Almost all our troubles with the Bakhtiari during the past years could be summed up in one six-letter word: *guards*. Although the Indian sepoys had helped, thievery remained a major problem. Land use was another, but one that would require the *khans* treating their *ryots*, the people who rented their land, differently than how they were treated for the past thousand years.

I had several friendly and confidential chats with the Sirdar and the other *khans* on questions of general interest. In light of the crisis in Tehran when the Shah abdicated and turned the government over to his twelve-year old son, they were as unsettled in their own minds as the country was unsettled.

I was disinclined to be disposed of with a parcel of empty talk and vain promises, at which the *khans* are true artists. When mention of the guards was made, I expressed the wish to the Sirdar to grant what I thought would be welcomed by the directors, by Reynolds, and by Captain Lorimer. Briefly put, I proposed the *entire* guarding arrangement be handed over at once into the hands of the CSL and Mr. Reynolds.

They eventually, in a roundabout and overly lengthy manner, told me they were ready to arrange a meeting as soon as possible with Reynolds and Captain Lorimer at either Camp Maidan-i-Napthun or at Malamir, and would finally settle this matter of local guards.

They asked me to use my influence and obtain for them the extra money which they said they were promised. To this I absolutely refused and hinted they need not trouble themselves. A Persian's capacity for mendacity, I had discovered, knows no bounds. They also asked for Reynolds to arrest payment of further installments until the position of the *Ilkhani* is made clear. It seems the Samsam, the Company's adversary and chief *khan* of all the Bakhtiari, had been deposed.

By the time I returned to Musjid-i-Suleiman, the weather had turned cold and windy. Snow flurries hid the higher elevations in a cloud-covered shroud. My assistants had secured the bottom of the dispensary tent to the ground so that frigid gusts could not penetrate the tent, but the stove provided only minimal warmth.

Mr. Reynolds was in camp to oversee the spudding of wellbore No. 5. When he heard of my return, he met me in the dispensary. A dog, a white Jack Russell terrier, followed him inside. I asked if the dog belonged to him.

"Yes," he said, "a chap brought him to me, and now he won't leave my side." He said this somewhat sheepishly, but I could tell he was attached to the dog, which commenced to sniff every corner of the dispensary.

"Dr. Young," he said, "I understand you met with the Sirdar."

"Yes, sir," I said, and explained the purpose of my trip to Malamir. When I told him of my conversation with the *khans* about the guards, he became excited.

"I do not intend to suggest I concluded an agreement with the *khans*," I told him, "but as I was in their company, I felt the subject should be broached."

"Dr. Young, you have done the Company a great service," he said, in a rare expression of pleasure. "I can handle problems with drilling, feuds, and floods, but the native guards have been a problem I cannot fix. Even with the assistance of the Indian Guards, we are unable to keep the natives from pilfering supplies or maintaining peace among the factions. Your medical work with the *khans* may solve our most difficult political problem."

I was pleased by his praise, but I assured Reynolds that a verbal understanding with the *khans* was one matter, and a signed agreement was another. Since he was in a good frame of mind, I thought this as good a time as any to express my doubts about an extension of my contract. The Scotsmen had not been very generous in their offer to extend my contract.

"I regret to say that I do not see my way to accept the terms which I understand to be conveyed in the telegram you showed me. Eight months leave during seven years of service is insufficient."

"The matter has not been decided," he replied firmly. "I will emphasize to the directors how your influence has changed our relation with the Bakhtiari. You have done more to serve the company than Captain Lorimer or the Legation."

In March Reynolds and his dog, which followed him everywhere but which he never called by name, and I set off for Malamir to meet with the *khans* for the purpose of negotiating the details of an agreement concerning the local Bakhtiari guards, and for compensation for more land. We reached Malamir on March 12th. The Sidar was most amiable, and expressed gratitude that I had cured his son.

The son of the new *Ilkhani*, head of all the Bakhtiara tribes who had replaced the Samsam, had just arrived from Europe, and gave unmistakable evidence of his dislike for the change. During the negotiations, the Sirdar showed Reynolds an anonymous communication he had received from Teheran disagreeing with turning the guards over to the CLS. Reynolds examined the document and laid it aside. Later when I asked what he thought of the document, he raised his eyebrows.

"I recognized the handwriting," he replied. "It was written by a former employee of the Company. I fired him three years ago."

Throughout the next five days, Reynolds was diplomatic and patiently worked through the specifics of an agreement, never confronting the *khans* with what he knew to be their false statements. When we left Malamir, an agreement was in hand which Reynolds said must be approved by Captain Lorimer and the Foreign Department, but which he assured them would re-set relations with the company and the *khans*.

In the next few months I was kept busy with healthcare at Musjid-i-Suleiman. More workers arrived, some for building a brick kiln for the construction of housing at the camp, some for surveying a pipeline route. Reynolds said that Abadan Island had been selected as the site for a refinery.

In April I was again called to Malamir by the Sirdar to care for another of his three small sons, and to examine the Sirdar's leg. The young son was suffering from cramping, which I treated with *belladonna* and urotropine. He responded to the treatment, and I left a week's dosage of sodium bicarbonate to be administered daily until all symptoms were past.

The Sirdar's leg was a different matter. He had punctured it on a sharp staff while riding. His medical man had applied a poultice and wrapped the leg in goat's skin. When I unwrapped the "bandage", it was evident that blood poisoning had set in. The wound was ulcerated and the leg was septic.

I cleansed the wound with pryogallic acid and carbolic and dressed the leg in an Unna's boot soaked in glycerine and zinc oxide. My concern was gangrene. Blood poisoning had spread beyond the wound. Time would tell if modern medicine could cure his very serious infection.

A week after returning to camp, I received a personal letter from the Sirdar expressing gratitude for my administrations and telling me that his leg was much improved. Had I arrived a day or two later, only amputation would have arrested the infection.

The last week of May, Reynolds and his Jack Russell terrier arrived at Camp Musjid-i-Suleiman to converse with Willans about drilling operations while he was on leave. He was accompanied by Mr. Crush, a man the Company sent to assist Willans.

George B. Reynolds (left)

After our trip to Malamir together, Reynolds seemed to show an even deeper respect for my work, no doubt because of my contribution to the new agreement with the *khans* regarding the local guards.

"As you know, Doctor, I will be leaving for England next week."

"Yes, sir."

"I received notice by telegram this morning." He pulled the telegram from his pocket and read its content.

We have arranged Lloyd of Shaw, Wallace and Co and Assistant Walpole sail to Karachi Mohummerah 16th *May with full authority to constitute Firm to act as Management Agents and make all necessary arrangements after consultation with you.*

He looked up. "I will soon report to agents. To *agents!*" he repeated.

I knew he had expected to be placed in charge of all operations, just as he had been for the past eight years. He lowered his head and shook it in dismay.

"Agents…who don't even work for the company!"

I didn't understand the implication of what he was saying. Surely the person in charge of the now enlarged operation would be a company employee.

"Oh, no. It's exactly as Mr. D'Arcy warned," he replied. "The Scots want their man in charge. Probably they'll send an incompetent who knows only how to nod his head and say 'aye, aye, sir'. All the effort, all the trouble and now with success, they choose an *agent* to run the operation. It's worse than ingratitude," he said.

I could only extend my sympathy, and said with sincerity that no other man could carry the baton. Reynolds looked down but when he looked up, he was again in command.

"How are the workers?" he asked.

He was referring to four drilling hands who had been gassed the previous night. The oil had a high sulfur content, and its associated gas probably contained hydrogen sulfide, a very toxic substance, heavier than air, which settled invisibly in lower depressions. Wellbore No. 6 had drilled into a high pressure zone that blew oil and water over the top of the derrick. After the blow subsided, the driller discovered that one of his men was missing. He gathered three others to look for the missing man. After finding him unconscious, the whole lot were gassed and had to be pulled from under the drilling platform.

"All but one have been released. I will observe him for a few more days."

"Thanks to you once again for your medical expertise," he said. "Only to be matched by your diplomatic talents."

"My diplomacy is my healthcare. Mr. Reynolds, do you remain optimistic about the field?" I asked.

"The field continues to expand. I am not enthusiastic about No. 5. The Numbers 1, 2, and 4 all found pay at approximately the same depth, just below a very hard cap. The No. 6, like the No. 3, is from a shallower depth. We are setting casing this morning at 710 feet. I'm not optimistic the shallower zone will be commercial. It depleted in the No. 3 within three weeks."

"And the lower zone?"

"Until the limits of the field are better defined, we cannot be assured of its size or of the commercial success of the entire enterprise. Committing to lay a pipeline and build a refinery without knowing the extent of the field is optimism."

"Have you heard from the directors about my contract?" I asked. "Did they accept my request for two months vacation each year?"

"Not yet, Dr. Young. In my last correspondence I noted that no mention of a new agreement with you had been extended. I will be returning to Ahwaz in the morning, and will send them another telegram."

Four days later I received word from Reynolds. The terms of my contract had been agreed to.

Chapter Fourteen

Lt. A. W. Wilson

In April 1909 Major Cox asked me to visit him in Bushire. I wondered why but waited to leave until competitions between my Indian cavalrymen and the Bakhtiari were held the following day. My Indians showed themselves to be just as good horsemen as the Bakhtiari and more adept with their rifles at target practice at four hundred yards. I also competed and did fairly well with rifle, sword, and spear.

When my servant and I left Camp Maidan-i-Napthun the weather looked unsettled. We rode thirty-five miles non-stop, intending to camp on the river under the stars. A sudden thunderstorm drenched us and pelted us with hailstones of a great size. I could scarcely restrain my mount from bolting on a road dangerously slippery by mud. We shivered in the rain until dawn when my baggage arrived, consisting of my Sunday suit for dress at Bushire and some books, now soaked with muddy water. The mule which carried them had fallen into a deep hole when crossing the river.

I put myself and my kit on a boat that was passing downstream after discharging a cargo of dried fish. It smelled abominably but I found some compensation because our craft was followed by a great flock of swifts. Whenever a sail flapped or I struck at the deck with my riding whip, a swarm of flies arose. The swifts swooped down with open beaks and provided great entertainment to keep my mind off our fragrance.

At midnight a sudden gale heeled us over. Our boat nearly grounded. As Malcolm's British bo'sun said on the Euphrates, *tears and prayers... proved no manner of use.* We dropped anchor, a heavy stone with a hole in it for the rope, and hoped for dawn while pitiless rain beat upon us. With dawn came the bright sun, and good coffee and good temper.

I had made a plane-table survey of the northern end of Abadan Island and had taken soundings along the bank. Based upon my maps, the Company made its decision to acquire land for the refinery. They thought a square mile would suffice.

When I arrived in Ahwaz, Major Cox was reported to be en route to negotiate the purchase of Abadan Island for the company. We met in Mohammerah, whereupon Major Cox asked me to move to Burshire and be his Personal Assistant. It would be a valuable experience, and was the most important and responsible junior job in the Foreign Department. I could only hope, not very confidently, that it would not damage my career. Little did I realize how important Major Cox' trust in me was to my future.

Major Cox had travelled much in the unknown parts of Persia himself, so he could criticize with knowledge and speak with authority. He knew much of birds and was a close observer of animal and plant life. His servant told me his house was filled with strange birds and animals. His Arabic was excellent and his bearing dignified.

During the week-long negotiations with the Sheikh, Major Cox enlisted me as his cipher clerk and secretary-typist. I was very closely cross-examined by him on every phase of the company's activities, and all that I had seen and done in the Bakhtiari country. It was my first experience with this kind of negotiation. Major Cox exercised great influence on the Sheikh, but was careful not to press him unduly. His patience was unbounded, and his temper unaffected by the great heat. He and the Sheikh sat on cushions on the floor, the later with his secretary at his side. Major Cox attached great importance to writing an agreement which should not give rise to disputes, and drafted a version in both Persian and Arabic. Only when it had been agreed to in the vernacular did he translate it into English. His ideal was that the Persian text should prevail.

For the Sheikh, the agreement was momentous. It called upon him to assist in the establishment within his bailiwick of a company which, as he foresaw, would eventually overshadow all other commercial interests and would eventually cause the Persian government in Teheran to seek to extend their administration to every part of Arabistan, a jurisdiction which hitherto belonged to him. As an Arab, he hated and feared such a prospect. Without a guarantee that we would assist him in maintaining his hereditary and customary rights, any such agreement would have been suicidal for him. The Home Government authorized Major Cox to give such assurances, and to extend them to his heirs and successors. The Sheikh therefore gave the Company full permission for the pipeline and sold them the land they required for the refinery with the understanding it would revert to him when the concession expired.

The Indian government turned down Major Cox' request that I be appointed his assistant. They said I was too inexperienced. However the government assigned me two surveyors and a free hand to survey anywhere I wanted. Major Cox was heartily in favor of my Intelligence Branch work, and wanted it extended. He thought that disorders in other parts of Persia would spread to these parts, and that my survey and reports on the local authorities was invaluable. He also told me that the Indian Guard would remain at least through July. I had another scorching summer in Persia to look forward to.

The CSL had recently been re-named the Anglo-Persian Oil Company, or A.P.O.C. I knew little of corporate matters, but based upon my discussions with Reynolds and others in the company, it was clear that the level of activity would increase. The Company had changed its name and embarked on a great task: to build a refinery and lay a hundred-fifty mile pipeline over two ranges of rugged hills from Musjid-i-Suleiman to Abadan Island. Even though I still saw a brighter future in India, the Company's and the Foreign Department's endeavor were significant, and in fact turned out to be historic.

PART III

Geopolitics

Chapter Fifteen

James Hamilton

"Gentlemen, I call the meeting to order," said Mr. Cargill, chairman of Burmah Oil Ltd.

Today was February 26, 1909. Glasgow was covered in a foot of snow. In spite of the weather, all the directors were present.

I read the minutes of last month's meeting. The motion to approve was quickly made and seconded, and a voice vote accepted the motion.

"As you gentlemen know, today's agenda is particularly important," said Mr. Cargill. "Sir Boverton Redwood is joining us to discuss whether our discovery in Persia merits the large expenditures necessary to develop the oil field. With your permission, Sir Boverton, may our directors ask questions as you proceed?"

"Certainly, certainly, Mr. Cargill," responded Sir Boverton. He looked around the room at the directors. "As you know, I have been involved in the search for oil in Persia since 1901 when Mr. William Knox D'Arcy acquired the Persian concession. Before your joinder in the project, Mr. D'Arcy drilled two wells at Chiah Sourkh near the village of Zorab."

Sir Boverton needn't review the painfully long process that brought us to the present, but he nevertheless continued with his summary.

"The No. 1 Chiah Sourkh was drilled to 2315 feet and in May 1904 was completed for twenty-five barrels per diem. The No. 2 was drilled to 760 feet at a more favorable location and was completed in January 1904 for two hundred barrels per diem. As a result of the gas pressure, it was impossible to completely arrest the overflow. According to a report of 24 April 1908, the oil has been flowing continuously at the rate of 150 loads of 175 pounds, or approximately one hundred barrels per diem."

He handed the Board a photo of the Chiah Sourkh No. 1. Sir Boverton did not mention that the two wells had nearly cost Mr. D'Arcy his fortune and that our agreement to continue the exploration efforts was prompted by the Admiralty, which contemplated a source of fuel oil and did not wish the

Concession to fall into the hands of a foreign company.

Rig at Chiah Sourkh

"From Zorab to the Marmatain district is a distance more than three hundred miles, which may safely be regarded as the two ends of an oil belt."

"Do you believe the entire belt, as you call it, will be productive?" asked Mr. Wallace.

"Yes, sir, I do," replied Sir Boverton.

"The two wells at Marmatain are not productive," observed Mr. Wallace.

"After the Consolidated Syndicate Ltd purchased an interest in the Concession from Mr. D'Arcy in 1905, the No. 1 Marmatain commenced on September 18, 1906 and the No. 2 on November 11, 1906. Both wells have been temporarily suspended before they reached a depth at which, in light of present knowledge, oil could expected to be found."

It sounded like a reasonable explanation. Until our most recent wells were completed, how could we know how deep to drill?

"Your company commenced the No. 1 Musjid-i-Suleiman on January 23, 1908, and the No. 2 on March 25, 1908. In May of last year the No. 1 was brought in at 1,180 feet for approximately 300 barrels per diem and has flowed intermittently since. The No. 2 was subsequently completed at 1,010 feet. The No. 3A was completed at 280 feet for 3,000 barrel per diem but after a few months became choked and bridged over. The No. 4 has been recently carried down to 1,033 feet at which the same petroliferous formation has been found. The No. 5 and No. 6 are now drilling."

The other directors listened patiently. I knew all of this from the reports sent to me by Reynolds, our field manager.

"In December of last year, at your direction, I sent Basil F. Macrorie to Persia to examine the oil field, to review the geology, and to look at additional exudations that might reveal additional oil fields. Mr. Macrorie's report will be furnished to you by mid-March. I will summarize his findings."

We had hoped for Macrorie's report before our meeting today, but understood that a written report with geologic maps might require some time to assemble. Macrorie had only returned earlier in the month.

"Do we know," asked Mr. Fleming, "what the productive formation is?"

"Not precisely," answered Sir Boverton. "In 1901 Mr. Burls examined the area and formed the opinion that the deposits occur in the same geological horizon, a gypsiferous series, which is a division of the Eocene according to Loftus. The lower part of the series is a distinctive Nummulitic limestone."

"Is it the objective?" asked Mr. Fleming.

"In 1903 my colleague, Mr. W. H. Dalton, was deputed to make an examination of the central oil fields. He observed that the Nummulitic limestone, which forms a considerable portion of the Persian Highland and appears from a distance as great elongated domes, is not known to be petroliferous in Persia, while the succeeding Oligocene series is the principal source of the Caucasian oil and appears to be entirely unrepresented in the Zagros range."

"What did Mr. Craig think?" I asked. It had barely been a year since, at Sir Boverton's request, we had paid for Mr. E. H. Cunningham Craig to review the geology of our Persian concession.

"Mr. Craig believes the oil shows are all exudations from the outcrop of limestones, but they only occur in low ground or river valleys."

"What does this indicate?" I asked.

"It indicates that the Nummulitic limestone exposed at the surface is sourced from a deeper sediment," he explained.

The other directors, myself included, were confused by this geologic discourse. Our hope was to determine if the oil was of commercial grade and sufficient quantity to justify the expenditure of large sums.

"I have examined the crude oil in my laboratory," Sir Boverton continued. "It is of a paraffin base, and yields the usual commercial products though it contains one percent of sulfur. It has been refined and been found to yield twenty-five percent water-white kerosene."

Since kerosene was the primary use for crude oil, this figure was encouraging. Mr. Cargill pressed Sir Boverton for a geological valuation of the quantity at Musjid-i-Suleiman.

"It is evident," Sir Boverton concluded, "that amply sufficient work has been done to demonstrate the existence of petroleum in good quality in abundance at a very moderate depth at the northern end and center of an oil belt extending from the Turko-Persian frontier to the Persian Gulf. At the central field, Musjid-i-Suleiman, the operations have passed from the stage of exploration to that of exploitation or development and the foundation of a commercial enterprise has been laid. The four wells that have been sunk are not mere trial borings. They will doubtless give a good yield for years to come. They prove a considerable area on which further wells may be drilled in the confident expectation of proportionately increasing the output."

Finally, he had said it. In spite of my own reservations, Sir Boverton, the most respected geologist in England if not in the world, believed we had discovered oil of sufficient quality and quantity to launch a large enterprise, and to sell shares to the public.

Mr. Cargill handed me a paper with a list of directors for the new the Anglo-Persian Oil Company, which in conversation we shortened to A.P.O.C. At the previous board meeting in which Sir Boverton gave us the encouraging information, we had voted to create a company and raise money for developing the Persian oil fields.

Lord Strathcona was to be chairman, and Mr. C.W. Wallace vice-chairman. Next was Mr. John T. Cargill, chair of Burmah Oil, followed by Sir Hugh S. Barnes, the lieutenant-governor of Burmah. W.K. Darcy, chair of Morgan Gold Mining Co and HSH Prince Francis of Teck were members of the Board, as well as William Garson, writer to the Signet Group in Edinburgh and legal advisor to Lord Strathcona. Next to last was a man with whom I was not well acquainted, C. Greenway, merchant. I was also listed as Director, Burmah Oil.

"Will Lord Strathcona agree to be chairman?" I asked. Lord Strathcona was elderly, eighty-eight years old, and one of the wealthiest men in England.

"He has already agreed. He will keep five percent of the new company, the same percent he held in CSL. Burmah Oil will own the remaining 95% of the ordinary shares."

"Lord Strathcona was recommended by the Admiralty," Mr. Cargill continued.

I understood the implication. Admiral Fisher had met D'Arcy at Marienbad in 1903, and had expressed an interest in keeping the concession in British hands.

"Who is C. Greenway?" I asked.

"Charles Greenway is a man recommended by Mr. Wallace. Until last year Mr. Greenway worked in India as a merchant for our agent, R. G. Shaw and Company. He and Mr. Wallace reside at Winchester House in our London office."

Ah, I thought. Mr. Wallace was closely associated with R. G. Shaw and Company and Greenway was his trusted colleague.

"Mr. Greenway returned last year from India. He rose in rank and reputation there as one of the leading men engaged in commercial development. We need someone on board with Oriental experience.

"How much money will the offering raise?" I asked.

"It is of course a decision for the Board," replied Mr. Cargill. "An initial capitalization of L2,000,000 will launch the enterprise, 1,000,000 ordinary shares at L1 per share and 1,000,000 participating preference shares at L1 each with 6% interest to the public. CSL and Lord Strathcona will be reimbursed L380,249 for their expenditures to present, which should leave sufficient funds to develop the oil field, lay a pipeline, and build a refinery."

Surveying the pipeline and purchase of lands for a refinery were already underway. Funding for them had been my primary concern. I expected the first refined products would not bring cash to the company for years.

"And what of Mr. D'Arcy?" I asked.

"After prolonged negotiations, Mr. D'Arcy will receive L203,067 from CSL and 160,000 ordinary shares of Burmah Oil in return for his remaining sixty-two percent of the Concession. Additionally he will receive 10,000 shares of Burmah Oil for his share in the Turkish Concession."

"And no shares in A.P.O.C.? Last May the Board told him if he would not pay half an additional L20,000, we would stop operations. He never responded. We came close to shutting down because of his unwillingness to contribute L10,000. Today we reward him with a fortune."

I didn't intend to question an agreement already made, but nevertheless wondered if we had not been premature in our valuation of D'Arcy's remaining interest in the Concession. Shares in Burmah Oil were publicly trading at L5.50.

"When CSL made the agreement in 1905 to fund the new exploration, Mr. D'Arcy was paid L25,000 with the proviso that if oil was not found in sufficient quantities, he would return those funds. If however oil was found as he predicted, CSL would reimburse him for the additional L200,000 he had expended before our engagement. Since our new company is as yet unproven, or shall I say not yet profitable, Mr. D'Arcy, perhaps cautiously, elected to take shares in Burmah. He will also serve on the new company's board."

"Why do you say 'perhaps cautiously'?" I asked.

"Have you read Macrorie's report?" Cargill replied, and handed me a thick document.

I picked up it and thumbed through the pages. Most of it was geological in nature.

"Read page 42," Cargill said.

I turned to the page. "He writes that Reynolds spoke of Cretaceous anticlines," I observed.

"Keep reading."

"About his summary?"

"Yes, please read it aloud, Mr. Hamilton."

"Summarizing," I read, "I am of the opinion that the Company will take over Musjid-i-Suleiman, a valuable *small* field." I looked up. I had emphasized the word "small" because Macrorie had written the word in italics.

"Go on," prompted Cargill. "He mentions your Mr. Reynolds."

I continued to read aloud. "I cannot conclude the Report without expressing my admiration of the wide topographical and structural knowledge of the country in general, as well as notice of interesting particular features, which Mr. Reynolds has acquired, all of which he has put freely at my disposal, besides volunteering information on details of development which he considered might be of value to my work and report. I owe him a great debt of gratitude for his excellent arrangements for my journeys and camping, both as expediting my work and giving me the maximum personal comfort under the circumstances. I am also indebted to him and Dr. Young for the photographs accompanying this Report. Signed Basil F. Macrorie March 18, 1909."

I looked up. "Reynolds impressed him," I said. It was not Reynolds' knowledge or diplomacy which concerned me. It was the word Macrorie used to describe Musjid-i-Suleiman.

"*Small* field?" I repeated.

"At this point, we must rely on Sir Boverton's expertise," responded Cargill emphatically. "His report is more reassuring."

"And will insure the shares are sold," I observed, to which Cargill made no comment.

CSL's discovery of oil in Persia based on Sir Boverton's report created tremendous public interest. Everyone seemed to want shares. On the day of the offering, lines of people five deep stood for hours to purchase shares. It was a momentous day. On April 14, 1909, A.P.O.C., the Anglo-Persian Oil Company, came into existence.

Two other companies were involved as well, to befit the requirements of the Concession and to satisfy the local chieftains. The First Exploration Company was formed in 1903 to acquire and develop a one-square mile area around any discovery well, this being specified in the Concession, a portion of the shares being granted to the Persian government. In March 1909 the Bakhtiari Oil Company was formed. A.P.O.C. owned its stock except for three percent set aside for the local Bakhtiari chieftains. If A.P.O.C. were to develop into a large enterprise, the national government and the locals who controlled the land needed to share in its success.

Many discussions were held about management of the new company. Burmah Oil had long used agencies as representatives in foreign countries. Reynolds was never considered. Last month I reprimanded him for using the title "Manager, Concession Syndicate Ltd", partially as a way of reminding him that decisions were made in Glasgow, and partially to prepare him to serve under an agency.

The Board looked for a suitable agent among firms already established in the Persian Gulf. Only one firm met their requirement of sufficient standing and repute to represent the company; however that firm had no knowledge of or experience in the technical side of the oil business. Therefore it was resolved that Burmah Oil's agent Messrs Finlay, Fleming and Co, and Messrs Shaw, Wallace, and Co, the Indian agents of Burmah Oil, would establish a new firm in the Persian Gulf to provide the company with the necessary organization of experienced men.

The firm of Lloyd, Scott, and Co was formed and chosen in May as our agent. At a later date the firm's name was changed to Strick, Scott, and Co when Mr. Strick, who owned large interests in the Gulf, was admitted as a member.

On May 14 the Board sent a telegram to Reynolds.

We have arranged Lloyd of Shaw Wallace and Co and Assistant Walpole sail Karachi to Mohammerah 16ᵗʰ May with full authority to constitute Firm to act as Management Agents and make all necessary arrangements after consultation with you. Please give every facility to them and arrange accommodation.

"How do you think Reynolds will take the new arrangement?" I asked Cargill. Reynolds had reported to me for the past four years. I knew how he would take it.

"Reynolds has no choice in the matter," replied Cargill. "A.P.O.C. will be managed by Lloyd, Scott and Company from their London office at Winchester House."

"Yes," I responded, "but who will be in charge *on the ground?*"

"John Black was hired as overall manager for the project."

"Reynolds will report to Black?"

"Yes. Reynolds will report to Black."

"Does Black know anything of drilling or refining or laying pipelines? Does he know anything of the local culture? Does he speak Persian or Arabic?"

"Wallace assures me that Black is one of his most trusted employees. He understands management and communications. The rest he will learn."

"Who will Black report to?"

"To Mr. Greenway in London."

I was relieved. Although Wallace, Cargill, Greenway, and I were all directors of Lloyd, Scott and Company, I did not want the responsibility to deal with the new and larger operation. Nor did I want to handle communications with Black. Dealing with Reynolds had been challenge enough.

Chapter Sixteen

Lt. A.T. Wilson

In June 1909 I explored the Karkhah River twenty miles west of Ahwaz. No European had been there in fifty years. Five years later I would be conducting the 12th Division under General Gorringe across this tract of country by night, preparatory to crossing the Karkhah in pursuit of the retreating Turks.

Shortly after Reynolds departed on leave, J. B. Lloyd and C. A. Walpole, aged 35 and 27 respectively, arrived at Mohammerah. They would act as Managers of the new Anglo-Persian Oil Company. Both were gentlemen. Lloyd had experience in business in India and England, but none in Persia. Walpole had little experience in either. Both would soon get more than they bargained for. They were on virgin soil here. New offices were to be built or leased, new Persian clerks to be recruited, and a wholly new type of work begun to which they and I and everyone else were strangers.

I wondered why the new company had hired men unfamiliar with the languages, customs, and local operations to run what was to become a huge undertaking. Captain Lorimer and I had discussed this issue. I told him Reynolds was the only man with the experience and knowledge for the task. Captain Lorimer expressed doubts, believing that Reynolds was unequal to the demands of such an enterprise. Based on my brief acquaintance with Lloyd and Walpole, I was convinced Reynolds was a better choice.

A telegram I received in July 1909 changed my assignment. It directed me to Mohammerah to take over temporarily as Acting Consul. Mr. McDouall, who had been consul there since 1891, had been re-assigned to Kermanshah, a change which caused great distress in his family. Although a devout Protestant, he had married a Moslem and had assumed he and their family would remain in Mohammerah. He was only 53, but had deteriorated both physically and mentally. Still, he was much respected and was not without influence locally.

Three days after receiving the telegram, I was directed to report to Major Cox in Bushire. The journey there was twelve hours by sea, followed by an hour over choppy shallows in a steam launch, ending with a six-mile drive along a barren island to the Residency. There I received a warm welcome from Mrs. Cox. After eighteen months in camp, it was delightful to spend forty-eight hours in a civilized environment.

I was puzzled that three months ago the Foreign Department in India had told Major Cox I was too raw, untrained, and junior to become Major Cox' assistant, but now was assigned a duty with much more responsibility. I owed the new responsibility to Major Cox, whom I had only met a month previously while he was in Mohammerah negotiating the land purchase for the refinery with the Sheikh.

Major Cox told me my assignment would last six months, after which I would be replaced by a senior officer. In the meantime, my pay was raised significantly to what, for a frugal bachelor, was a liberal figure.

While in Bushire, I met some of the British colony as well as the even smaller foreign colony. One morning while I was drinking coffee near the bazaar, a German about my age named Wilhelm Wassmuss approached me and said how he was impressed with my language skills. I found it odd that he knew I spoke Persian. He was curious about my new assignment and asked many questions about our activities at Abadan. I evaded his questioning but mentioned his inquiries to Major Cox.

"Wassmuss?" repeated Major Cox, and raised his eyebrows. "Yes, we met last month. He is the new German consul. He informed me his primary assignment is to establish shipping rights in the Gulf for Wonckhaus, a German trading firm.

"Why would he be questioning me about Abadan?" I asked.

"Because he is a German spy whose objective is to interfere with British interests and to rouse Persian hatred against the British."

Such frankness from Major Cox was unexpected. Circumspection was his trademark.

"I tell you this, Lieutenant Wilson," he continued, "so that you will be aware of German intrigues with your Bakhtiari friends. My informants tell me that Samsam, the recently deposed *Ilkhani*, has met with Wasmuss."

I knew how much the Samsam disliked the British. Reynolds had told me many stories about the Samsam's activities against the oil company and British citizens.

"Since the Bakhtiari marched into Tehran and forced Muhammed Ali Shah to abdicate, we have solicited their support. A few, however, respond with enthusiasm to German and Russian persuasion."

"Is the new Shah anti-British?" I asked.

"He is only a boy of twelve. People in our Legation believe his advisors, especially Nasr ul Mulk, remain our friends. But the crisis in the central government can create opportunities for the Germans and the Russians. If you hear of meetings between foreigners with any Bakhtiari *khans*, please report them to me immediately."

Mrs. Cox was a marvelous hostess, a stately person who was the quintessence of kindness. She treated me like a mother and spared no pains to make life tolerable for all Europeans in the social sphere.

Major Cox directed me to write a report setting forth my ideas of what the Mohammerah Consulate required in view of the growth of the oil company. I spent many hours preparing the dispatch, and worked on the wording as carefully as a sermon, and about as long. Major Cox reviewed it and altered it but little.

Thankfully I was allowed to take my own initiative. It took a fortnight to take over the consulate. Mr. McDouall had saved copies of every Foreign Office letter, keeping them in bundles folded twice and docketed on the back. Each bundle was tied with red tape and had its own pigeon-hole. When it grew too bulky for the hole, it was wrapped in brown paper, tied with white tape, and shelved. He wanted to review the entire history of his term with me. Even though his family thought me to be a villain, I encouraged him to move along and did all I could to make things easy for him.

After a year-and-a-half of living and eating like a Bakhtiari, I quickly transformed into a respectable householder, dressing most evenings for dinner, and blessed with a decent cook who kept up the mark when I was visited by a succession of guests. *Punkah* fans suspended from the ceiling were hand-pulled for my guests but not for myself, as I was accustomed to the heat. I could not help but wonder whether the Arab boy who pulled the string was not weary, as the very thought of his monotonous occupation made me tired.

I initiated a Sunday morning church service in the Consulate. A mixed gathering of British, Armenian, and Portuguese guests attended the service, as well as an American female missionary, who became rather a thorn in my side, as she was anxious to convert me to American fundamentalism.

In October I surveyed the marshes along the Karkhah River with twenty guards and a score of chainmen. I had to swim from rock to rock with a line round my neck to haul a tape measure or a chain. Within ten days I had a good set of rough drawings, which I sent to Simla for reproduction. Beni Turuf, the local tribesmen, speared us great carp in the narrow channels of the marsh. We could have shot some wild pig, but in a Moslem country, this would be folly. I bagged some rock pigeons, quail, and black partridges. We thus had better than normal fare for dinner. I also brought coffee beans to keep all the Arab guards and chainmen supplied. They roasted and ground them in a mortar and provided us with all we wanted.

In working through issues with the oil company, I did not like the system under which it was managed locally by an ad hoc commercial firm which also did general business outside the oil company's needs. Lloyd, Scott was not only representing A.P.O.C., it was looking to represent other companies as well, including Hamburg-America, the German shipping company. Past discussions with Captain Lorimer had raised my suspicion of anything German in the Persian Gulf. I made it clear to Mr. Cox and the Foreign Department that such a system seemed to work in India, but it created divergent interests here.

A.P.O.C. had begun hiring what would soon be thousands of employees to build the refinery and lay the pipeline. A manager's hands would be full simply managing the company's construction and drilling activities.

I am not sure what Reynolds expected. In November he returned from leave in England out of sorts with the new arrangement. He had left Persia just as the new A.P.O.C. organization was getting underway. By the time he returned, a new hierarchy had been established, workers of many nationalities had been hired by the hundreds, and the movement of men and material was ratcheting up at a furious pace.

"And how is it, Lieutenant Wilson?" he asked me, "working with the agents of A.P.O.C.?"

I didn't express my doubts, but replied that since he had left in June, the company had certainly increased in size and level of activity.

"There are more ships arriving every day," I explained, "delivering materials for the refinery. Thousands of tons of pipe are being dropped at Nasiri. Only the *Shushan* can carry it upriver, which bottlenecks the equipment at Ahwaz.

I had to remind the Governor of Shushtar that the Concession granted the oil company the right to navigate the Karun, and that no duties were to be imposed. He wanted to exact a fee for offloading at Dar-i-Khazineh. Indeed, every *khan* for a hundred fifty miles has his hand out."

"Yes, well," replied Reynolds, "the smell of money attracts all breeds, does it not? I see you have shaved and are wearing Western clothes."

He said this with a slight smile that seemed nearly mocking.

"Yes sir, but I kept a mustache. The government still allows me a free hand to continue surveying. I spent a week exploring the old mouths of the Karun which enter the Khor Musa north of the Shaatt-al-Arab bar. The place had not seen a European since the 18th century."

"One foot in one era and one in another, Lieutenant," he replied. "Like myself. Tell me about these agents. Do you work with them?"

"John Black is the agent's local manager. He does not speak the languages or know the customs, but works through assistants. Ahmed Khan interprets and handles local issues for him. Charles Ritchie is in charge of laying the pipeline. Willans is in charge of the field operations at Musjid-i-Suleiman. Walpole is his understudy."

"The Scots leave no pence unturned," he replied. "Mr. D'Arcy offered insight into our new leadership. It seems Lloyd, Scott was created to run the show here for a fee, a fee which covers all their costs plus a payment for each gallon that leaves the refinery. Through its relation with A.P.O.C., the arrangement should be highly profitable for its owners, which include several members of the A.P.O.C. board who serve on Lloyd's board as well."

"Really?" I replied. I did not understand the workings of corporations, but thought this might be perceived as a conflict of interest.

"Your Mr. Hamilton, Mr. Cargill, and Mr. Greenway serve on both boards. And Mr. Lloyd, who is in charge of the agency, serves on the board of R.G. Shaw and Co with Mr. Greenway. Agencies are a means to rake money from a public company into the pockets of its directors. Scots keep their money within the clan, don't they?"

I worried that Reynolds' attitude might not fit in with what had become a different organization. Before he took leave, his attitude toward the directors had been one of facetious acerbity. Now, since he no longer would be the sole authority, his attitude seemed more cynical. It was not easy for me to advise him. He was old enough to be my father. His son was with me at Clifton.

"And what of the Indian guards?" he asked. "Are they still protecting the camps?"

"Bad news on that front," I replied. "In spite of Major Cox' recommendation to keep them, the Company said they were no longer needed and would not reimburse the India government for more expenses. Costs for the eight months of January through August ran *L*174, which included Lt. Ranking's and my salary. They returned to Ambala in August."

He shook his head at this news.

"I understand that the Kurds at Camp Maidan-i-Napthun are causing trouble with the local guards," I said. "Same old story between Shia's and Sunni's.

"Well, well, some things never change," he replied.

We had dinner together in the evening, and afterward a smoke in the garden, which was behind the house and surrounded by a high mud wall. The trees in the garden belonged to an old *sayid*, a reputed descendent of the Prophet. The days were cooler now, and the evenings pleasant. I asked Reynolds about the prime minister. He said the Liberals budget was ill suited for peacetime. I told him I believed their policy of redistributing wealth by means of taxation was oriental in its simplicity, and did not increase prosperity over a long period.

Reynolds, as I anticipated, did not work well with Black. Rather than simply grant Reynolds the authority to run Musjid-i-Suleiman and the drilling operation, Black held the strings of authority tightly, probably to insure that his own authority prevailed. He questioned any decision Reynolds made. He disrespected and disavowed his own assistant, Ahmed Kahn, even though without his help he could not understand or handle situations with the natives or with the Sheikh or with local *khans*. When Lloyd, Scott hired Charles Ritchie to oversee the pipeline construction, trouble soon arose between Black and Ritchie as well.

In July I visited the oil field for the first time in nearly a year. The level of activity was surprising. Three rigs were now running. Additional workers had been hired to build steel storage tanks. Dr. Young's dispensary had doubled in size. I asked him what he thought of the growth.

"It's not the same," he replied. "The more workers, the more health problems. We've outgrown the clinic and dispensary. We now have three more assistants and a Brit physician."

"Are you too busy to help the natives?" I knew how much they depended on his medical service, and in what reverence they held Dr. Young.

"Yes, but I can no longer see as many patients. My work involves as much coordination as treatment. The directors have talked favorably of my request to build a hospital on Abadan. It will be the first medical facility in southwest Persia."

The prospect of a hospital excited Dr. Young. I had never a met a man so dedicated to the cause of providing healthcare to all persons who needed it, whether European or native.

One evening I climbed the hill on which I had so often sat when I lived here. From the hill's elevated viewpoint, the activity level was nothing less than astounding. Camp Maidan-i-Napthun had turned into a huge field operation.

I gazed toward the old ruins of Musjid-i-Suleiman and saw shadows flickering against a wall. Curious if it was the old holy man, I left my aerie and walked to the ruins.

He was there just as I had seen him before, squatted over a flame. The light from the flame cast deep shadows in the furrows on his wrinkled face. His skin, in sharp contrast with his white hair and beard, was the texture and color of a leather hide. I greeted him in Persian, "*salam aleikum*, peace be with you", to which he replied "*aleikum salam*, with you peace."

I will never forget our conversation.

"At the beginning was fire," he said.

I did not respond, but waited, squatting beside him, staring into the flames. Science has explained too many mysteries of the ancient world. Who now looks intently at a flame, or gives thought to the ethereal nature of fire, or ponders its mystical dancing luminosity?

"*Ahura Mazdah*, the Wise Lord, lit the truth with fire to show man the path to pure existence."

"How does one attain pure existence?" I asked.

"By practicing righteousness."

I asked him if I was on the path to righteousness. He turned and stared at me for a long time.

"The struggle ends with the triumph of good," he said. "You will fall from the sky and perish in flames in the truth of righteousness. The righteous will meet in paradise."

Perish in flames, I thought. What could he mean?

The refinery and pipeline now employed more than two thousand men. Reynolds was running the drilling operation at Camp Maidan, but he told me his position was untenable. In Ahwaz, Black told me how Reynolds had bungled negotiations with the *khans*. I asked about which negotiations. Black's answer was not specific but stated that Mr. Greenway agreed with him. My recommendation to Reynolds was for him to resign. I saw, perhaps clearer than Reynolds, that he no longer fit the organization.

I was kept busy with my new assignment, especially with the details of building the docks and refinery. The Sheikh of Mohammerah expected compensation for everything, from removing date palms to deepening the river channel. These and other issues required a cultural diplomacy which I was unfamiliar with. Our discussions were held in the Sheikh's palace, where I would sit with the Sheikh on cushions arranged on the floor. We talked what seemed to me endlessly of details which mattered little. His secretary, Mirza Muhamad, stayed at his side and occasionally whispered comments in his ear. Oriental negotiations tested my patience.

Major Cox was a steady hand in overseeing how I dealt with these and other thorny issues. He had the good sense to know when to allow me free hand and when to hold the reins. He warned me of excess of zeal, but I could not do less. Things move quickly. One must be ahead of the march of events or be crushed by them, or which is almost as bad, be passed by. With his help in guiding my new responsibilities, my respect for Major Cox grew immeasurably.

Major Cox did nothing carelessly. He was never in a hurry. If needed to, he worked sixteen hours a day, doing thoroughly what he might have done in an hour superficially. Every notable local was indexed and cross-indexed. Every town and village identified and placed on a map. Every old file searched to confirm statements that might well be taken for granted. His staff had an unbounded admiration for him, as did the Navy. The government might differ from his conclusions and reject his advice, but they scarcely ever disputed his facts or his deductions.

A.T. Wilson (left) and Sir Percy Loraine

One of my guests, E. B. Soane, was a remarkable man who had been living in Kurdistan disguised as a Persian. He had at least one Persian wife and was dismissed from the Imperial Bank of Persia, its directors not holding with mixed marriages. He was penniless but understood most languages and cultures of the region. I asked him to stay and write a full account for the government of all he knew of Kurdistan, which he agreed to do. Upon my recommendation, he was hired by A.P.O.C. to look after their interests at Chiah Sourkh.

Black often visited the consulate. He told me he had recommended to Mr. Greenway that both Reynolds and Ahmed Khan be dismissed. Black enlisted my friend Soane to write a letter about Reynolds' inadequacies. Soane echoed Black's recommendation. Reynolds was not respectful of Soane, whom he considered a vagabond.

Since I was not part of A.P.O.C. or the agency yet was familiar with the oil company's personnel, Black asked me to make an enquiry into the condition of the entire camp and specifically into the conduct of Ahmed Khan. I wrote Black and the directors a report after confidential conversations extending over three day with all the principal European and native employees of the company at Musjid-i-Suleiman, in regard to the measures to be taken to put things right, and to prevent further troubles, whether with the Staff or with the guards. My report:

Things at Musjid-i-Suleiman, though perhaps not so black as they have sometimes been painted, are in a very unsatisfactory way, and radical changes are necessary. The position of affairs is such as to be a matter of grave concern to me, and I offer the following suggestions for your careful consideration.

Mr. G.B. Reynolds, General Field Manager: This gentleman expressed his deliberate opinion to me that his position in the camp is untenable for reasons into which I do not enter, and that he was unable any longer to hold it with credit to himself or with profit to the Company. Things have plainly gone too far for any substantial improvement to be made by administration adjustment. He said to me, "I suppose that the outcome of this enquiry will be that you will try to get me out of it. I am quite ready to resign. If the Company makes a reasonable offer, I shall raise no difficulty." This suggestion on his part was entirely unsought by me. He read over it in writing and approved of it being shown to anyone I thought fit.

Ahmed Khan: He was anxious to resign forthwith, but Mr. Reynolds dissuaded him from doing so at present. Were Ahmed Khan to leave at once, Mr. Reynolds would be gravely inconvenienced, and his departure would indubitably be looked upon as a victory for the guard, who would be more difficult than ever to be dealt with. Ahmed Khan has informed me he will apply to the managing agents for permission to resign when Mr. Reynolds goes on leave.

I have little doubt that he has to a large extent brought the enmity of the Europeans upon himself by posing as Mr. Reynolds' confidant and personal assistant. But I am satisfied that he is not guilty of the charges brought against him. The real fault is with the arrangement which places him in a position of authority where he inevitably has to come in conflict with Europeans. With men of the class of Mr. Willans, Blackwell, Dunn, Turnbull, Bird, and Coy the mere fact that Ahmed Khan is a native of India is enough to make them treat him with contempt.

Much of the evidence obtained from them indicated that

racial prejudice was at the bottom of their objections and complaints. "I don't see why Mr. Reynolds should treat a b____y niggar like that, better than a white man." "I don't see why a niggar should ride a horse and a white man a mule." "He is only a black man and goes around giving orders to native workmen a if was a Sahib." "He doesn't treat me with proper respect, being only a native."

On the other hand, Mr. Reynolds replies that Ahmed Khan is a more companionable and civilized person than his detractors, better educated, better manners, cleaner habits: a point of view which has my sympathy. The mistake was to introduce such a person into a camp consisting of rough engineers.

Greenway's response was not to question Black or Soane, but to send out a letter stating that there can only be one boss, and that boss was the managing agent. I could only imagine how Reynolds reacted to the letter.

On May 6, 1910, unexpected news plunged us into genuine gloom. King Edward VII had died. I hastened to send official notifications in the prescribed form, and to drape the consulate in black and to fly the flag at half-mast. I warned all British subject to wear mourning clothes and all consulate employees to wear black bands.

The new century, which his inauguration had heralded, was abruptly transformed. In hindsight, his death was the coda to the previous century, with all its pomp and circumstance, its monarchies and empires, and its struggling classes. Upon his death, a new era had begun.

Chapter Seventeen

Sir Admiral John Arbuthnot Fisher

Admiral Fisher

Lord Esher brought the news to me at Kilverstone Hall, where I had retired this past January, on my seventieth birthday. What an *inexpressible* sorrow! How we both knew the loss. What a great national calamity! The King was dead!

I really couldn't get over the irreparable loss. Treves gave me an account of the King's last day. I rather think the King was coming to see me here, had he remained at Sandringham.

The funeral was attended by Europe's royalty: nine kings, seven queens, five heirs to the throne, forty royal highnesses, dukes and ambassadors representing seventy nations. It was the greatest assemblage of rank ever gathered in one place. I walked alone in the cortege in my admiral's uniform, decorated with medals pinned to my breast by the very hands that now were silently crossed in the casket. I mourned not alone. The streets were lined ten-deep with our countrymen, all dressed in black, silent and apprehensive.

He was a noble man and every inch a King. God Bless Him! I don't say he was a Saint. I know lots of cabbages that are saints. They couldn't sin if they wanted to.

We all knew, I think, that the King's death changed the world. The King's nephew, Queen Victoria's oldest grandson, Kaiser Wilhelm II, rode at the head of the cortege next to George V, his cousin, our new king. Kin or not, I had known since 1905 that England would fight a war with Germany. Few believed me, and many questioned my judgment, but I knew it was coming.

Later in the summer Lord Esher came to Kilverstone to discuss the Navy. Even retired, I was consulted by friends who knew my sole purpose in life had been to reform and to advance the Navy. My enemies knew it as well!

"What of McKenna?" asked Lord Esher. "Will he continue your programs?"

McKenna was First Lord and had just been here on his second visit, so he liked the first visit, I suppose!

"He has shown me various secret papers. He is a real fighter, and the Navy Haters will pass over his dead body! If our late Blessed Master was alive, I should know what to do. But I feel my hands tied now. Perhaps a kindly Providence put us both on the beach at the right moment! Who knows?"

"Some are pushing for have an inquiry into ships designs," said Lord Esher. "What is their purpose?"

"Their purpose is delay, delay, delay! I shoved my colleagues over the precipice about water tube boilers, the turbine, the Dreadnought, the scrapping of ships that could neither fight nor run away, the nucleus crews, the redistribution of the fleet. In each and all it was *athanasius contra mundrum*, but each and all were a magnificent success. Two immense episodes are doing Damocles over the Navy just now! Delay would be insanity!"

"Sir John, what two items are you speaking about?" asked Lord Esher. "Our Naval Program has been supported, even by the Liberals. We have twice as many dreadnoughts as Germany and a number greater by one than the whole of the rest of the world put together. Lloyd George had rather spend money on Old Age Pension than on the defense of the Empire. But our Navy rules the waves. What else could you hope for?"

"Oil engines and internal combustion! Since July 11th Bloom & Voss in

Germany have received an order to build a motor liner for the Atlantic trade with *no engineers, no stokers, no funnels, and no boilers!* It requires only a damned chauffeur! The economy is prodigious! As the Germans say, *kolossal billig!*"

"It's a passenger liner, not a ship of the line," replied Lord Esher. "Surely a passenger ship is no threat to our Navy."

"No threat? It will prove to Germany the speed and efficiency of a diesel engine. No more coal! Why, all the past pales before the prospect! I've been pushing and shoving to convert to fuel oil since '03. I said to McKenna, shove'em over the precipice!"

"Yes, yes, well, I'm on your side, Admiral," replied Lord Esher. "Shoving worked when you had the King at your side. Now we must proceed with caution."

"Caution be damned! What would Nelson have done? Caution is not a strategy for war. It's a policy of congenital idiots!"

"You mentioned two items held over the Navy."

"The second is that a democratic country won't stand ninety-nine percent of their Naval officers being drawn from the upper ten. It's amazing to me that anyone should persuade himself that an aristocratic service can be maintained in a democratic state."

"It's been the case since long before Nelson. Meritocracy still rises. Look at yourself."

"The true democratic principal is Napoleon's: *la carrier ouverte aux talents!*" The democracy will soon realize this. The twentieth century leaves no place for a tradition that favors sending sons to serve the Navy because they are from the right family. The Navy, indeed the world, demands meritocracy! The secret of successful administration is the intelligent anticipation of agitation. I said to McKenna, "Shove! *Shove them over the precipice!*"

"How can we change a policy that has been a tradition for two hundred years?" asked Lord Esher.

"It is essentially a political question rather than a Naval question. Only the damned Tory prejudices stand in the way!"

"Tory prejudices?" Lord Esher's back stiffened at the statement. "Tory prejudices?" he repeated.

"I am greatly inclined to move out in the open on these two vital questions," I replied. "The one affects its fighting efficiency as much as the other. Meanwhile I'm doing the mole. Certain upheavals will appear soon. It wants a leader in the open!"

"It wants a *political* leader," said Lord Esher. "Which wouldn't be Jacky Fisher. You have more enemies than a vineyard has grapes. Surely you are not thinking of a run for Parliament."

I did not feel compelled to reply to such a statement. Of course I wasn't. Seventy years old and more enemies than a vineyard has grapes. Ha! But shall I count my friends? What Britain needs is a First Lord of the Admiralty with some fortitude.

"It needs someone to shove'em!" I concluded.

I've loved dancing and singing all my life. Neither compromises fidelity. When I repeated the wedding vows, I swore on the Bible. Dancing and singing are not unfaithful. I've danced all night many times over the past fifty years, and recently danced with a sweet and truly delightful American til dawn. It keeps the brain sharp. Even though now nearly as old as Dandolo, I don't feel any lesser than at nineteen. Dandolo after an escapade at the Dardanelles became conqueror of Byzantium at eighty years of age. And Justinian's two generals, Belisarius and Narses, were over seventy. Dolts don't realize that the brain improves while the body decays, provided of course that the original brain is not that of a congenital idiot, or of an effete poltroon who never will run risks.

Once at a very dull lunch party given in his honor, I sat next to King Edward. "Pretty dull, Sir, this," I said, "hadn't I better give them a song?" He didn't say otherwise so I sang a delicious Cockney tune, with an introduction.

"Two tramps had been camping out in Trafalgar Square. They lean against each other for support. 'Too much beer!' says one. They look upward at Nelson on his monument," and in an inimitable and beery voice I sang:

> We live in Trafalgar Square
> With four lions to guard us,
> Fountains and statues all over the place,
> The Metrolpole staring us right in the face
> We own it's a trifle draughty,
> But we don't want to make no fuss.
> What's good e-nough for Nelson
> Is good e-nough for us!

One of my critics at *The Times* says I am not modest. I never said I was. The next day, Sir Alfred Yarrow mentioned perhaps the most momentous thing I ever did – the introduction of the Destroyer. And the following day, Sir Marcus Samuel writes that I am the godfather of oil, and oil is going to be the fuel of the world.

In a life of some sixty years on actual Naval service, with but three weeks only unemployed, from the time of my entry into the Navy to the time of Admiral of the Fleet, I still enjoy suet pudding and treacle with a pleasure. I remember on July 4th, 1854, when I went on board H.M.S. *Victory*, 101 guns, the flagship of Trafalgar of Admiral Lord Viscount Nelson. Yes! My thankfulness is equal to but hardly as wonderful as that of the almost toothless old woman who, being commiserated with, replied, "Yes, I only 'as two left, but thank God they meet!"

When asked at the Hague Peace Conference, I was one of the British delegates, what are the amenities of war, I replied war has no amenities. It's like two innocents playing singlestick. They agree when they begin not to hit hard, but it don't last long! Like fighting using only one fist against the other man with two, the other fist damn soon comes out! "All's fair in love and war" enunciated a great principal.

War is the essence of violence. Moderation in war is imbecility. *Hit first! Hit hard! Keep on hitting!* In war you want *surprise*. To beget surprise you want *imagination* to go to bed with *audacity*!

When asked why modern nations should ever conduct war, since our business interests are so closely intertwined, and therefore everyone loses. Because, I said, two qualities rule the world: emotion and earnestness. I have said elsewhere, with them you can move far more than mountains. You can move multitudes. Brains never yet moved the masses. Emotion and earnestness will not only move the masses, but they will *remove* mountains! As I told Queen Alexandra on seeing the King's dear dead face for the last time, his epitaph is the great words of Pascal in the *Pensees*, chapter 9. *The heart has reasons that reason knows nothing about!*

It's the personality of the soul of man that has immortal influence. Printed and written stuff is but an inanimate picture – a very fine picture sometimes, no doubt, but you get no *aroma* out of a picture. Fancy seeing the Queen of Sheba herself, instead of only reading of her in Solomon's print!

Chapter Eighteen

James Hamilton

In January 1910 Greenway took over as Managing Director of A.P.O.C. at the recommendation of Mr. Wallace, who said a younger man than himself need fill the position. From a merchant working for Shaw, Wallace & Co in April to Managing Director of the Anglo-Persian Oil Company in January was quite an increase in responsibility for Greenway, He accepted the position with relish.

By the summer of 1910 the European staff had increased to thirty-seven and the native staff by several hundred. Black, the on-the-ground manager, was challenged by the build-up in personnel and delivery of equipment, and complained to Greenway that both Reynolds and Ritchie did not willingly comply with his directions.

"I am sorry to see that Ritchie, too, has now joined the band of people who are disputing Lloyd, Scott's position," Greenway told me. "For the sake of discipline and the dignity of our firm in Persia, I think you should make it clear that this system of attacking them behind their backs, which is foreign to all my ideas and experience, and which if permitted will make it impossible for us to retain any self-respecting men in Lloyd, Scott's employ, will not for a moment be tolerated. The Managing Agents in Persia must have *supreme control* in all local matters."

"Black seems to have difficulty with his managers," I observed. "Perhaps *he* is the problem."

Greenway dismissed this with a comment about the chain of command being paramount to personalities. I wondered if he thought the chain of command trumped competence, but did not contradict his concern.

The next week he telegrammed Glasgow from London that I should instruct Black to give Ritchie a "free hand in all matters relating to the pipeline and water problems outside political negotiations" and that "Ritchie must have an entirely free hand and that every possible assistance must be given him in carrying out his special work."

I wondered if this was not sending crossed signals to Black, who was told he was the Managing Director and all direction should flow through him.

In October Black asked to be relieved if the directors would not give him their full support. Greenway told the Board he was not satisfied with the supervision or the progress of our field operations, that Black was not up to performance levels, and that the Board should accept his resignation.

The Board approved Ritchie's appointment. Greenway next recommended that he travel to Persia to evaluate the progress of our operation. The directors approved his request and added that I accompany him in order to add a perspective and to assist in writing a summary report. Greenway further recommended that Reynolds be absent from the field during our inspection. He feared Reynolds presence would intimidate employees from expressing themselves freely.

The trip to Persia was the most strenuous of my life. The passage to Persia on the P&O was delightful, but as soon as the ship's lines were secured to the dock in Mohammerah, I could smell the fetid land. Date palms waved a doleful greeting. The town gave testament to a civilization long past its days of glory. Instead of the palaces of Darius, before us stood a hovel of mud huts.

The next two months were arduous beyond endurance. Even in January the humidity and heat were oppressive. The acting consul, Lieutenant Wilson, tried his best to make our evenings more comfortable by placing us at dinner under fans pulled by *punkah wallahs*, but sleepless nights under mosquito netting on the rooftop left me groggy and lethargic.

The company staff in Ahwaz complained bitterly about tinned food, the need for a club, and inadequacy of direction. Ritchie I found to be impetuous and unlikeable, a bully of a man who lacked leadership qualities. The horseback ride from Dar-i-Khazineh to Camp Marmatain was stressful, thirty miles on a dusty cart path to a place as desolate as any on earth. Gas flares and the smell of sulfurous rotten eggs at Musjid-i-Suleiman made me think, instead of oil, we had discovered Dante's inferno.

Greenway seemed enervated by the scale of our operations. He dismissed the climate and nineteenth century transportation systems as nuisances. Mainly I think he wanted to validate his conclusion that Reynolds had to go. When we returned to England, he bound his report and presented it to the board.

Charles Greenway

Greenway's report accused Reynolds of deliberately delaying work, of sabotaging operations, and of myriad acts against the best interests of the company. Greenway sent a telegram from Ahwaz to London stating Reynolds should be terminated forthwith. After a brief interview, he fired Ahmed Khan, whom he described in the report as "dangerous".

In Persia, as in England, Greenway took the reins of authority with confidence and self-certainty. By the time he left Tehran, there was no question who was in supreme control of A.P.O.C.

On my return to Glasgow I stopped in London and reported to Mr. Wallace. He updated me on the termination of Reynolds, stating that he was sorry it had turned out as it did.

"Before you and Greenway left for Persia, I wrote Reynolds, asking for his version of the allegations against him. I used the words 'it would appear' because I will not accept the *ex parte* reports of anybody high or low without having the version of the others. He responded by saying Black obstructed his work and overruled his decisions."

"It's a sad state," Mr. Wallace continued. "I spoke with Reynolds here. We discussed his complaints. He could not work for Black."

"Did you terminate him on the spot?"

"I wrote him a letter on Feb 10, explaining that based on Greenway's telegram from the field, he was terminated. He responded by letter."

Mr. Wallace handed me a letter dated February 13 from Reynolds. It was brief and stated he "considered it most inadequate and ungenerous treatment", but he was disposed to accept it if could have a quick answer as he had another opportunity of taking up important work.

"What were his terms?" I asked. Several years remained on his contract.

"To pay him L3250."

His salary was L2000. Later I calculated he was owed for vacation at full pay and his contract had two years and three months remaining.

"Did you accept his proposal?" I asked.

"Cargill thought it outrageous," replied Mr. Wallace. "He felt strongly that you and Greenway had proof of his negligence, and stated he would not pay the man a penny. Those were his words."

"So you fired him without compensation?"

"Cargill relented and authorized me to offer L1000, which Reynolds accepted. Cargill believed his quick acceptance proved beyond a doubt that he was guilty as accused and the L1000 was a final extortion fee."

Rumor had it that Reynolds accepted a position in Venezuela. We never saw him again.

Chapter Nineteen

Dr. Morris Y. Young

While he was in Persia, Mr. Greenway appointed me the Anglo-Persian Oil Company Political Officer. He thought that my good relations with the Persians would be beneficial to the company far beyond my work as a medical officer. I recommended to Mr. Greenway that the appointment be kept unofficial so that *khans* and the locals would continue to look at me as a medical officer rather than as a political officer.

My first assignment as Political Officer was to purchase land from the *khans* at Musjid-i-Suleiman covering the limits of the oilfield. Although Reynolds had reached agreement with them in November 1905 on the use of their lands, at the time it was never contemplated that a large oilfield would be found. The agreement never pinned down cultivated lands and *cultivable* lands. It assumed the *khans* owned the land, which was not completely true. The *ryats* who farmed the land believed it to be theirs, for which they paid an annual rental to the *khans*. Thus operations had been carried on without any very definite understanding on land ownership.

Dealing with the *khans* on any basis is difficult. They do not draw a distinct line between truth and falsehood. They expect to be compensated for every piece of ground, whether we drill on it, build on it, or travel on it. They regret what they signed in 1905 and were doing their best to retreat from the terms already agreed upon, which was a payment of L5000 for use of the lands. At the time of the 1905 agreement, Reynolds told me, although the 1901 Concession gave full rights to the minerals, it did not specify surface rights. If the company did not pay for the use of the surface, the Bakhtiari *kahns* threatened to withdraw all the native laborers from the project. The payment, which covered the right to drill on their lands, was actually to prevent them from carrying out their threat to stop work.

The ordinary Lur depends for his livelihood on the few acres given him to cultivate, and knows, as well as we did, that the *khans* will pocket every available *kran*, even if it be for land he, his father, and forefathers have been cultivating. He knows further that once a settlement has been arrived at with the *khans*, he will be expelled from the place and told to go and find a place "elsewhere". It is not an easy matter, as every piece of ground in any way cultivable is already taken up.

Such a Lur, and he has many followers, can be no friend of ours. To his simple mind it appears that we have robbed him of his land, of his crops, of all he possesses, and not only have we not paid *him* for it, but have actually been the cause of his expulsion from the place altogether. We can hardly blame these people since they are left uncompensated and unprovided for in every way. The owner of a piece of land which we were to acquire for a pumping station told us that he would see his wife's and children's throats cut before the *khans'* eyes rather than give up the land in question.

In this way, we are breeding enemies who take advantage of the slightest incident to cause a row. The Company retaliates by complaining to the *khans*, who subject these people to harsher treatment. The Alawands, in whose midst we live, very often take the law into their own hands.

Not only do they plough uncultivated land, but they do so on drilling sites. They have even gone to the extent of encircling machinery laid ready for erection of a rig, knowing perfectly well that we must find a way to the site. It is done in order to obtain compensation for the crops which we will eventually destroy in crossing to the place. Why no effort has been made to stop them I cannot understand. Outside of our camp, some have taken to plowing part of our road, which we have been using for years without trouble. In a sentence, ever since that sum was paid, all the *khans* and their *ryats* exercised greater activity and vigilance, anticipating our need of certain plots of ground.

It is in this context that I had been appointed Political Officer to negotiate with the *khans* over the Company's use of lands. I looked forward to the negotiations in Malamir with some trepidation.

Negotiations with my acquaintance, the *Ilbeghi* Sirdar Mutusham, lasted three weeks before breaking down. Lt. Ranking, the vice-consul at Ahwaz, Mr. Scott, who had surveyed the lands for the Company and had brought detailed maps of the lands under discussion, and I were greeted each morning with much ceremony and led to cushioned seats. After formal inquiries about our health and dispositions, tea was brought in silver teapots and served in small glasses. Then coffee was offered, and finally a *qalyan* or water-pipe was passed round the assembled company.

Following the formalities, discussions ensued on each point of negotiation. The *khans* must have rehearsed their play in Teheran. The Russians had given them the prices of land in Baku, which had no bearing on the prices here but set the stage for debate.

"Mr. Reynolds paid the Amirs £5000 last winter, do you acknowledge?" I said.

Yes, there was no argument about the payment. The issue was what it had covered.

"It was agreed to be the earnest money for £50,000."

Of course this was nonsense. I showed them the 1905 Agreement signed by the *khans*, granting the oil company use of their lands, with payment for cultivated land, old fallow land, and non-arable land.

"Mr. Reynolds promised to pay us 50 *tomans* per *jarib*. Why then should you desire it for less?"

This was a complete falsehood, but to drive a precedent out of a Bakhtiari's head is no more possible than to break a wall by ramming one's head against it. From this starting point, I directed the discussion to each issue. We all agreed the definition of cultivated land included what was under cultivation at present or had been under cultivation every second or third year. It was the custom to cultivate a patch one year, and then to let it lie fallow for two to three years.

Heated discussion followed about old fallow land, lands that were cultivable but which had not been under cultivation for several years. The *khans* denied the existence of such land and maintained that their *ryats* cultivated not only all the flat land within recent years, but even the sides of hills. The tribes, they said, migrated a good deal and a plot of land may be left fallow for a few years, but either the same or another tribe returned to cultivate it. Mr. Scott, with an experience in these matters spread over a period of forty-five years, could not conscientiously say that what he called "old fallow" had not been cultivated within recent years. He informed me that practically all the flat land had been under cultivation at some time or another. In the face of such conflicting evidence, it became a most difficult matter to lay a hard and fast rule between new and old fallow, especially as related to flat land.

Grazing and non-arable land was another thorn in both sides. It was true that the 1905 agreement made a point of cultivated land, but there was no clause whereby they were bound to supply non-cultivated land free of charge.

In the Persian text, the meaning of the word "give" does not necessarily convey the idea of a *free gift*. In reply to our contention that the hills were useless to us, they replied, "We do not force you to buy them. Buy as many *jarib* as you like, but our tribes will use what is left."

There were heated discussions, but we were very careful to keep them respectful. After three weeks, though, it was clear we could not reach agreement on a price, so we broke off discussions altogether. The very day we broke off, I had the *khans* over to lunch at our house as if nothing had happened. I really thought they would excuse themselves, but they came. Nevertheless, we all knew very well what it might mean to us were these people to leave in a rage and with the land question unsettled. We told them we would wire London for instructions.

Although we had no official meetings until replies reached me, we had a good many unofficial ones, and the final price arrived at was 20 *tomans* for arable land and three *tomans* for non-arable. Ultimately they gave me two-thirds of the total area of non-arable for free. This meant 3,064 acres free of charge.

We finally closed at L22,000 on the condition that two thousand pounds out of this sum be given to the themselves as agents for the sale of the lands. This we agreed to do, but noted in the agreement the price was L22,000.

Thus we bought about 9½ square miles or 6,131.38 acres for a price of L3.12 per acre. I am advised at least seventy-five percent of the land can be drilled on with ease. The *khans* realized they could not obtain money from the *ferringis* by merely stretching out their hand. They told me that I was hard on them. I wish I could have been harder and would to goodness this undertaking had been in our hands last year instead of this year. I should mention that the original Persian text of the agreement is much more solid than the English translation, and gave us full rights to do anything we liked with the land we had bought.

Chapter Twenty

Lt. A.T. Wilson

In January 1911 my assignment as Acting Consul in Mohammerah ceased with the appointment of Major Haworth of the Indian Political Department to the post. In 1910 I had pushed my surveys from the seacoast to the creeks. I had made the acquaintance of Colonel Cox and the Royal Navy. I had gained experience in handling men of my own kind and race as well as Indians, Persian, and Arabs, and in the spheres of local politics and diplomacy. I had made progress in learning Persian and Arabic, and was glad to leave Mohammerah for fresh adventures in the mountains.

The growth of the German trade was causing concern, as was the tendency of the Russian consular and diplomatic officers to increase their activities in the Neutral Zone. I heard rumors confirming what Major Cox had told me that the old *Ilkhani*, Samsam-es-Sultana, was meeting with German agitators who spoke harshly about the British presence in the Persian Gulf.

Before I left the post two directors of the oil company, Mssrs. Greenway and Hamilton, came out to see things for themselves. Neither of them was as able as John Lloyd, but held large ideas within certain rather narrow limits. They did, however, settle a few outstanding issues. I wished they had come out sooner.

In February while I was in Bushire visiting Colonel Cox, I learned that Reynolds had been terminated. Since last year when he returned from leave, he had been unable to adjust to the new organization.

In many ways Greenway reminded me of Reynolds. Both were self-assured. Both by their nature commanded authority. For Reynolds, no challenge was too great to tackle, or to resolve. I could not speak to Greenway's competence, but he seemed a more ambitious man than Reynolds, and with a large sense of importance. Authority compels some men to expect loyalty and deference, and to wrap themselves in a cloak of self-importance.

While I was in Bushire reporting to Colonel Cox, the indefatigable Mrs. Cox tried teaching me to dance. My Consul replacement, Major Haworth, enjoyed dancing, playing the guitar, singing, and gardening, and was in many respects my opposite. Mrs. Cox thought I should learn the finer arts of socializing, but my heart was in action and exploration.

Railways in the Middle East were part of a diplomatic game being played by Russia and Germany. The Germans were financing and helping the Turks build the Berlin-to-Bagdad railroad. The Persians preferred to have no railway rather than one not under their control. Our concern was to see that our strategic interests in India were safeguarded. Germany's aggressive presence in the Middle East was perceived as a challenge to our interests. The termini on the Persian Gulf should be under our control and the railways, if built, should serve to assist British and Indian trade.

It was thus that I received my next assignment: to survey possible routes for railways from Mohammerah through the Zagros Mountains to Burujird and Hamadan. I relished the work.

Before leaving with the surveying party, I spent a month in Bushire working with Colonel Cox and studying all the official papers on the subjects. His insights showed the usual foresight, for he had been pressing for years the need for safeguarding our position at this end of the Gulf. He cautioned me to be aware of German influences. Rumors abounded that a German whom I had met briefly, Wilhelm Wassmuss, was actively fomenting revolt among the Bakhtiari against our interests.

While I was in Bushire with Colonel and Mrs. Cox, Captain Lorimer and his new wife dropped in for a visit on their way to his new assignment. Now that he was married, Captain Lorimer's life had taken a new direction. No longer would we converse for hours, sharing interests in culture, poetry, religion, and politics. Those days in Ahwaz were gone. Time had pressed forward.

I asked Captain Lorimer about the Pusht-i-Khu. He offered valuable advice about tribal factions in the mountainous region where I would be surveying and cautioned me to take along a force of soldiers.

"Tribes in the Pusht are a warrior class from Biblical times," he said. "They live by blood feud and will kidnap and hold for ransom any foreigner who penetrates their strongholds."

I took his advice seriously, but Colonel Cox overruled an armed guard. He wanted the information and sanctioned the endeavor, but attaching an armed guard to a survey party would require central government sanction that would be impossible to receive.

I departed Bushire for Ahwaz and spent Easter in Shush haggling with Lur chiefs over supplies and men for the journey into the Pusht-i-Kuh. Few Englishmen had penetrated their lands. In the 1800's, Rawlinson had crossed the mountains, as did a trader, Mackenzie. Lord Curzon wrote of the region in 1890. Otherwise, it was unexplored.

I set about learning everything possible about the country and the tribes, believing that forewarned is fore-armed. The outstanding source of discussion in southwest Persia was resentment among Lurs and Arabs alike against the Bakhtiari *khans*, who appeared to aim at replacing the Qajar dynasty. No one objected to the Qajar's mild and weak rule, but the prospect of being governed by men whose forefathers were petty tribal leaders was intolerable.

In Shush I was introduced to Mulla Ma Taqi Dirakwandi, an old man who had influence with all the tribes. He gave his age as seventy-five, but he had an accurate recollection of Colonel Rawlinson's expedition in 1844. He was thin, white-haired, his face deeply furrowed, but his teeth and eyesight were perfect and his fund of stories inexhaustible. I filled a notebook with his detailed accounts of local land revenue, crops grown, ownership of various tracts, tribal rights and feuds. If A.P.O.C. should bore for oil in the region, such data would be of great value.

Mulla Ma Taqi had a remarkable memory. He gave me a list of all the governors of Luristan for nearly a century. Some were princes of the blood royal; others were Lur chiefs; some hanged robber chiefs and tortured malefactors; some brought armies and some brought peace. Luristan today, he told me, was as bad as at any time in his life. Nothing would improve it but trade from opening of the road or building a railway. But that would mean domination by the central government, which had always treated the tribes with cruelty. In the end, the government would weaken and the tribes would take their revenge. Ten times he had seen this happen. The road was dotted with ruined forts. The hillsides were strewn with graves.

An immediate arrangement for my journey to Kharamabad was impossible. The more I pressed, the higher the price they asked. After a week of hunting expeditions into the area, which were short trips to the edge of Luristan proper, my plans began to mature.

Three chiefs of the Qalawand agreed to convey me in safety to Kharamabad for about L50. My best manuscript Quran was produced. I wrote our agreement with a fine red pen and India ink upon the flyleaf. With great ceremony, the seals of the three signatories were produced from a silk purse and affixed by the Mullah who had engrossed the deed. Each signatory kissed the Quran in turn, and placing his right hand upon it swore "by the faith of the glorious word of God" to abide by the letter and spirit of the bond.

On April 20th all my plans were upset. The Qalawand women leaving Dizful for their weekly picnic and bath in the river were robbed of all they possessed and stripped naked by the Baharwand. Fresh raids across the river added to the prevailing insecurity. There was intermittent firing all night round my camp, and several attempts made to steal my horses and mules.

I was unmoved and left Dizful on the 25th, transferring my camp to the old barracks on the right bank. On the way I climbed a 4,500-foot hill, and during a three days' halt made miserable by heavy rain, drew maps of the region. I was struck by the nervousness of my escort. From the moment we left camp, they were clearly afraid of being attacked.

As we moved into the Pusht, I worked on my maps and took careful geological notes, too. On May 2nd we travelled to Tirado, where the Zal River breaks through the Chinara or Kialan range in a deep gorge, passable on foot year round and with mules when the water is low.

At Qafilajah we had to halt for a day to bury a man killed in a tribal dispute. The dead man's toes were tied together. A Mullah read prayers as six young men carried the body on a rough bier shoulder high to the grave, dug in a cemetery so old that some of the graves were, by their orientation, pre-Islamic. The body was buried in the blood-stained shirt in which he had met his death, his feet towards Mecca. The men were solemn; the women wailed aloud. Some relatives tore at their *hari* and rent their tattered garments. The cries of the man's children were dreadful. His death meant that little was left for them but slavery within the tribe.

On May 5th we halted near Pul-i-Tang, where the Karkhah River runs in a deep gorge so narrow at the top that it is spanned by a single arch. Close by, only twelve to fifteen feet separated two projecting rocks, one on either side. The tribal chiefs with me said that the young men of the tribe often jumped, rifle in hand, across the gorge.

"If they can do it, so can I," I told them. "Let me see them do it and I will follow."

They took it as a challenge and called for volunteers. None came forward. Anxious to prove my mettle, I declared that I would jump it myself. They begged me to do no such thing. It would be a terrible thing for them if I should miss my footing. I had no fears, though, for I wore the Persian *givah* or cloth shoe. I took a short run and leapt across the chasm. It was certainly worth doing, for the fame of it preceded me to Burujird, where the chasm was described as at least thirty yards across.

I enjoyed this life to the fullest. The tribe, with its flocks and herds, moved only thirty miles or so a week, which left me time to climb mountains and survey the route. I was now fairly fluent in the Lur dialect and could converse freely on what interested my hosts. They were helpful but uncouth and overbearing, regarding themselves as good Moslems, naturally superior to pale-faced Christians, though I was tanned as deep a shade of brown as they, and wore a solid black beard. My food was just what they eat, neither more nor less. I slept always on the ground, as a safeguard against robbers and against being shot as one lies in a bed.

One night as I sat on the hillside below my camp I witnessed at close quarters a little ceremony which must have dated back to pre-Islam, perhaps to Sumerian times. Half a score of young women came in single file along the rough path to a *pir* or sacred place, marked by a few graves, some pre-Islamic, and a great pile of small stones. Here they formed a line, facing the Kuh-i-Shahzada Ahmad, a massive mountain which stood out clear-cut against the light of the moon behind it. Two of the women lit little oil lamps and placed them upon the ground in front of the party. They waited for a time, then as the moon rose above the crest of the hill, one of them began to pray aloud.

"O Shahzada Ahmad, O Shahzada Ahmad, our guide and defender, answer our prayers, protect our men, give health to our children, guard our flocks, and make them fruitful."

Then they waited in silence until the last of the lamps flickered and went out. With a final deep obeisance, they returned by the same path, murmuring prayers as they went. Some minutes later one woman returned alone. She too lighted a lamp and prayed aloud, "May my next be a boy."

There is no place in Islam for women in public prayer. Nowhere else in Persia or Arabia did I in later years witness or hear of such a ceremony.

I came to regard the wives and daughters of he tribesmen with whom I was living with real admiration. Their powers of endurance were a perpetual source of wonder to me. They bore, quite literally, the burden of the day, in heat and bitter cold, though far less well-clad as their men. They bore, too, many children, carrying them often for great distances. They and they alone milked the sheep and goats, prepared the food, wove carpets and tent cloth and many more items. They helped to load and unload the pack animals, but went afoot more often than they rode. Without a wife, a man was as helpless and useless as half a pair of anything else, and he knew it.

On May 7th we crossed the western end of the Kialan Mountain to Jaidar. On the way, I climbed 2,500 feet to the top of Do Furush, accompanied by one man who carried my plane table. I reached the summit long before he did and was amply rewarded. A great Lammergier eagle with its claws lowered to strike swooped down again and again to within a few feet of a rock. Coming up silently in my cloth *givahs*, I peeped over the rock to see what quarry it was after, and saw an ibex standing guard over two kids. Down came the eagle again, wing feathers rustling like wind among leaves. The kids ran under their mother, who butted the eagle boldly with her horns. The moment the eagle had passed, the kids ran out and began to graze, only to take shelter again when the bird made another snatching dive at them. This was repeated three or four times until it saw me and flew off.

Next day at Walmiyan, near Jaidar, news came that the Baharwand Mirs, the same who had attacked Captain Lorimer, had seized the next pass and barred the way against us. They demanded *rahdari*, road toll, to the amount I had promised my friends for the whole trip from Dizful to Khurramabad. To give way to them would be to ensure a repetition of such tactics all the way to Burujird.

I formally refused to pay, and held my hosts to their bond. We pushed on a few miles farther to Badamak, where a council of war was held. The Mirs had shown that they were in earnest by seizing some flocks of goats and sheep belonging to my friends. The possibility of a compromise was discussed. The Kurd Aliwands had joined us, so we were now the stronger party.

The greybeards took me into their confidence. They did not wish to fight, but would not give way to blackmail, else there would be no passage for them in future years. I was a good shot and had a good rifle. Would I fight?

"Yes," I said, "gladly!"

"Ah, but it would be fatal," one said. "He would kill a man and start a blood feud and no foreigner coming up the road would be safe from vengeance." He quoted a verse from the Quran. *By killing your father, you sow seeds of malice; having killed your father, when will come reconciliation?*

"But you will pretend to fight?" one asked me.

"Yes," I agreed, "I will pretend to fight."

"He might be killed," said a third, "and the British government would demand our blood. He must not expose himself. That would be madness."

Thus they bandied words and balanced arguments until a man rushed into the tent with the news that the Mirs had again seized a flock and had cruelly beaten his son. A minute or two later came news that they had killed a man of the tribe.

Women wailed. Shouts of indignation came from outside the tent in which we sat. The leading greybeard, a man of great stature and presence, arose and swore a great oath.

"By Baba Buzurg and by this holy Quran," and he placed his hand on the sacred book slung across his shoulder in a satchel, "it shall be blood for blood and no more words. We will fall upon these dogs and sons of dogs, bastard spawn of dishonored mothers. They shall remember this day."

The tribesmen ran to their tents, where they cast down any superfluous garments, and emerged a moment later, lithe, barefooted, half-naked figures, and with extraordinary skill and speed, ran up the rocky slopes that lay between them and the enemy. They formed themselves into groups, each with a recognized leader, usually an older man, one of whom was pointed out to me as "a lion" who had killed twelve men.

The fight began soon after midday. The total number of engaged was not more than three hundred. By nightfall, two or three of the enemy had been killed or wounded. The flocks were collected close to our camp, and after they had been milked, were watched by shepherd boys, assisted by women who had heaped quantities of dry thorn and long grass next to small fires.

One of my hosts, Kadkhuda Baruni, took me with him to the top of the pass, which our men had seized shortly after the firing began. Two boys with us brought bread and dried cheese for the sentries who lay invisible under boulders or in crevices, listening rather than watching the slopes before them.

At dawn there was more shooting and we learned that an enemy leader had just been killed and one of our young men mortally wounded. We had captured a large flock and four men, and had taken their rifles and felt coats, but not their lives.

At midday, firing ceased to see what was happening, I walked to the top of a low hill which dominated the camp and was perhaps eight hundred yards from the front line. I raised my binoculars and focused on a section of the enemy line. Suddenly a cry was raised from our side.

"*Tilism daravurd*! He has cast a spell upon them! Let us go forward!"

I lowered my glasses, and up rushed Baruni, leaping from rock to rock, his *aba* or cloak flowing in the wind.

"Put up your arms again!" he shouted to me. "Do not lower them. Hold the spell!"

"My arms will tire," I said.

"I will send men to uphold them," he replied, and shouted for two men. The tradition was from the days of Joshua in Exodus:

Joshua fought with Amalek, and Moses and Aaron and Hur went up to the top of the hill. And it came to pass, when Moses held up his hand, Israel prevailed, and when he let down his hand, Amalek prevailed. But Moses' hands were heavy, and Aaron and Hur stayed up his hands, the one on the one side, and the other on the other side. And his hands were steady until the going down of the sun. And Joshua discomfited Amalek and his people with the edge of the sword.

Fascinated by this historical parallel, I let the men hold up my hands. Our side cheered and went forward, leaping form boulder to boulder. A few long shots spattered the ground on which I stood. The greybeard shepherds on either side comforted me.

"It matters not," said one. "The talisman is working. The medicine has turned their hearts to water."

An hour later, the fight was over. On balance, we had won. Our dead were three to their four. Our captured sheep and goats three hundred to their one hundred. *Sayids* in blue turbans headed by one who was also a *Haji*, as shown by his green waistband, went forward under a tattered flag. As they left our camp, they began to chant from the Quran the opening verses of the *Sura* used at the Burial of the Dead.

As the procession left camp, our warriors were silent. The hush was broken only by the bleating of unfed lambs and by the wails of mourning women within the tents.

The greybeards from each group discussed terms of the armistice. The Mirs offered six mares and two rifles as blood money, but still demanded the right to take me to Khurramabad. The terms were indignantly rejected and the Mirs left, abusing me, the *farangi*, the Frank.

Just before dark, news came of an intended night attack. It was a full moon. A shot was fired. Women screamed and flocks of goats began to scatter. The panic soon died down. The shot had been fired by one of our side who had mistaken a returning patrol for an enemy band.

The rest of the night passed without incident and the next two days were spent in negotiations, which were extended to cover all outstanding blood feuds and claims on both sides. The *mirzas* of both sides, peaceable men skilled with the pen, sat by the chiefs and gave details of unsettled debits for the past two years or so. The proceedings were marked by a great show of courtesy, lest trouble should start afresh. Agreement was at length reached after some twenty hours of talk, during which I was an interested but silent listener.

The Mirs were to hand over two mares, two mules, three rifles with ammunition, and two women of good family to be given in marriage to the sons of Baharwand leaders, as a commitment of future friendship. I was to remain with the Baharwand, but was to soften this blow to their enemies by a present to the Mirs of *L*20 when I was safely in Khurramabad. On the way, I was to be free to survey and go where I wanted.

The day after the battle I witnessed the burial of our dead. The ceremony lacked nothing of dignity or pathos. The burial ground held the bodies of many men who had died thus in battle. Some graves were marked by stone lions roughly, almost grotesquely, cut from pieces of solid limestone. Others had a headstone on which was carved an invocation to Ali, patron saint of the Shias, above crossed swords to indicate a fighting man, "a mighty man of valor", as the Old Testament put it.

Nearly a fortnight later, just before I entered Khurramabad, I was present at the final stages of the tribal settlement. Mares, mules, and rifles had been handed over, after much dispute as to quality, but the question of brides had still to be adjusted.

The greybeards sat in their long tent and the first of the two women was brought before them, a girl of some eighteen years, shapely, comely with fearless eyes, the daughter of a black-bearded Mir of fierce mien who sat in the assembly, eyeing her with pride. Opposite him sat the prospective bridegroom, nervously fingering his robe. He was the son of one of my hosts, who sat on his left.

The presiding *sayid* extolled his virtues and those of his father and ancestors, whose lineage he traced through ten generations or so to the eponymous head of the tribe. He had a good tent, fine herds of sheep and goats. His father had given him a mule and half a mare. He was an ideal match.

The Mirs delegate said as much and more of the girl's ancestry and of her noble father, a lion in battle, a statesman in counsel, a lamb in society, devout in religious practices, esteemed in the market place, a travelled man who had visited many shrines, including Karbala and Narjaf, Meshed, and Qum.

The assembly listened with obvious enjoyment to their eloquence, feeling themselves to be vicariously ennobled by their tributes. The contrast between the proceedings and the fierce outbursts which marked the armistice negotiations a fortnight earlier was impressive. The speeches were formal, and not perhaps wholly sincere, but they did much to smooth the path of the peacemakers.

The girl's father then spoke in measured tones. His daughter had never lacked handmaids. She had never gone afoot. She had never ridden save upon a fine mare. Not for her was the drudgery of milking cattle. She made carpets such as only her mother could make, carpets for which the merchants compete eagerly. She was a mullah, could read a little and write well. She could keep accounts and was more than a match for the hucksters of the bazaar. She must have better pots and pans, quilts and pillows, than her future husband could offer.

The youth's father took up the challenge. His tent lacked nothing. He would see to it that the bride's establishment was furnished as well as his own.

After an hour of parlaying, conducted with great courtesy, I helped both parties reach agreement by presenting a wedding gift to the bride of a pair of silver dessert spoons and L2 cash.

"Well done!" cried the assembly. "God give you luck!"

The case of the second bride was less spectacular, but eventually assurances were given and satisfaction reached.

The remainder of my journey was less eventful until the last stage. In this region, as everywhere else in southwest Persia, were remains of paved roads, probably of Sassanian construction from more than a millennia earlier. Here and there may have been remains of yet more ancient tracks upon which the Sassanian road builders superimposed their own handiwork. The old tracks zigzagged up the same hillsides on steeper gradients.

The Sassanian paved road was often built across limestone slabs deeply furrowed for centuries by the feet of flocks and pack animals. Here and there, too, often running across the Sassanian road but never across the older track,

I saw the foundations of earlier buildings, consisting uniformly of large uncut boulders as heavy as a man can lift, laid on a rectangular plan.

My mapping was interrupted before reaching Khurramabad when, after a long climb to well above 8,000 feet snow level, I found that my muleteer had been set upon by two Mirs who had incised his throat, the cut being slowly made with a blunt knife. They told him it would be deeper unless I paid for the right to cross the barren hills.

My servant, Mirza Daud, had played a man's part during the journey, but with the goal in sight, his heart failed him and he urged compromise, which I refused to consider. If I gave way now, I could never return, and my successor's path would be even thornier than mine.

I roundly upbraided my hosts, declaring that they might cut my throat and take my poor belongings, but not a penny would I pay. The dispute waxed loud and long. At length, they relinquished and agreed to forego any claims.

Before riding into Khurramabad, I put on my best Persian cloths, had my servants don their best frock coats, and threw a pair of handsome carpets over the backs of the two mules which bore my camp kit. The Kadkhudas with me were now all smiles and compliments. They made their mounts caracole on either side of mine. The galloped at full speed, aiming their rifles backwards Parthian fashion to shoot at a rock or stone, which they often hit, and vowed undying friendship.

Five miles outside of town the British Consular agent, Mirza Ali Akbar, met me. Two miles farther on, the governor of the town awaited me with a large mounted escort. My hosts were suspicious and would not approach the townsmen until the agent had arranged and vouched for a temporary truce to enter the town, which turned out to receive us, thronging the gates and crowding the narrow streets, while Mirza Daud and Nabi distributed largesse to blind and maimed beggars at my expense, receiving in return the conventional assurance that God would regard their liberality as an act of merit and atonement for tyranny.

Thus I was able to map an area hitherto un-surveyed. In early June I explored the almost completely unknown country west of the Kashgan. I traveled fast, carrying a rifle and a rucksack that cut sores in my back. In one deep gorge I discovered an oil spring, which I examined with proper care, taking samples in bottles, and specimens of the rocks whence it emerged. Finally I made it to Karmanshah, where I met my old colleague McDouall, who I found well content with his life and his garden.

Finally I travelled to Baghdad, where I was the guest of bank managers, missionaries, and consuls. I called upon the Belgian director of customs, the Russian consul, and upon other Europeans. They were all watching my closely. It amused me to note their surprise when I paid my call and told them what they doubtless already knew of my movements. A fortnight later I was back in the comfort of the Residency in Bushire under the genial inspiration of Colonel Cox and the motherly care of his wife. Soon the sores on my back were cured, and I put on eight pounds.

Chapter Twenty-one

Sir Admiral John Arbuthnot Fisher

I knew it when the German gunboat *Panther* dropped anchor at Agadir, Morocco in July 1911. France protested. By virtue of our 1904 Entente with France, Britain supported France. Until then, until July 1911, Lloyd George was a Germanophile. After Agadir, he switched. Finally he understood who was the enemy. He elucidated it at the Mansion House, "If a situation were to be forced upon us in which peace could only be preserved by the surrender of the great and beneficent position Britain has won by centuries of heroism and achievement, by allowing Britain to be treated, where her interests were vitally concerned, as if she were of no account in the Cabinet of nations, then I say emphatically that peace at the price would be a humiliation intolerable for a great country like ours to endure…"

How wonderfully Providence guides England! Just when there is a quite natural tendency to ease down our Naval endeavors, along comes Agadir! *Time and the Ocean and some Guiding Star, in high cabal have made us what we are!*

One consequence of Agadir was a change within the Cabinet. McKenna was replaced as First Lord of the Admiralty by young Winston Churchill, thirty-six years old. He said he opened the Bible at random to the ninth chapter of Deuteronomy: *Understand therefore this day that the Lord thy God is He which goeth before thee, as a consuming fire he shall destroy them…*

Now, Winston said when he became First Lord, he could lay eggs instead of scratching around in the dust and clucking.

Wasn't it the Emperor Diocletian who doffed the imperial purple to plant cabbages? And damned fine cabbages, no doubt! So don't blackguard me for leaving the Admiralty of my own free will to plant roses!

After retirement I never did a wiser thing than coming abroad and remaining abroad, and working like a mole. My métier is that of the mole! Trace my upheavals! Just after retirement, I communicated with Winston. He sent me by return post a most affectionate letter and said I was the one man in the world he really loves! Well! I really love him because he's a great fighter! In October he was appointed First Lord, and asked me to Reigate Priory in Surrey. I was there three days with him and Asquith and Lloyd George.

Winston told me he intended to prepare for an attack by Germany as if it might come the next day. God bless him! He plied me with questions. I poured out ideas he said "like a veritable volcano"!

I told him in 1899 at the Hague Conference, I walked the sands of Scheveningen with General Gross von Schwarzthoff. The Kaiser said he, Schwartzhoff, was greater than Moltke. There was no German Navy then. He expatiated on the role of the British Army, how the absolute supremacy of the British Navy gave it such an inordinate power far beyond its numerical strength, because 200,000 men embarked in transports was a weapon of enormous influence, and capable of deadly blows – occupying Antwerp, or Flushing, or landing ninety miles from Berlin on the fourteen-miles of sandy beach in Pomerania, impossible of defense against a battle fleet sweeping with devastating shells the flat country for miles, like a mower's scythe, no fortifications able to withstand projectiles of 1,450 pounds.

On Trafalgar Day 1904, I became First Sea Lord. I was already working like a mole subterraneously about the submarines, and there were already upheavals in consequence. In 1905 we designed a new class of ship that revolutionized naval warfare. The *H.M.S. Dreadnought*, our first all-big-gun ship, armed with ten guns, each firing a shell twelve inches in diameter and weighing 850 pounds was built in record time, *in twelve months*, by the Royal Dockyard. By the time Winston arrived at the Admiralty, eighteen dreadnoughts with 13.5 inch guns had been launched, laid down, or authorized, but none had gone to sea. Winston immediately included in the Naval Estimates for five more ships, each to hurl a 15-inch 1,920-pound projectile more than six miles. All powered by *oil*!

Winston and I talked three days while the Prime Minister and the Exchequer listened. From what Winston has since said to a friend of mine, I think I did right in going. Without doubt, McKenna is a patriot to have encouraged *me* to help Winston, who said his penchant for me was that I painted with a big brush, and was violent! I reminded him that even the Kingdom of Heaven suffereth violence, and the violent should take it by force!

I returned to Lucerne, but three weeks later Winston called me back to Plymouth. We spent three days on the *Enchantress*, the First Lord's yacht, three days of continuous talking and practically no sleep!

Because of my recommendations, he brought eighty-eight percent of the entire Fleet to the North Sea -- *and made its future battle ground in the North Sea its drill ground!* Oh my God! Winston's work. My recommendation. He's my beloved Winston till charcoal sprouts!

Sixteen admirals were scrapped! I am more popular than ever!!!

A lovely woman two days ago sent me this riddle: why are you like Holland? Because you lie low and are dammed all around. But there it is. With the sixteen shoved over the precipice, Jellicoe will be the Admiralissimo. He has all the attributes of Nelson, imagination and audacity, except *one*. He is totally wanting in the great gift of *insubordination*. Nelson's greatest achievements were all solely due to his disobeying orders! But when the Battle of Armageddon comes along in September 1914 -- as I predict it will -- Jellicoe will be Commander-in-Chief. That date suits the Germans. Both their Army and Fleet then mobilized and the Kiel Canal finished and their new ships complete.

In April I broke off talks with Winston. He promoted three admirals close to Beresford, one of the baying hounds when I brought home 160 vessels in '05, vessels that could neither fight nor run, whose officers were shooting pheasants up Chinese rivers and giving tea parties to British consuls. Brought'em home from all over the world! How those consuls did write! And how agitated was the Foreign Office. *Sweep'em out!*

In April when he sailed the *Enchantress* to the Mediterranean to tell the admirals and Kitchener we would move the battleships to the North Sea, he and Clementine and Asquith and his lovely daughter Violet dropped anchor in Naples harbor and invited me to lunch. I was nearly kidnapped and carried off. They were very sweet about it. My old cabin as First Sea Lord all arranged for me! I had a good time and came out on top! I took it up with Winston again, and heard the lovely Violet say to Winston, "he's melting"

"What's melting?" I demanded.

"The butter," replied Violet.

I danced on deck the next morning with Violet. What a lovely twenty-five year old lady! Between her dancing and Winston's charm, and the prime minister dead on for my coming back, with great reluctance I agreed to re-enter the battlefield.

Speed! Speed! My constant cry was for speed. Do you remember the recipe for jugged hare in Mrs. Glasse's Cookery? *First you catch a hare…!* The first of all necessities is speed so as to be able to fight *when* you like, *where* you like, and *how* you like!

Oil fuel meant speed. Oil was already in use in submarines. They couldn't run on coal. By Winston's arrival we had seventy submarines and fifty-six destroyers, all run on oil. I love the Americans! They already had two battleships, the *Oklahoma* and the *Nevada*, to run on oil. But America had its own oil.

Winston needed advice. He needed facts. He asked me to return to England to preside over a Royal Commission on Oil Supply. His letter to me was irresistible:

"The liquid fuel problem has got to be solved. It requires a big man. I want you for this, to crack the nut. No one else can do it so well. Perhaps no one else can do it at all. I will put you in a position where you can crack the nut, if indeed it is crackable. Your gifts, your force, your hopes, belong to the Navy. As your most ardent admirer and as the head of the Naval Service, I claim them now, knowing you will not grudge them. You need a plough to draw. Your propellers are racing in air."

How could I resist?

Chapter Twenty-two

James Hamilton

D'Arcy met Admiral Jacky Fisher, now Lord Fisher, at Marienbad back in '03. D'Arcy told me he spent a weekend later that year with Lord Fisher a short time before he talked to the Rothschilds in Cannes about the Concession. The meeting aboard their yacht was shrouded in mystery, but whether it was D'Arcy's discussion with parties outside the Empire with the Rothschilds and The Shell Group, or whether it was Lord Fisher's push to convert the Navy from coal to fuel oil, shortly afterwards the Oil Committee of the Admiralty was formed.

Indeed it was First Lord of the Admiralty Pretyman who brought the Persian Concession to the attention of Burmah Oil back in 1905. It was First Lord Selborne at the Admiralty in 1909 who earnestly insisted Lord Strathcona be named chairmen of A.P.O.C. And it was the Admiralty in December 1911 that called upon Lord Strathcona and Mr. Greenway to report on the results of their Persian oilfield development. After his meeting with the Committee, I asked Mr. Greenway what the Admiralty was looking for.

"Captain Parkenham said the Navy was looking at all sources of supply for fuel oil either in British territory or elsewhere."

"Was he interested in our Persian project?"

"He asked about oil sources in Burmah, Canada, Egypt, Nigeria, and Trinidad. I told him what I knew, that our production in Burmah had peaked and except for Trinidad, the quantities found in the other locations were small. Lord Strathcona and I assured the panel that A.P.O.C. had found an inexhaustible supply of oil in Persia."

"Inexhaustible?"

Mr. Greenway straightened his back. "Inexhaustible. I said we were developing only one field, but there are ten to twenty fields we know of, and probably fifty fields with, so far as can be judged, an *endless* supply of oil at various points between the Northwest Frontier of Persia right down to Bander Abbas."

"Was Mexico mentioned?" I asked. Recent discoveries there had excited the public, and if true, were far superior to our Persian production.

"Mexico was not mentioned. Had they asked, I would have predicted ruin for Lord Cowdray and his Mexican Eagle. The country is undergoing revolution."

"Did the committee ask about our pipeline and refinery?"

"Yes, I told them the pipeline had been completed and the refinery should be in operation within three months. Admiral Riley asked about its capacity. When I told him four million gallons per month, he thought this adequate for the needs of the Navy."

"Is the Admiralty looking to purchase oil for their ships? Encouraging, don't you think, Mr. Greenway?"

"We discussed the viscosity of the oil and other characteristics which would make it suitable for Naval ships. They also inquired about the politics of Persia. I told them we had a little problem two or three years ago with the Bakhtiari, but had sent guards from India for a period of twelve to eighteen months. When the necessity for the guards no longer existed, we let them go, but if trouble arose again, the Government of India would be quite prepared to send them again."

"Well, well. The prospects for selling our refined fuel oil has just risen, do you think, Mr. Greenway?"

He smiled. "I told the committee the problem our company faced was not in securing a quantity of oil, but in securing a market for our refined products. The only markets open to us are small markets on the east coast of Africa. Consequently we are considering joining ranks with The Standard Oil or with the Royal Dutch to help in marketing our refined products."

"What did they say to this?" I asked.

Mr. Greenway smiled again. "It is not in the Admiralty's strategic plan, they told me, for the Persian Concession or for the refined products to be in foreign hands. Perhaps," he concluded with another smile, "there is a deal in the making."

Chapter Twenty-three

Lt. A.T. Wilson

I left Isfahan for Ahwaz on the first day of January 1912 in deep snow, travelling very light, with two servants. We generally found shelter for ourselves and our beasts in caravanserais, or in some headman's house in a village, for the cold was intense on the Isfahan plain, which is about 6,000 feet above sea level. We travelled fairly fast from dawn to dusk, until we reached the first of the three lofty passes by which this once much-used track crosses the Zagros. We were told that the snow on the higher slopes and on the summit was so deep that even an experienced guide would probably lose it. Moreover, it was soft snow, and no caravan had passed for three weeks.

At last we found an old Bakhtiari who knew the road well, and who wished to reach the low country whither his family had already gone. He promised to lead us if we would let him ride half the way. He insisted on leaving four hours before dawn, as he hoped that our beasts could be led over the snow without plunging into it.

It was a clear moonlit night when we started out. I have never in all my journeys seen a more beautiful or awe-inspiring sight than that which met my eager eyes at early dawn from the summit of the highest pass, about 9,000 feet, after four hours of steady walking over crisp, crackling snow. Range after range was visible in the clear air, the farthest at least a hundred miles distant. *The roseate hues of early dawn, the brightness of the day*, in the words of the hymn, lent brilliance and color for a time to these forbidding hills, utterly deserted of all life. Even my stolid Persian servants were moved by the magnificence of the view spread before them, and piously murmured "Allah Akbar" God is great, partly in recognition of the majesty of nature, partly in relief at finding that, despite the warnings and forebodings of our friends, the snow was hard enough to walk over.

We arrived next day at Ardal, a village set in a mountain valley where the Bakhtiari khans of one of the leading families make their summer headquarters.

I intended to go to the caravanserai like an ordinary traveller, but was told by my guide that the mother of one of the senior chiefs was in residence in the little castle there and that I should be a welcome guest. We had spent the previous night in our tiny tents upon a patch of frozen earth between two deep drifts in a bitter wind with temperatures in the twenties or thirties.

The lady was most gracious and hospitable. I was given the best room, richly carpeted and tapestried with the product of local looms, and was given a dinner worthy of a great London club. After I had dined she came to see me, and after the usual polite preliminaries, began to cross-examine me.

I have never met any Persian of either sex better informed or so well-balanced in the expression of political views. She told the story of her father, a famous *Ilkhani*, who like her grandfather, had been treacherously murdered by a Persian Governor-General, the Zill-us-Sultan, uncle of the present Shah.

Persia, she said, would not recover till the Qajars were ousted. God would decide in his own good time who should replace them. It could not be the Bakhtiari *khans*, who were playing a leading part at Teheran at the moment. After tea and coffee had been brought in, in silver urns and served in silver cups on silver trays, she withdrew. Her place was taken by her major-domo, who I suspect had been listening at the door. The bluff, hearty old rogue came with a bottle of good shiraz wine and two glasses, and drank with me the health of his mistress.

We did not leave Ardal till three hours before midday. We rode hard that day, continuing till long after dark, and again the next day, spending the night in a *sarai* without windows or doors. On the second day, with great effort, we reached Malamir plain. A bitter wind blew with such violence that it lifted fine gravel, which stung like hail. Then the rain came. I was less well-clad than my followers and decided to walk to keep myself warm. I drew ahead of them, and found out later that they had been forced to stop to renew a broken girth. My horse was lamed by a stone fixed underneath the broad plate which, in Persian, takes the place of the traditional horseshoe. They had to take off the plate, remove the stone, and replace the plate.

Trudging on in the dark in heavy rain, I saw lights ahead and hoped for food and shelter. The lights went out and I saw them no more. An hour later, tired and hungry, despairing of finding shelter, I took refuge in a rough shed. Hearing heavy breathing I struck a match, which revealed some cows lying close together. Here was warmth, which I needed more than food.

I lay between the cows and went to sleep. When I awoke it was dawn. I struggled to my feet and went back to the main road. Less than an hour later I saw my caravan approaching. We pushed on to Kala Tul, a romantic little fort in the center of a small plain at the foot of the western slopes of the Mungasht, made famous by Sir Henry Layard's account twenty years earlier. We fed our animals, got some bread and buttermilk for ourselves, and pushed on to Jaru, where we were well-known and well-treated.

To the northwest the sky at night was lit by the great flares of burning gas from the oil wells at Musjid-i-Suleiman. The headman told me all the local gossip, much of which centered round Dr. Young, whose medical skill was doing much to reconcile the local people to the rising prices, rising wages, and other changes which such sudden development must always bring. The next day we rode to Weis, a long and dreary march with tired beasts, where I put on clean clothes, washed and shaved, polished my saddlery and did my best to appear presentable. I walked into the Ahwaz consulate as if I had just returned from a morning ride.

I was welcomed by Captain A.J.H. Grey and his new wife. She was a sprightly French girl who dressed "better than we should advise". Grey told me the latest news. It was not good.

Disturbances were still reported from every quarter. The oilfield might be affected. Anxious as we were to avoid intervention, it might be forced upon us, as in Egypt in 1881, by events over which we had not control.

Persia has been decaying for years. The Constitutional movement, started by men who were trying to stop the rot, has hastened it. The Anglo-Russian Agreement of 1907, designed to retard the rot, has not succeeded.

I paid calls on the Deputy Governor and upon all local European residents. The river steamer was not due to sail for a week, so leaving my servants and animals to rest at the consulate, I put my small belongings upon an open sail boat returning to Mohammerah, and arrived just in time to catch the little B.I. steamer to Bushire, where I was informed I was not at present to go to India, but was to remain in the Gulf "on special duty", as a sort of spare horse.

Chapter Twenty-four

Sir Admiral John Arbuthnot Fisher

In March 1912 Winston introduced his first Naval estimates to the House: four dreadnoughts, eight light cruisers, twenty destroyers, and an unspecified number of submarines. For decades, our naval strategy required the maintenance of a fleet capable of defeating the fleets of any two other naval powers. Winston changed the strategy. Henceforth, the goal of our construction was to maintain a sixty-percent superiority over any *single* nation which threatened us. We cannot have everything or be strong everywhere. It is futile to be strong on the subsidiary theater of war and not overwhelmingly supreme in the decisive battle. In the North Sea! We turned over the Mediterranean to the French.

Newspapers claimed our preoccupation with the North Sea had lost our hold on the Mediterranean, "the carotid artery of the Empire". O.M.G.! Did they not see the threat! The hounds keep baying at the moon but get no answer! Didn't Solomon and Mr. Disraeli both say that whatever you did you were to do it with all your might? You can't do more than one thing at a time with all your might – that's Euclid. Mr. Disraeli added something to Solomon. He said there was nothing you couldn't have if only you wanted it enough.

I have only had one idea at a time. I have been a humble and an unostentatious follower of our Immortal Hero Nelson. Some venomous reptile in the press called Nelson vain and egotistical. Good God! Some nip-cheese clerk at the Admiralty wrote to Nelson for a statement of his services, to justify his being given a pension for his wounds -- his arm off, his eye out, his scalp torn off at the Nile. Let us thank God for that clerk! The Almighty has a place for nip-cheese clerks as much as for the sweetest wild flower that perishes in a day. How this shows one the wonderful working of the Almighty Providence, and that fools are an essential feature in the great scheme of creation. Whenever the words *fool, ass* and *congenital idiot* are used, they should be printed in large capitals!

In March 1912 Lord Cowdray submitted to the Admiralty a report on his

Mexican Eagle oil discoveries in Mexico. His oil wells, although significant producers, were within the geographic sphere of American predominance. In November I chaired a committee at the Admiralty to question the manager of A.P.O.C. about their Persian concession, which is within the British sphere of predominance.

"Mr. Greenway," I asked, "will you kindly tell us what you wish us to know about Persia?"

"We are of the opinion," he replied, "that we hold the biggest oil concession, not only in British, or British-controlled territory, but also perhaps in the world. The concession, as you probably all know, is rather a unique one, inasmuch as it covers nearly the whole of Persia."

"Will the whole of Persia produce oil?" I asked.

"I brought a map with me in order that you may appreciate the extent of it. This is the map of Persia and our concession is that apart which I have colored in red. Our opinion is that the whole of the hills running from the northwest down to Bundar Abbas, more than eight hundred miles, are more or less oil-bearing."

I looked at my colleague Sir Boverton Redwood, who sat on the committee with me.

"Do you agree, Sir Boverton?"

Sir Boverton nodded. "It is all prospective," he replied. I took his answer to be more positive than negative.

"Mr. Greenway, please continue."

"The various geologists who have been there, Mr. Burls, in the first place, Mr. Reynolds later, and Mr. Cunningham Craig and others have only seen a little bit of it from time to time. But our knowledge of the whole area is to a great extent based upon what we know of their investigations, upon what has been seen by our employees, and upon the reports of officials and others, including myself, who have travelled over the country."

"And your development? You are developing an oilfield at present?"

"Indeed we are, Lord Fisher, at Musjid-i-Suleiman, here at this spot on the map." He pointed to a point north of the head of the Persian Gulf.

"What is its extent?" asked Vice Admiral Sir Henry Oram. Sir Henry was my protégé and an engineer.

"We believe we have got a proved area there of oil territory of about eighteen square miles," replied Mr. Greenway.

I had perused his testimony a year earlier in which he claimed the area to be three and a half square miles. Since then the field had expanded, but not by five-fold. Greenway's point was, even if somewhat exaggerated, that we had discovered a very large field.

"What kind of producing rates have you encountered?" asked Vice Admiral Sir John Jellicoe. Jellicoe is always to the point, a gunnery expert and my designee, if merit and talent matter, to command the Great Fleet.

"We have not had a sufficient experience yet to judge what the producing capacity of those wells is, but several of them began at about 3,000 barrels a day, and the ones that we have had producing, Nos 4 and 5, we have had to limit our output because we have not had our refinery working, so we have only been able to produce them to a very small extent. So far as I can judge, all the wells we put down there can be regarded as producing wells capable of yielding from 400 up to 800 barrels per day. How long their life will be at that rate we do not know."

"What do you wish the Admiralty to do, Mr. Greenway?" I asked. "If your company has found such an enormous supply of crude oil, is there not sufficient quantity to provide the Navy with fuel oil?"

"The intention, or rather the belief in the minds of the directors of the Anglo-Persian Oil Company, and of the people who associated themselves with it originally, Lord Strathcona, Mr. D'Arcy, and others, has been that it was the desire of the British Government that this field should be developed and exploited for the benefit of British interest. It has been carried on purely from that point of view up to the present time, the directors always having had the belief that when the Company came to the producing stage, the Admiralty would desire in some form or another to exercise control over the field."

"Yes, yes," I responded, "in some form or another. What are you suggesting?"

"We have got to make up our minds whether we are to attach ourselves to the Admiralty, or whether we should join hands with the Shell Company. Yesterday the Shell Company requested to have an interview with us. The object of the interview was to renew the threats which have been made from time to time that if we did not come and join hands with them they would start a war of rates and make the Anglo-Persian Oil Company lose money. They suggested that we should come to an all-the-world arrangement with them."

"An all-the world agreement?"

"They are carrying on negotiations with a view to securing control of Lord

Cowdray's Mexican Eagle Oil Company, the Texas Oil Company, and other concerns which are at present independent. We know they have recently secured control of the Union Oil Company and are in progress with the German Imperial Company."

"Undoubtedly," inserted Sir Boverton, "I think that this German Imperial Oil Company has been engineered, to use a familiar phrase, by the Royal Dutch Company, and I believe it is a fulfillment of the threat which Sir Marcus Samuel has been making publicly, again and again, during the past few years."

My friend Sir Marcus Samuel, I knew to be a patriot. But combining the Anglo-Persian Oil Company with his and Mr. Deterding's Royal Dutch Shell would mean foreign ownership of what is now a strategic commodity for the Navy. I asked Mr. Greenway what was Anglo-Persian's alternative, if not to join with Shell.

"I propose an alliance with the Admiralty," Mr. Greenway replied.

"Have you any concrete ideas as at to how an alliance as you have mentioned between the interests of the Admiralty and the interest of the Anglo-Persian Oil Company could be carried out?"

"There are many ways it could be done. For instance the Indian Government could lend our Company $L100,000$ per annum, which we could repay in oil."

"Have you put that forward to the Indian Government?" I asked.

"No, I put it forward to the Admiralty in my interview with Sir Francis Hopwood the other day."

"Could you see your way to guarantee half a million tons a year at the expiration of, say, three years from now?" asked Sir Boverton.

"I think so, without the slightest doubt," answered Mr. Greenway.

"Suppose that the Admiralty made a contract without any question of subsidy. Does that not give you security enough?" I asked.

"No, because how are we to get it out? We want that amount either guaranteed or advanced in some shape or form to enable us to get the capital we require."

I finally understood what he meant: the Asian-Persian Oil Company has the crude oil but does not have the money to increase the production of fuel oil in quantities to satisfy the needs of the Navy.

"Can you let us have a copy of this map?" I asked.

"Certainly," he replied, and handed me the map. "I hope that the information I have given you," he continued, "will have been of a convincing nature, at any rate as to the desirability of retaining British control."

"There is no doubt the Anglo-Persian Company is very patriotic," I replied, and adjourned the meeting. Now that I understood their situation, a full Admiralty review of the oil fields was needed. The Navy needed its own evaluation.

Chapter Twenty-five

Lt. A.T. Wilson

The Indian Government nominated me for a survey of the Luristan country, however I was delayed by fresh troubles at Bushire. An attempt was made by a Persian, under the influence of the heady wine of Constitutionalism, to murder the Belgian Director of Customs. It might be the precursor of other attempts, and so was necessary to devise such practical measures as would reassure foreign residents without committing ourselves to intervention.

I went first to see the Bakhtiara *khans* at Ab-bid on the Karun above Shushtar -- big men with big escorts and small minds, but able as no one else to keep the tribes they govern from fighting with each other. Their faults are many, but they have made it possible for the oil company to develop their oilfield at Musjid-i-Suleiman without a day's interruption of work. That would have been quite impossible anywhere else in Persia except Arabistan, where the Sheikh of Mohummerah is supreme.

I went next day to Dizful, where a feud had broken out between rival factions. While I was negotiating agreements for the survey party which has just reached Mohammerah, I heard that I had been appointed as Deputy British Commissioner to an International Commission to "delimit" and "demarcate" the Turco-Persian frontier from Fao to Ararat. Over the greater part of the length, some seven hundred miles, the line follows watersheds or rivers, or crosses barren stretches of desert. There we have to "demarcate", i.e. put up boundary pillars and mark them on maps. There are some stretches where the frontier line has to be settled. In the event of disagreement between the Turkish and Persian Commissioners, the British and Russian Commissioners have been invested with arbitral powers to reach a decision on the spot.

I am to go home at once, make all arrangements with the Foreign Office and the India Office for the equipment of the Commission, which will have an escort of Indian, Russian, Turkish, and Persian cavalry. After the boundary has been demarcated, I am solemnly promised a tour of duty in India.

I returned to Bushire, stopping on the way at Ahwaz, where I stayed with Charles Ritchie, the new manager for Lloyd, Scott and Co, which runs the oil company's business. He has something of Reynolds in him, but without his experience of men and things. I wish Reynolds were here as General Manager.

After a busy fortnight at Bushire, I regretfully said farewell to Sir Percy and Lady Cox, but gladly saw from the deck of the mail steamer the sandy wastes of Persia fade on the horizon. On the way home from Bombay, it was suggested that I should stoke a ship home, in order to try my strength to the limit. The idea took possession of me. It would save me the cost of my passage by P & O and put some money in my pocket.

The stokers were a rough lot, given to the use of words which are conventionally regarded as obscene. Their physique was not good. They had long spells of leave ashore on return to England. While waiting for the next ship to start a fresh voyage, they spent their time and money for the most part in miserable doss-houses. The seemingly endless routine of shifts and rest periods, four hours on and eight hours off, day and night, seven days a week, predisposed them to seek solace when they set foot on shore in the temples of Venus and Bacchus and Euphrosyne, goddess of song, who brought to them, as Milton puts it, *jest and youthful jollity.*

We were twelve days from Bombay to Aden. It was the height of the monsoon season. I soon found out how to wield a shovel and how to spread the fine coal over the length of the grate. I learned to time my stroke to follow the heavy pitch or roll of the vessel, and when and how to rake the bars.

At first my mates would not believe me capable of standing the heavy work. They "knew my sort". We always ended by going sick and having others to do our work. One man picked a quarrel with me, as a blackleg with a white collar, which ended in blows. I retorted that I would do a double shift to decide the question. That settled it. The others separated us and I did my double shift under the watchful eye of the charge-hand, whose job it was to see that the steam was kept up.

The spirit of emulation was strong upon me. I would show them that I could beat them for once at their own dread and dreary trade. I asked the Chief Engineer to let me do double shifts to Suez, and to draw double pay for the extra shift. I retorted that if I failed to do double shifts to Suez, I was willing to forgo the extra pay and would take the ordinary hourly rate for all overtime worked. He offered me pay and half for the extra shift. This I refused. I would not be a blackleg.

I took bets and gave the cook $L1$ extra to provide me extra meat, for I should have to work sixteen hours a day, eight on and four off twice the first day, and four on and four off the second day, alternately, until we reached the Canal.

It was the hardest ten days I have ever spent. I could not have stood the strain had not my mates, who had wagered four to one against me, made things easy for me when I was off duty. They put my mat under the wind sail and made it easier to rest by laying two of their own mats below it. They brought me food into the stoke-hold when I was on the eight-hour shift and water as cool as the wind would make it. I stoked and ate and stoked again, went up to doze or sleep and went down to the stifling damp heat of the boiler room, forgetful of nights or days but spurred on by the sight of a chalked calendar on which we marked our progress.

We reached Suez exactly on time. The Chief Engineer sent for me and shook hands. The Captain came off the bridge and said I was a "tough bugger", a word I reproduce without apologies, for in good English, it is a term of endearment.

At Port Said most of us had a night on shore. My mates declared they would stand me dinner "and the rest" to celebrate the occasion. I had the thought of leaving the ship here, but after this touching tribute, I put the idea aside. It was my first complimentary dinner. None other has given me quite so much gratification.

A stoker "knew a good place". It was a brothel with a veranda on the ground floor, brightly lit with oil lamps. We were served the best food we had tasted since we left Bombay, and strong Italian wine by a genial bevy of friendly young women whose lot was not more unfortunate than that of those whom they served. There was music and song. T.E Brown has described the scene, as I remember it, in one of his poems:

> Ah, naughty little girl,
> With teeth of pearl,
> You exquisite little brute
> So young, so dissolute –

It must have been such women, too, that he wrote

> So these that want to hold Jove's offspring on their knees
> Take current odds
> Accept life's lees,
> And wait returning Gods

We were *life's lees* to them, and they to us. We left Port Said with a few headaches, but feeling life was worth living a little longer.

While in London I had conversations about the affairs of the Anglo-Persian Oil Company with Charles Greenway, and with Lord Cowdray regarding the Luristan Survey. I also renewed my acquaintance with Admiral Sir Edward Slade, who was deeply interested in the future of the oil company, and in such matters as the dredging of the Shatt-al-Arab from the Gulf to the juncture of the Tigris and Euphrates.

After a few weeks in London, Admiral Edmond Slade asked me informally whether I would like to go with an Admiralty Commission to Bahrain and other places on the Arab side of the Persian Gulf to examine and report upon the prospects of finding oil there. I said casually that there was nothing I should like better if it did not clash with Luristan and the Frontier Commission. By some mistake the Foreign Office and the India Office were not told of the proposal by the Admiralty until preparations were far advanced, and I was unofficially rebuked for trying to serve three gods in Whitehall instead of as hitherto only the Foreign Office and the Indian Office.

Chapter Twenty-six

James Hamilton

The Admiralty report relieved some of my anxiety. Anglo-Persian's funds were nearly exhausted. The Abadan refinery continually experienced difficulties with processing the high-sulfur crude. Our options were limited, but we held hopes for a long-term agreement with the Admiralty. Following our trip to Persia in 1911 and Greenway's responses to the Admiralty Committee, the Navy sent Admiral Slade to Persia to evaluate Musjid-i-Suleiman. The report was the result of his four-month investigation. I handed Greenway a bound volume: *The Admiralty Commission on the Petroleum Resources of the Countries Adjoining the Persian Gulf* 28 November 1913 by Admiral Edmond J.W. Slade.

"Have you read it?" Greenway asked.

"Yes," I replied. "I found the report to be generally accurate."

"Yes, good news, Hamilton, good news," replied Greenway with a smile. "And supportive of our position that an arrangement must be forthcoming in order to increase the pipeline and refinery capacities to supply the Navy with sufficient quantities of fuel oil. Did you read the part about the quantity of crude oil supply?"

"Yes, Admiral Slade's report agrees that we have found enough crude oil to supply the Navy until at least 1930, even if all of the Navy's ships are converted to oil. A long-term supply is their biggest concern, don't you think?"

"Walpole seems to think so," he said. "The Admiralty endorses our position that Musjid-i-Suleiman is a significant oil field," Greenway continued. "Although the report states it covers only 3½ square miles, they agree that the oil-bearing rocks are at least 2,500 feet thick, and that the field contains enough oil to supply the Admiralty with 500,000 tons of fuel oil per year for twenty years. We would of course have to enlarge the refinery."

"Now that the Admiralty has made its independent evaluation," I asked, "do you believe they will in some manner advance A.P.O.C. the funds to secure a stable source of fuel oil for the Navy?"

"Yes, in some manner. And at the same time," he smiled, "secure A.P.O.C. a stable source of revenue."

We all knew A.P.O.C. was out of funds. If we ever needed capital, it was now.

"Yes, Hamilton," he continued, "with this report, I believe there is a deal to be made that will be profitable for all of us *and* for the Government."

"A subsidy, do you think?" I asked.

"No, not a subsidy. I intend to propose that the Government buy a fifty-one percent interest in the Company, which would give them control of both the Company and of their oil supply."

"You are suggesting the government invest in a private company...?" I was somewhat incredulous. "Has the Government *ever* purchased a private company before?"

"Only on the Suez project. Here."

He handed me a two-page typed summary. I thumbed through it quickly. "Did the report mention the Strick, Scott agency fee?" I asked.

We all knew what this meant. The owners of Strick, Scott were paid a five percent commission on all refinery sales, plus a reimbursement for all costs. If the Admiralty provided the capital to enlarge the refinery capacity, it would make the owners of Strick, Scott, which included Greenway and myself, wealthy men.

"Certainly," replied Greenway. "Full disclosure is paramount. I told Admiral Slade, Lord Fisher, and the others that legal contracts are in place which must be honored."

"Did they mention the high-sulfur crude?"

"Not a problem, it seems."

In our negotiation with Shell Oil to distribute Abadan's fuel oil, they discounted the price because of the sulfur content. I had worried that the Admiralty might think the fuel oil not suited for their ships.

"It sounds to me like the Admiralty report is a major step. Do you agree?" I asked.

Greenway removed his cigar and nodded. "Yes, a major step. With this report, the terms of any agreement rest upon a political question. For the answer, the First Lord of the Admiralty will ultimately put the question to the House. You might say our future is in the hands of the Mr. Churchill."

Chapter Twenty-seven

Admiral Sir John Arbuthnot Fisher

Mr. Holt Thomas was a valued witness before the Royal Commission on Oil and Oil Engines, of which I was chairman – a sad business for me financially. I only possessed a few hundred pounds and I put it into Oil. I had to sell them out, of course, on becoming chairman of the Oil Commission, and what I put those few hundreds into caused a disappearance of most of those hundreds. When I emerged from the Royal Commission, the oil shares had more than quintupled in value and gone up to twenty times what they were when I first put in.

The Regular Army, as distinguished from the Home Army and the Indian Army, should be regarded as a projectile to be fired by the Navy! The Navy embarks it and lands it where it can do most mischief. Instead of our military maneuvers being on Salisbury Plain – ineffectually aping the vast Continental armies – we should be employing ourselves in joint naval and military maneuvers embarking 50,000 men at Portsmouth and landing them at Milford Haven or Bantry Bay. This would make the foreigners sit up! Fancy! In the Mediterranean Fleet we disembarked 12,000 men with guns in nineteen *minutes*! What do you think of that! We strain at the gnat of perfection and swallow the camel of unreadiness!

On New Year's Day 1914 in an interview in the *Daily Chronicle* Lloyd George attacked Winston's Naval Estimates. He reminded readers that Lord Randolph had resigned rather than agree to "bloated and profligate" budgets for the Navy. Bloated and profligate! Winston had the support of the King, of Edward Gray, and of the Prime Minister. Lloyd George didn't want to raise taxes. Oh My God! Did he not care about the survival of the British Empire?

Winston said, "I am the slave of facts." Facts and realities! On March 7 he presented his Naval Estimates to the House. For two and a half hours his eloquence held them spellbound.

Our naval strength is the one great balancing force which we can contribute to our own safety and to the peace of the world. We are not a young people with a blank record and scant inheritance. We have won for ourselves, in times when other powerful nations were paralyzed by barbarism or internal war, an exceptional, disproportionate share of the wealth and traffic of the world. The world is armed as it was never armed before. All the world is building ships. It is sport to them. It is life and death to us.

The Naval Estimates passed: four more battleships with 15-inch guns, four more light cruisers, and twelve destroyers.

We must have faster ships. No brainy man ever sees that speed is armor. The atheists are all brainy men. I hate a brainy man. All the brainy men said it was impossible to have aeroplanes. Directly the brainy men got a chance they clapped masses of armor on what are known as the "Hush-Hush" ships on account of the mystery surrounding their construction. They couldn't understand speed being armor, and said to themselves, "Didn't she draw so little water she could stand having weight put on her? Shove on armor! Isn't it called handicapping? Isn't it the object to beat the favorite – the real winner? There really is comfort in the 27th verse of the 1st chapter of 1 Corinthians, where the Foolish are wiser than the Wise.

There is absolutely nothing in common between the fleets of Nelson and ours today. Sails have given way to steam. Oak to steel. Lofty four-decked ships with 144 guns to low-lying hulls like that of the first Dreadnought. Guns of one hundred tons instead of one ton. Torpedoes, mines, submarines, aircraft. And now even coal being obsolete! And, unlike Nelson's day, no human valor can now compensate for mechanical inferiority.

What! A battle cruiser called the *Furious* going forty miles an hour with 18-inch guns reaching 26 miles! Take the damn guns out and make it an aeroplane ship! Yes, and we still have ancient Admirals who believe in bows and arrows! There's a good deal to be said for bows and arrows. Our ancestors insisted on all churchyards being planted with yew trees to make bows. There you are! It's a home product! Not like those damn fools who get their oil abroad! Winston said it best. His inimitable words demand repeating.

> For consider these ships, so vast in themselves, yet so small, so easily lost on the surface of waters. Sufficient at the moment, we trusted, for their task, but yet only a score or so. They were all we had. On them, as we conceived, floated the might, majesty, dominion, and power of the British Empire.
>
> All our long history built up century after century, all our great affairs in every part of the globe, all the means of livelihood and safety of our faithful, industrious, active population depended upon them. Open the seacocks and let them sink beneath the surface, and in a few minutes – a half hour at most – the whole outlook of the world would be changed. The British Empire would dissolve like a dream.

Chapter Twenty-eight

James Hamilton

The evening of July 7, 1914 was the most important in our Company's history. The Committee had passed a resolution to be put before the House:

That it is expedient to authorize the issue, out of the Consolidated Fund, of such sums, not exceeding in the whole two million two hundred thousand pounds, as are required for the acquisition of share or loan of capital of the Anglo-Persian Oil Company.

Mr. Greenway and I sat in the public gallery. Lord Fisher and members of the Admiralty were in attendance as well. The House and public gallery were filled in anticipation of the debate and vote.

Mr. Gretton: The matter of expending a large sum of money on Persian oil was debated at length in the Committee of the House, but there were certain aspects of the question, which were not in the time available, thoroughly investigated. A map has been issued is covered with a large number of green dots, showing the places where oil is stated to be, but where no wells have been bored and no supply of oil has actually been proved to exist. This investment of L2,200,000 upon one well and one proved supply is an investment which the House ought not to accept without further inquiry. The First Lord has based his case entirely upon the fact that certain oil companies have formed a ring or trust, and that the Admiralty, in consequence, has not been able to buy oil on fair terms. Any businessman going to an assembly of businessmen to obtain sanction to an investment of this magnitude would have given some figures, at any rate, to support such a statement. The First Lord has absolutely abstained from doing so. He has never told us at what price he would have been forced to buy oil in consequence of the operations of this trust. The whole matter is covered with a veil of impenetrable secrecy, and the First Lord appears to glory in the secrecy with which he has shrouded this operation.

He assumes that the oil is there. Upon that assumption he asks for L2,200,000 to be expended upon one well and upon forming a depot in one harbor at the head of the Persian Gulf, which is blocked by a formidable bar, can only be entered by steamers of a limited size and draught, and then only at certain states of the tide. It is not a business proposition, as it has been stated to the House of Commons. We should have further information.

Lord Charles Beresford: I would like once more to raise my protest against what I consider a gambling transaction – a transaction in which we have no security whatever, because the First Lord of the Admiralty himself acknowledged that the Mediterranean route might probably, or possibly, would be blocked and we should have to send oil derived from this new source round by the Cape. There is another point – that is the security of the pipeline. There is no doubt that the locality will be the focus of disturbance for some very considerable time; and there is no doubt that friction may occur with Russia with which at the moment our relations are perfectly amicable. I think the sum of money is far too large and I do not think there is any security for it.

Another point is that the question of the defense of the oil fields and the routes by the Mediterranean and the Persian Gulf should be explained by the First Lord of the Admiralty before the House of Commons is asked to sanction the expenditure of this enormous sum of money without knowing whether the oil routes will be adequately protected once this becomes British property.

Colonel Yate: There is one question I should like to ask the First Lord of the Admiralty. It is a question I put to the Secretary of State for Foreign Affairs the other day, namely, will he give the country a distinct guarantee that this L2,200,000 now to be paid over to the Anglo-Persian Oil Company will be devoted by that Company wholly and solely to the development of the works in Persia, and not used for any other project in any other country whatsoever?

Mr. George Lloyd: I wish to refer to a statement made by the Foreign Secretary in reference to the oil contract. The right honorable Gentleman said he wanted one question answered, and the contention he put forward was: "I must have oil, and unless anybody could show me a better and less dangerous place than the one we are now going to, our proposition holds good." We are still not quite clear on this point. Does the Government absolutely intend to defend the whole of this *L*2,000,000 and all it involves once they have gone into Persia? Our fleet has never before been so weak in the Mediterranean.

Sir A. Markham: Are we to have no figures put before us as to what price the Government are paying for oil at the present? The House has not been told. It has been kept, as it always is kept by all Government Departments, in absolute darkness as to the price which is paid for all supplies bought by the Government. I want to know how the right honorable Gentleman justifies the maintenance of the veil of secrecy over this contract when the Shell Company has definitely stated in a letter to the press that they are anxious and desirous their price should be stated.

Mr. Rupert Gwynne: The First Lord of the Admiralty spent a great deal of his time when he introduced this measure to the House in casting aspersions on certain people interested in the oil industry, but he expended a very little time in supplying information as to the contract entered into. It is a growing habit with him to say that he will give no information because it is not in the public interest. The difficulty, as the right honorable Gentleman told the House in March last, is not in obtaining oil, but in getting it at a fair price.

Mr. Churchill (First Lord of the Admiralty): When I had the honor of presenting this proposal first to the Committee I made a very long speech and endeavored to give a comprehensive and connected argument, stating the case in its entirety which had led the Admiralty to press this matter first upon the Cabinet and, after they had been convinced of the propriety and necessity of the measure, then pressing it upon Parliament. I certainly do not feel, although I have been asked a great number of questions ranging over every conceivable aspect – military, commercial, Parliamentary, and technical – connected with this subject that I could present the arguments for the Anglo-Persian oil contract by answering all those questions in any manner which would do justice to the subject equal to that contained in the original arguments which I submitted to the House. I have taken the greatest possible pains to lay the argument in its fullness before the House. Now I find, of course, that there is the noble Lord Beresford who says it is a gambling transaction; the honorable Member George Lloyd who says the tribesmen are very dangerous and that we shall be led into great military ventures, from which he recoils; the honorable Member Sir Markham who wants to know all about the price; the last speaker, who asked a number of questions, and the honorable Member who opened the discussion, all of whom raised a great number of questions and objections to our doing anything in this direction.

Here are all these innumerable objections; if any one of which is seriously entertained by the House, the whole thing drops. (shouts of "Hear! Hear!") That applause would seem to indicate that the House as a whole would like to see this contract dropped. I do not believe for a moment that Parliament would allow a proposal put forward in this manner, and dealing with issues of such importance, and offering prospects so promising and so assured, to drop. The financial provision the House is asked to make would secure for the State the control and development of this enormous metalliferous area and this great region of natural oil supply for the Fleet over routes which we can control and in a country which compares in the particular circumstances with any other competitive area. If the House found a difficulty in finding this money, do you suppose for one moment that it would not be possible to find it from other quarters by going upon the market? It would be a perfectly easy thing to do, but then we should not get the advantage of having the control which is so essential to our arrangement, nor would the State get the fair returns and profits which they are entitled to in virtue of the supply contract which they are bound to make for Persian oil.

(After further debate, amid shouts and calls from the bench, the Prime Minister calls for a vote)

Question put, "That this House doth agree with the Committee in the said Resolution."

The House divided: Ayes, 228; Noes, 48.

Three weeks later, on August 4, 1914, Great Britain was at war with Germany. In 1911 Admiral Jacky Fisher had missed predicting its onset by one month.

Chapter Twenty-nine

Lt. A. T. Wilson

The Frontier Commission, which had the authority of four governments – Turkey, Persia, Russia and Britain -- began its work to define the boundary in October 1913. The Turko-Persian Frontier was of great antiquity. From Mt. Ararat southwards it follows the great watershed between the Tigris and the Euphrates to the west, and the Oxus and the inland lakes of Persia to the east. At some points, such as Kel-i-Shin, the present boundary line is where it was in the earliest recorded history of Sumeria and Assyria. At other points, especially in the region of the foothills, it has moved forwards and backwards according to the relative strength of the neighboring tribes. Frontier incidents aroused little interest in the capitals of Turkey or Persia, for the mountain ranges along which the frontier ran had always been grazing grounds of semi-nomadic Kurdish tribes who owned only nominal allegiance to Shah or Sultan. The idea of a territorial boundary was secondary to the allegiance of the tribes who, in their wanderings in search of grass, could not be expected to conform to an artificial frontier line.

The main chain of the Zagros, as formidable and well marked as the Pyrenees, was the boundary between Assyria and Medea, and though swept aside by invaders such as Alexander and Genghis Khan and penetrated by the Arab invaders of Persia in the seventh century, it has always after a lapse of a generation or two reasserted its historical role.

The Turkish and Persian Empires came into contact early in the sixteenth century when Persia was lifting her head after the devastation suffered at the hands of Mongols, who probably killed half the whole adult male population within a few years and reduced Persia to a state of desolation from which it never recovered. At that time Turkey was an aggressor state. Her armies were at the gates of Vienna, her fleets in almost every port of the southern littoral of the Mediterranean. They were titular masters of Arabia and exercised authority on the coasts of Africa as far as Zanzibar. Sultan Suleiman, known as "The

Magnificent", took the provinces of northern Kurdistan and Azerbaijan and finally conquered Baghdad in 1534. Then the tide turned in favor of the Persian Shah Abbas, a man who played as great a part in the East as Charlemagne in the West. Stability was only reached when Sultan Murad IV won Baghdad for Turkey, ousting the Persians, and settled the frontier by treaty upon lines which differ little from those in force today.

Two hundred years later Britain and Russia became involved in a succession of Turco-Persian frontier disputes. In the early years of the nineteenth century, Russia forcibly seized great areas from both Turkey and Persia. British commercial interests in the Persian Gulf and Turkish Arabia, as Mesopotamia was officially called, were important and rapidly growing with the advent of steam vessels. Frontier incidents between Turkey and Persia became increasingly serious. An Anglo-Russian Commission met and after four years, signed the Treaty of Erzerum in 1847 which settled most major issues.

After peace had been declared following the Crimean War, survey work began. In 1869 the British and Russians surveyors produced, at vast cost, a map of the region on either side of the frontier. The frontier remained, a strip some twenty-five miles broad. The Turkish and Persian governments agreed that the boundary line would be found "somewhere" upon this map.

After a small-scale invasion of Kurdistan and Azerbaijan by Turkish soldiers in 1906, Britain and Russia redoubled their efforts to procure consent to a definite boundary line from Fao on the Persian Gulf to Ararat on the north. The aim of Britain and Russia was to promote peace between Persia and Turkey both in their own interest and in those of other countries.

The frontier by this time had become a matter of the greatest importance to Britain. The D'Arcy Oil Concession covered all that part of Persia bordering on Mesopotamia. It seemed likely that the oil-bearing region might be wholly excluded from Persia according to one interpretation. Alternatively it might be wholly excluded from Turkey according to another. For Britain, it mattered less where the line should lie than it should be laid down definitely somewhere.

The Anglo-Persian Oil Company held oil rights to Persia. Another company held a concession for the *vilayets* of Baghdad and Mosul. The respective rights of these companies would be determined by the boundary and all four governments agreed that the verdict of the Commission would be final. Such was the background of the Turko-Persian Frontier Commission, to which I had been attached.

In July I read with intense interest of the acquisition by the Treasury of a controlling interest in A.P.O.C. It is a strange reversal of the established order that such a step should be taken by a Liberal government.

On August 4th the Great War began. The news reached us on August 12th. Our action in supporting France and Russia has taken most foreigners here by surprise.

We were near Ushnu, camped near a Russian detachment. The Archbishops of Canterbury's Mission to the Nestorians was nearby. Two English priests, Spearing and Barnard, very High Church but very pleasant persons, unassuming, sociable, and glad to see us, came out to camp with us for some days. I went to communion in their little church.

The news of the war eclipsed all else. Only persons willfully blind to facts refused to see that Germany was intent on fighting us. I knew enough of diplomacy to be convinced that she has for years been a danger to the peace of Europe. It has always been, I believe, an article of faith with the Germans that the neutrality of Belgium, though guaranteed by a treaty signed by Germany, could be infringed with impunity.

From an internal point of view, a war may do good by forcing everyone to face the realities of life. There will be a lowering of the standard of comfort all round from some years, and a vast loss of life. But we don't deserve our present prosperity and it may do good. The best thing that can happen is for Germany to be unable to make headway in Europe, lose her colonies, commerce and fleet, and then make peace. It will give a crushing blow to militarism. If this is affected, the war will have been worthwhile. I do not want to see Germany crushed altogether on land. I think, and I may be quite wrong, that she is a necessary equipoise to Russia.

The Russian commissioner Minorsky is as determined as I am to finish the boundary job, war or no war, by the end of October. All the officers on the British Commission are military officers except Hubbard. We here are in close and friendly touch with the Russian Army, with whom we dine and dance Cossack dances and – I am sorry to say sometimes -- drink. I introduced a whole brigade to the prophylactic virtues of the "prairie oyster", a raw egg in a wineglass with Worcester sauce and red pepper, as a counterblast to excess of vodka.

The last protocols and maps of the Turco-Persian Frontier were signed not far from the foot of Mount Ararat on October 27, 1914. Of the British

Commission, only Colonel Ryder and I remained. We had brought to a successful conclusion a task which had defied the efforts of at least four international bodies during the preceding century.

A few hours after the signing ceremony, the Turkish officials must have had news by telegraph that a declaration of war between Turkey and the Allies was hourly expected. I had sent Colonel Ryder ahead to cross into Persia with the precious map and supplementaries and relative protocols, intending to follow him with the tents and animals.

The Turks raised objections to my leaving. They said they wanted an extra copy of the protocol. I saw clear indications that I should be forcibly prevented from leaving and held prisoner. I instantly agreed to stay, saying I was in no hurry, and invited the Turkish officials to lunch with me the next day. I returned to my camp, only four hundred yards away, and waited until 6 p.m. Then, telling my servants, all local men, that they need not prepare food for me, as I should dine with the Turks, I walked out into the darkness towards their camp. Once out of sight of my camp, I turned at right angles into a ravine and made for the frontier between Persia and Turkey some eight miles distance.

The trip home was a series of escapades that brought me to Tiflis and thence ten days by train to Archangel, which was ice-bound. We waited only one day at Archangel for a ship. A Canadian ice-breaker came up, broke the ice round us, forcing the great slabs to slide over the frozen surface of the river, and followed it to open sea. We were the last ship to leave Archangel that winter.

In London I reported at once to the Foreign Office, and handed them our copy of the boundary maps and of protocols. I then went directly to the India Office, and learned, much to my joy, that I would be sent to France to join my regiment. I was given leave for two days at home before embarkation. While there, a telegram reached me that changed my billet and my future. I was to go to Basrah immediately to be Sir Percy Cox's assistant.

It was a sore disappointment to me, for I did not believe that the Mesopotamian campaign would involve much fighting and feared that I should be doomed to an office stool. But Sir Percy had asked for me by name and his word was law.

I had foreseen, and who could not, that the discovery of oil would change the world in the course of time. I could not see that within six years of its discovery we would be fighting a war in Mesopotamia, and to maintain the supply of oil essential to the Navy, England would rely upon the Arab and Lur chiefs whose acquaintances I had cultivated.

Chapter Thirty

Dr. Morris Y. Young

During the war I was kept busy with political endeavors as much as with overseeing the medical needs of A.P.O.C. A modern company hospital was built at Abadan. The clinic at Musjid-i-Suleiman was enlarged and staffed with capable assistants. In spite of the disruptions in medical supplies and personnel caused by the war, we were able to continue administering to the needs of the locals and the Europeans, as well as tend to those wounded in the war.

Early in the war, German agents induced anti-British Arabs and Bakhtiari to join a *jihad* against British interests. In February 1915, Wassmuss was in Shustar stirring up discontent among locals and barely escaped capture by the British, who had been informed of his activities. The same month, the Bawi tribe cut the pipeline in two places north of Ahwaz. Supplies of crude oil to Abadan fell by 600,000 barrels during the four months required to repair the line. In March, Wassmuss was captured but managed to escape, and spent the rest of the war near Bushire, fomenting sabotage against British interests.

In February 1915, A British force under General Gorringe was sent up the Karun to Ahwaz to prevent a threatened Turkish advance towards the oilfield. Lieutenant Wilson was assigned to General Gorringe's division as a political officer, but because of his intimate knowledge of the marshy terrain, became the expedition's military scout. His daring exploits on the advance and capture of Asmara and Nasiriya became legendary.

In April 1916 when the 14,000-man British force at Kut surrendered to the Turks, anti-British sentiment among the Bakhtiari waxed. I intervened with the *Ilkhani* on behalf of the British. When Kut was recaptured in February 1917, all the *khans* eagerly professed allegiance to the British. Their loyalty was influenced by who would pay the most *tomans*, and by which side they believed would be victorious.

After Reynolds left the company in 1911, the management of A.P.O.C at Mohammerah and Ahwaz rotated continuously until February 1921 when my colleague, the recently knighted Sir A.T. Wilson, took the reins as Managing Director in Persia, Mesopotamia, and the Persian Gulf for Mssrs Strick, Scott and Co, the Managing Agents of A.P.O.C.

Sir A.T. and the London management supported most of of my recommendations and allowed me a free hand with medical practices. In 1924 I was appointed head of he Medical Department, dealing not only with Persia, but with medical questions that arose within the Company's worldwide operations. The following year, Greenway's son, Captain Charles K. Greenway, was appointed Deputy Director of the General Department, comprised of four general service branches, including the medical branch and political branch. I was attached to both branches, even though the dual responsibility covered widely different subjects and practices.

In 1927 Greenway retired as chairman, and was honored with the title Lord Greenway. The same year, the agency agreement with Strick, Scott and Co was terminated, and the Board of Anglo-Persian assumed management of the company. I was appointed Deputy Director of the General Department, and was tasked with paying visits of inspection to the various spheres of operation. On my recommendation, special attention was paid to preventive medicine, particularly to the maintenance of safe water systems.

In 1921 by a military coup, Riza Shah seized power and deposed the Qajar Dynasty. He had a domineering personality and a dangerous temper. Persians who disputed his authority or met with his displeasure were summarily shot, hanged, or sent into exile.

In 1932, the Shah cancelled the D'Arcy Concession. As a result, I accompanied Mr. Cadman, the new chairman of A.P.O.C., to Persia to serve as his advisor in negotiations with the re-named Iranian Government. After an international outcry and lengthy negotiations, a new sixty-year concession, which reduced the concession area to 100,000 square miles and increased payments to the Persian government, was signed on January 1, 1933.

Sir A.T Wilson retired from A.P.O.C. in July 1932 and is now a Member of Parliament.

I served the Company for twenty-six years. My interests and talents are not in managerial responsibilities of a large and growing company, but in serving the medical needs of people. I am most interested in inoculations for diseases. When offered the opportunity to work with Professor Sir Alexander Fleming at St. Mary's Hospital in London, I accepted the position, and retired from

A.P.O.C. on 28 June 1933.

In 1907 when I accepted a position for one-year with Burmah Oil's subsidiary in Persia, I thought it would be an adventure, and took a gamble that it might lead to greater opportunities. Fate and good fortune proved it to be a rewarding challenge. Today Anglo-Iranian Oil Company, its new name, is one of the world's largest oil companies and one of Britain's most successful corporations. I played a role in its early stages, and hope that readers will find interesting the story of its inception.

Dr. Morris Y. Young
London July 1933

The End

EPILOGUE

Solomon's Temple is written in the genre of an historical novel. I attempted to write it as historically accurate as possible. All the characters were real people. All the events actually happened. Except for the public thrashing in Ahwaz, which was described by J. Jameson on June 26, 1913, all the events are accurately dated.

Wherever possible, I used the characters' own words. Consequently, the book is as much a compilation as an original work. Many of the words of Dr. Morris Young and George Reynolds were derived from reports written by them to the directors of the Consolidated Syndicate Ltd (CSL) and the Anglo-Persian Oil Company. Entire passages were taken from Sir A.T. Wilson's autobiography *Persia – A Political Officer's Diary*. Nearly all of Admiral John Fisher's words were from *Memories*, his autobiography. Many of Charles Greenway's comments were extracted from reports he wrote to the managing directors of Lloyd, Scott & Co and from his testimony before Admiralty commissions. The debate on the vote of the government's purchase of a majority interest in A.P.O.C. was transcribed from Hansard. Wherever practical, I also used actual reports and letters. If a paragraph is indented, it is authentic.

The intent of the book is to depict the many challenges facing the men who first discovered oil in the Mideast, as well as the historical and geopolitical context in which the story played a major role.

Anglo-Persian Oil Company

By 1914 the company was out of money. Funds raised in the 1909 stock offering plus an additional L300,000 had been expended. Although the Admiralty had contracted to buy 200,000 barrels of fuel oil, the company needed a large infusion of capital. In addition to the government purchasing a majority interest in the company, the Admiralty signed a contract for forty million tons of fuel oil over the next twenty years. Without the L2,200,000 injection of new capital provided by the government and the Admiralty contract, it is likely the company would have merged with Royal Dutch Shell.

Production from Abadan increased from 200,000 barrels in 1913 to nearly five million barrels per year by the end of the war.

A large share of the retail market for petroleum products sold in Britain was controlled by a German company named British Petroleum. It was confiscated during World War I by the Public Trustee for Enemy Property and in 1917 was purchased by the Anglo-Persian Oil Company.

In 1921 Riza Shah staged a coup against the Qajar Dynasty, which had been in power since 1796. He quickly eliminated the semi-autonomy of the Sheikh of Mohammerah and of the Bakhtiari *khans* by killing and imprisoning them, and forcing them to sell their lands and interest in the oil fields. In 1926 he was crowned Shah and chose Pahlavi as the dynastic name.

In 1928 Henri Deterding of Royal Dutch Shell invited Walter Teagle of Standard Oil of New Jersey, William Mellon of Gulf Oil, Colonel Robert Stewart of Standard Oil of Indiana, and John Cadman of Anglo-Persian Oil Company to meet at Achnacarry Castle in the Scottish Highland, where they agreed to a formula to control world oil output by fixing their market shares, which became known as the As-Is Agreement. However the worldwide Depression decreased demand and even with the As-Is Agreement in place, the price of crude oil plummeted.

As the Depression spread and the price of crude oil dropped, the Persian government's revenue from the D'Arcy Concession fell. British accountants hired by Riza Shah claimed that the company underpaid Persia based on the interpretation of "sixteen percent net royalty payments". In 1932 Riza Shah, in need of more revenue to support his regime, cancelled the D'Arcy Concession.

After lengthy negotiations, a new sixty-year concession was agreed to, effective January 1, 1933, with a guaranteed minimum payment of L750,000 per year and the royalty based on tonnage. Payments to the Persian government increased from L1.8 million in 1933 to L3.5 million in 1937.

The country was re-named Iran in 1935 and in the same year the company was re-named the Anglo-Iranian Oil Company.

At the beginning of World War II, Abadan was the world's largest refinery and was producing 135,000 barrels per day. By the end of the war, Abadan was producing 345,000 barrels per day and was critical to Britain's successful conclusion of the war.

In January 1944 Everette DeGolyer, on a mission for the U.S. government, visited the oil fields of the Middle East and reported that "the center of gravity of world oil is shifting from the Gulf of Mexico-Caribbean area to the Middle East – to the Persian Gulf area – and is likely to continue its shift until it is finally established in that area."

In April 1951 the Shah signed a law implementing the nationalization of Iran's oil industry. In 1954 the Anglo-Iranian Oil Company agreed to join a consortium and signed a 25-year agreement to operate the oil field and refinery. In the same year the company changed its name to British Petroleum.

During the Thatcher administration, the British government sold the last of its shares in British Petroleum. Today BP is one of the world's largest private corporations and produces more than 4 million barrels of oil per day.

Musjid-i-Suleiman Oil Field

Only ten wells were producing oil when the British government purchased a majority interest in the field. By the end of 1919, 48 wells had been drilled. By 1948, more than 248 wells were producing oil.

The British Admiralty's report of 1913 determined that the field covered three and a half square miles. When it was fully developed, the field covered fifty-five square miles.

The surface geology is complicated by thrust faulting in shallow horizons. The Zagros orogenic belt is bounded by two stable platforms. On the southwest is the Arabian platform where shelf sediments overlie the metamorphic rocks of the Arabian shield. On the northeast is the pre-Cambrian metamorphic basement of central Iran.

The gypsum beds which are expressed on the surface at Musjid-i-Suleiman are known by geologists as the Incompetent Group. When movement of continental plates shoved the Arabian plate onto the Iranian platform, the Incompetent Group detached along evaporitic beds above the more competent Miocene Lower Fars limestones. The resulting surface features, although aligned along a northwest-southeast axis that parallels the Zagros Mountains, were contorted, flexed, and folded without relation to the enormous northwest-southeast folds in the underlying Competent Group. Thus surface dips and strikes did not mirror the underlying deeper structures.

Geologists sent by Sir Boverton Redwood from 1901 until 1914 to examine the surface geology of southwest Persia were unable to map beds in the underlying Competent Group based on surface exposures. It was ten years after the discovery of the field that geologists finally recognized that the main pay was the Asmari limestone.

Additional wells at Chiah Soukh resulted in six more dry holes. Several more wells at Marmatain eventually found a small producer. Despite drilling many exploratory wells at the site of other seeps across the concession, it was fifteen years after the discovery of oil at Musjid-i-Suleiman before another discovery was made.

By 1998 Musjid-i-Suleiman had produced 1.4 billion barrels of oil. In March 2007 terms were reached with China National Petroleum Corp (CNPC) for an enhanced oil recovery (EOR) project. It is estimated an additional 5 billion barrels of oil remain in place

Dr. Morris Y. Young (1882 – 1950)

Dr. Young retired from British Petroleum on June 28, 1933. His contribution to A.P.O.C. as both a medical officer and as a political officer played a critical role in establishing and maintaining good relations with the local sheikhs, the Bakhtiari *khans*, the tribes, and the peasants. The hospital on Abadan Island became the largest and most modern medical facility in the Persian Gulf.

Following retirement from A.P.O.C., he spent the next six years engaged in research at the Inoculation Department of St. Mary's Hospital, London, where he was closely associated in the bacteriological research with Professor Sir Alexander Fleming and Sir Almorth Wright.

From 1939 to 1945 Dr. Young was closely involved with Professor Fleming in the development and application of penicillin.

Sir A.T. Wilson (1884 – 1940)

During World War I, Lt. Wilson was assigned to the Indian Expeditionary Force (IEF) D as Deputy Chief Political Officer serving under Sir Percy Cox. Although Persia was a neutral country, protection of the Abadan refinery and the Musjid-i-Suleiman oilfield was paramount to British military interests. With the assent of the Persian government, a British force was sent up the Karun River to Ahwaz to prevent a threatened Turkish advance.

Lieutenant Wilson, although a political officer, served with distinction as a military guide under Major General Gorringe in the 12th Division's advance from Ahwaz to Amara on the Tigris and on to Nasiriya on the Euphrates. John Marlowe, his biographer, wrote that "his tireless industry, his imposing presence, his gallantry on the Nasiriya expedition, his physical toughness, his knowledge of the country, his all-pervading efficiency, his influence with Cox, his habit of Latin and scriptural quotation, his Johnsonian air of omniscience in the Political Mess, had already made him famous throughout the IEF."

For his efforts and his gallantry, he was awarded the Distinguish Service Order (D.S.O.).

In April 1918 when Sir Percy Cox was called to Britain and later to Teheran, Captain Wilson took over as Acting Civil Commissioner of Mesopotamia. He was responsible for establishing a civil government in what today is Iraq, Kuwait, and Saudi Arabia. Gertrude Bell, renowned Arabic scholar and friend of Arab leaders, was assigned to the political staff reporting to Captain Wilson. She described A.T. Wilson as "a most remarkable creature, 34, brilliant abilities, a combined mental and physical power which is extremely rare. Never without a classical book in his pocket, he quoted Bacon, Shakespeare, Milton, Virgil and Socrates in his dispatches home and mesmerized his dinner guests with Persian poetry or Indian dialects."

Establishing a civil government out of the disparate and warring tribal cultures was a challenging task. Differences arose between Captain Wilson's vision and Gertrude Bell's and T.E. Lawrence's vision for the future of Mesopotamia. Bell and Lawrence believed in and promoted Arab nationhood. Wilson believed Mesopotamia should be a British protectorate. Realities of the cost to support a protectorate eventually led Britain to support Mesopotamia becoming a League of Nations mandate, which transitioned the new countries of Iraq, Kuwait, and Saudi Arabia to nationhood with the support of British professionals as advisors.

In October 1920 when Sir Percy Cox returned as High Commissioner of Iraq, Captain Wilson returned to London, where he received a knighthood at the hands of King George V. On February 17, 1921 he had lunch with Winston Churchill and Charles Greenway. Two days later he resigned his commission in the Army and accepted a job as Managing Director in Persia for Mssrs. Strick, Scott, and Co, the managing agents for the Anglo-Persian Oil Company.

In 1922 he married Rose Carver, who had a daughter Ann by her first marriage to Lt. Robin Carver, who was killed during World War I. Rose and A.T. had two children, Sara and Hugh.

Sir A.T. and Rose lived in Mohammerah until 1927 when they moved to London and A.T. was put in charge of A.P.O.C.'s worldwide exploration program. He resigned in 1932 and in 1933 was elected as a Unionist member to the House of Commons. He was deeply interested in social problems and wrote a book on workman's compensation. He was also interested in industrial assurance and penal reform.

While an MP he met with Franco and Hitler, and believed an accommodation with Hitler was the best course for Britain. He strongly supported Neville Chamberlain's goal of appeasement. When accused of being a Hitler sympathizer, he responded, "We must face the facts. Europe, released from Hitler, may fall under a bondage worse by far. Stalin is more deadly to religion and more dangerous to civilization than Hitler. When Germany takes a country over, they put the pieces together again and carry on and establish some ordered kind of government. When Russia takes over a country, it is like a fire sweeping over it."

When Hitler invaded Poland in September 1939, Sir A.T stated that his efforts to keep peace with Hitler had failed.

"I have failed. We have all failed to find any means by which we could live at peace with Hitler. May I also remind you that I was also a front-line fighter. I hold the D.S.O., which was awarded for gallantry in the field. From now on, I am pledged to one thing, and to one thing only…to bring the war to a successful conclusion."

He tried unsuccessfully to rejoin the Army, and was also rejected for a commission in the Navy. He was, however, able to join the Royal Air Force and in December 1939 was posted to Gunnery School. Upon graduation he was assigned as an Air Gunner to Wellington Bomber Squadron 37.

On May 7, 1940 he received leave from the squadron to attend the House of Commons debate on Norway, which led to the fall of the Chamberlain government. That day he made his last speech in the House of Commons:

"Within an hour, I must rejoin my unit... The men with whom I work have flown up and down the Valley of the Shadow of Death again and again, and they will go on doing so, until victory crowns their efforts, or until that Valley claims them."

On his sixth bombing raid the night of May 31, 1940, Sir A.T. Wilson's Wellington Bomber was shot down. His body was identified by his many medal ribbons and by his advanced age. He was fifty-five years old. On his grave is a wooden cross with the inscription:

So he passed over, and all the trumpets sounded for him
on the other side.

George Bernard Reynolds (1853 – 1925)

The son of a vice-admiral in the British Navy, George Reynolds attended the Royal Indian Engineering College, which trained engineers for the Indian civil service. From 1875 until 1897 he worked for India's Public Work Department. In 1895 he retired from Indian civil service and started work in the East Indies for a Dutch oil company. In 1901 William D'Arcy hired him to lead his oil exploration effort in Persia.

In 1911 after he was summarily dismissed by A.P.O.C., George Reynolds was hired by Royal Dutch Shell and sent to Venezuela to oversee their operations near Lake Maracaibo, where conditions were hazardous and tropical diseases rampant. A Standard of New Jersey geologist said that anyone who was there for a few weeks "is almost certain to become infected with malaria or liver and intestinal diseases." Hostile tribes made conditions even worse. By 1922, after years of small success and expenditures of millions, Royal Dutch Shell finally made Venezuela's first significant oil discovery. Their Baroso well in the Maracaibo Basin blew out at an estimated rate of 100,000 barrels per day and became the discovery well for La Rosa Field, establishing Venezuela as one of the world's foremost oil producing countries. Shell's local field manager on the La Rosa discovery was George B. Reynolds.

In August 1927, John P. Hamilton, a long-time friend of Reynolds, wrote to

John Cadman, chairman of A.P.O.C., that George Reynolds was "the soundest of the sound. I could tell you lots about him, and greatly to his credit, although we know many did not like him. He was one of the ablest men that was ever born."

In his diary, A.T. Wilson wrote that "the service rendered by G.B. Reynolds to the British Empire and to British industry and to Persia was never recognized. Yet the men whom he saved from the consequences of their own blindness became very rich, and were honored in their generation."

James Hamilton

Director of Burmah Oil, of the Consolidated Syndicate Ltd, of Lloyd, Scott & Co, and of the Anglo-Persian Oil Company. From 1905 until 1909 George Reynolds reported to James Hamilton from Persia. Four volumes of their correspondence reside in the BP Archives. James Hamilton was still a director of A.P.O.C. in 1921. No further information about him was uncovered.

Lord Greenway (1857 – 1934)

In 1885 Charles Greenway went to work in India as a merchant for Shaw, Wallace & Co, agents in India for the Burmah Oil Company. In 1908 he returned to London to work in the same office with Charles William Wallace, a director of both Shaw, Wallace & Co and the Burmah Oil Company. When Anglo-Persian Oil Company was formed in April 1909, Charles Greenway became one of the original directors. In January 1910 he was appointed managing director. In 1914, after Lord Strathcona died, he became both managing director and chairman of the board. In 1927, at age 70, he retired from A.P.O.C.

During his tenure Lord Greenway oversaw the rise of A.P.O.C. from a minor underfunded oil company with only four wells in Musjid-i-Suleiman into one of the world's largest petroleum corporations.

Charles Greenway was knighted in 1919 and ennobled in 1927. His successor, John Cadman, wrote of Lord Greenway, "It was he who was responsible for the main structure of the great Company of which we today are so justly proud."

Lord Greenway was also noted for his lavish hospitality at his estate, Standbridge Earls.

Lord Fisher (1841 – 1920)

John Arbuthnot Fisher entered the Royal Navy at age 13 and was posted to Lord Nelson's former flagship, *HMS Victory*. His 60-year naval career spanned the transformation of the British Fleet from sail to dreadnought and submarine. He was singularly responsible for much of the transformation.

As sail gave way to ironsides, he recognized the threat of submarines to Britain's centuries-old strategy of blockade of enemy ports, and introduced submarines to the Royal Navy, as well as destroyers to counter submarine warfare. His improvements to British warships included increasing the range, accuracy and firing rate of naval gunnery. He was an early proponent of mines and torpedoes, and early-on recognized the value of naval aircraft.

Lord Fisher was a faithful and devoted husband, and a religious man. When ashore he attended church regularly, sometimes two or more services in a day. In 1877 he took up dancing and insisted that officers in the fleet learn to dance. Heads of state, leading politicians, ladies of influence, and foreign naval officers were charmed by his energetic enthusiasm and engaging personality.

His Naval reforms made many enemies. Robert K. Massie wrote that "Fisher, the tempestuous builder of the modern Royal Navy, rushed through life from one seething, volcanic controversy to the next." He befriended King Edward VII and Queen Alexandra. The King's support and close friendship sustained him through many battles at the Admiralty.

In the 1882 Anglo-Egyptian War, his landing party successfully overran the Kedive's palace, which gained him instant fame. While serving on shore duty in Egypt, he became seriously ill with dysentery and malaria, and was not cured until taking the baths at Marienbad, where he met William D'Arcy.

Fisher was the driving force behind the development of the battleship. He chaired the Committee on Designs, which produced the *HMS Dreadnought*, the first modern battleship, constructed under his direction in a record time of twelve months.

He was First Sea Lord from 1904 until his retirement in 1910. When World War I started, First Lord of the Admiralty Winston Churchill re-appointed him First Sea Lord. With Churchill's support, he initiated a six-hundred ship building program. He and Churchill soon differed over sending the Mediterranean Fleet up the Dardanelles. Lord Fisher warned it would cost at least twelve battleships to breach the strait. When the Gallipoli campaign turned into a military debacle, Lord Fisher's relationship with Churchill suffered. In May 1915 he retired from the Royal Navy for a second time.

In 1911 Admiral Fisher predicted within one month the commencement date of World War I. His prediction was based upon the completion of widening and deepening the Kiev Canal, which provided German battleships a safe passageway to the North Sea. To prepare for the eventuality of a great sea battle with Germany, he re-stationed the bulk of the British fleet to the North Sea.

On May 31 and June 1, 1916, the Battle of Jutland was fought between the Royal Navy's Grand Fleet and the German High Seas Fleet. In the largest naval battle of the war, Britain's 151 combat ships faced Germany's 99 ships. Although Britain lost more men and ships, as a result of the battle the German fleet was confined within the Baltic Sea, thus protecting British troop and material movement across the English Channel and on the high seas, and preventing Germany's re-supply by sea of needed materials.

Lord Fisher was one of the first to fathom the threat to the British Empire presented by Germany's naval build-up. His efforts to construct more, larger, and faster ships prepared the Royal Navy for war with Germany. *More speed* was one of his credos. Faster ships required that they be fueled by oil.

After the war, he wrote that he admired "the great words of Dryden" as being appropriate to the close of a busied life:

> Not heaven itself upon the past has Power,
> What has been has been, and I have had my hour.

Appendix One

The journal of A. L. Marriott

In February 1901 I was asked by Mr. D'Arcy if I would undertake a journey to Teheran, as his representative, to endeavour to obtain from the Shah of Persia a concession for the oilfields believed to exist in that country. I accepted the offer and left London on March 23rd, being joined at Paris by Monsieur E. Cotte, who was to accompany me and assist me, in conjunction with a Persian official, General Kitabji Khan by name, who had preceded us by a few days, in the negotiations with the Persian Government.

Mssr. Cotte had paid three previous visits to Persia having obtained the "Reuter" Concession in 1872, one for the Imperial Bank of Persia in 1888 and assisted in securing the concession for the tobacco "Regie" in 1892.

The existence of oil springs in Persia was known to the ancients, and they were used by the fire worshippers, the ruins of whose temples still remain near many of the springs. In later times these springs or wells have been worked in a very rough manner to supply their own wants.

Some few years ago Monsieur de Morgan, who was in charge of the French Government Scientific Mission to Persia, was asked by a Persian Chief to explore the territory for ozokerite, which is a waxy residue of petroleum. M de Morgan, who is an eminent geologist, did not find ozokerite in payable quantities, but he discovered the unmistakable indications of widely-extended deposits of petroleum itself. He imparted his information to his friend M. Cotte. The latter together with General Kitabji Khan, who had come to Paris as Persian Commissioner at the Exhibition, visited London in search of a capitalist who would take the matter up, and eventually brought it to the notice of Mr. D'Arcy. General Kitabji is by birth a native of Georgia in the Caucasus and a Christian, but has been for many years in the service of the Persian Government, and was at one time Director-General of Customs.

M. Cotte and I left Paris on Monday March 25th at 8 p.m. traveling by the Orient Express via Munich, Vienna, Buda-Pesht, Belgrade and Sofia to Constantinople, which we reached without changing carriages about 10 a.m. on Thursday March 28th. We had been advised to stay at the Grand Hotel, but found it very poor.

We left Constantinople about noon on Saturday March 30th in the SS "Ceres" of the Austrian Lloyd Co., and very glad we were to get away from the dirt, dogs, and beggars. Steaming down the Bosphorus toward the Black Sea, we passed many heavily-armed forts, at one of which I counted over forty modern guns.

We arrived at Batum early on Thursday morning, the 4th of April, having called at several ports along the coast of Asia Minor. What we saw of the country appeared very fertile and well-wooded with a rich red soil reminding one of Devonshire.

We stayed a day and night at Trebizond, the capital of the former Kingdom of Armenia. During the Armenian Massacres thousands of men, women, and children were butchered there. Our captain told me his company had a steamer lying there at the time and those on board witnessed the massacre.

It had been arranged beforehand by the Turks that the opening of the post office, for the delivery of the mails brought by the steamer, should be the signal for commencing the attack on the Armenians, most of whom would be waiting to get their letters, as the principal commerce of the place was in their hands. Accordingly those unfortunate people – all unsuspecting and therefore unarmed – were suddenly set upon by hundreds of armed men, and the work of butchering began, and continued until almost every Armenian had been killed; only a very few escaping who were hid by Turkish friends.

When the infuriated Turks had tired of shooting, stabbing and beating to death, they caught the rest of their hapless victims alive and, carrying them up to the top of the steep cliffs, threw them over onto the rocks below. Many who tried to escape to the steamer by swimming were ruthlessly shot in the water by the *gendarmarie*.

Among our saloon passengers was an old Armenian gentleman who was at Trebizond at the time; but he was among those hid until the massacres were over.

Russia is credited with preventing the Powers interfering to help the Armenians, as she herself has a lot of Armenian subjects in the Caucasus, and feared the latter might join their compatriots. She was also afraid that the buffer Armenian state under the protection of the Powers might be created between her and Turkey, and so stop her designs of gradually extending her territory along the southern coast of the Black Sea. She is said to be greatly eyeing Trebizond, and to be waiting for an excuse to seize it. This place would be the most important acquisition for her, both commercially and strategically.

On arrival at Batum we were subjected to several hours annoyance by the Russian customs officials, who regarded a large map of Europe which I had with great suspicion. They also looked at my diary and account book most carefully, but did not seem to get much enlightenment from the perusal of them. My folding pocket Kodak was I think suspected of being some kind of infernal machine until its use was explained; and finally my saddle was pounced upon, and I was mulcted for *L*2 duty, though it was a second-hand one and I was only passing through the country.

Batum is an uninteresting town which has sprung up principally in connection with the Russian oil trade. The oil is brought over the Caucasus Mountains by rail, in tank-trains, from Baku, an is then refined at Batum ready for shipment in tank-steamers.

When Russia acquired the Caucasus at the close of the Turko-Russian war in 1878, it was expressly stipulated in the Treaty of Berlin that she should not fortify Batum, but with her usual contempt for treaties when it does not suit her to adhere to, she has built a long line of forts armed with large long-range guns commanding every approach.

Notation from M.Y. Young: The steady increase of Russian influence in Central Asia pre-occupied the Foreign Office and Indian Government almost more than any other single issue in the late 19th and early 20th century. The Anglo-Russia play for hegemony in the area is now referred to as The Great Game. In this respect, the position of Persia was critical to Great Britain for the defense of India.

Leaving Batum, the trans-Caucasus railway skirts along the coast for some miles, with beautifully wooded hills on the right. The trees were in lovely spring foliage and in places there were masses of rhododendrons in full bloom. On striking inland the line ascends a long gently-sloping valley with great ranges of snow-capped mountains on either side. Farther on it follows the course of the River Rion. When some thousands of feet above sea level, the railway passes through a long tunnel and emerges on the other side of the mountain range onto a great plain.

The weather was glorious and after sunset there was a brilliant moon. At all the stations there were crowds of Caucasus tribesmen in their wonderfully picturesque costumes. Every one of them is armed by special permission in the treaty concluded between the Russians and the Prince of the Caucasus at the close of the war. Their belts, often of beautiful silver work, are stuck all over with highly ornamental daggers and pistols and they wear cartridge belts across the chest. They are remarkably handsome and fine-looking men, many of them being as fair as Englishmen.

Tiflis, capital of the now Russian province of the Caucasus and seat of the governor-general who is a Grand Duke and cousin of the Czar, is quite a large city. It is built in a basin, surrounded by hills, on both banks of the river Kour. We stayed there three nights at the comfortable Hotel d"Orient, being detained by difficulties in getting a visa for Persia, without which we should not have been allowed to leave the country. We only succeeded with great difficulty. We were questioned and cross-questioned, as we were evidently looked upon as most suspicious characters. The fact of a Frenchman and an Englishman traveling to Persia together appeared to make them fear some deep design which they tried to discover. In the end, they gave us permission to proceed, most reluctantly.

We left Tiflis by train on Monday April 8th, arriving at Baku at 8 a.m. the next day. Near Baku the country is very bare and desolate-looking, and the town itself, situated on a peninsula on the western shore of the Caspian Sea, is a most uninviting place with its all-pervading smell of petroleum.

The oil area is only about ten square miles and the aggregate value of the properties is said to exceed one hundred millions sterling. I was shown the works of an English company purchased by them a few years ago for five million rubles, roughly L500,000 and now said to be worth ten times that amount. These works owing to their isolated position escaped damage in the last fires which caused immense destruction and great loss of life. The wonder is that there are not more fires as in all directions there are large open reservoirs of the highly-inflammable naphtha or crude petroleum, into which the oil is pumped before being refined. The wells vary from about 200 to 1000 feet in depth.

We left Baku the same day by one of the Russian steamers which carry the mails between Baku and Enzeli, a Persian port in the southwestern corner of the Caspian.

The ways of their steamers are, to say the least, odd. We paid for our tickets and went on board, naturally supposing that we had nothing further to pay except for wine; but on going to bed we found there were no bed-clothes in our cabins. On our asking for them we were told they were an extra and must be paid for – so we paid. Then there were no towels. They were quite an extra! Finally on leaving the steamer we were presented with a bill for our meals as we had eaten three meals in the day and only one was given free. As might be expected when towels were an extra, everything was very dirty on the steamer.

The day after leaving Baku we touched at Lenkoran and Astara, the latter being the Russo-Persian frontier, and early the following morning we reached Enzeli after a voyage of thirty hours.

The Caspian Sea, which is over seven hundred miles in length from north to south and varies from about two hundred to three hundred miles in width, is some eighty-five feet lower than the Black Sea. Although fed by several rivers, including the Volga (longest in Europe and equal to the Nile, being 2,400 miles in length) and yet having no outlet, the Caspian is becoming lower every year. It is now entirely dominated by Russia; no vessel being permitted to sail on its waters except under the Russian flag. This is one of the many humiliating concessions exacted from Persia by the government of the Czar.

We were favored with calm weather and a bright sunny morning. From the deck of the steamer the scene was very lovely; the smooth, blue sea and the picturesque village of Enzeli among its orange gardens, making a charming foreground to the mighty range of the Elburz mountains, coated in a fresh covering of snow, and whose distant peaks seemed to penetrate the sky.

We were met by the Swiss proprietor of the hotel at Resht, M. Albert, to whom we had telegraphed from Baku. As soon as we had gone through the Customs formalities without much difficulty, we started off in his boat. Passing through the narrow channel dividing the two long horns of land, we sailed and rowed across the bay to the mouth of a small creek, up which we were towed by our boats crew to Peri-Bazaar, which was reached two hours from Enzeli.

Peri-Bazaar is the principal landing place from the Caspian for all passengers and goods going to Teheran and the other northern towns of Persia. A more hopeless scene of confusion cannot be imagined. Merchandise and goods of value lay strewn about in the mud, exposed to sun and rain, there being practically no wharves or quay. I understood why it sometimes takes about a couple of years for things sent from England by this route to reach Teheran, and why they are often good for nothing when they do arrive.

We were carried ashore through the knee-deep mud on the backs of the sailors, and bundled bag and baggage into some ramshackle little Victorias which seemed principally held together with bundles of string. These were drawn by the sorriest-looking steeds I had hitherto met with, though they compared favourably with those we had afterwards to make use of on our drive to Teheran. An hour's drive along a very bad road brought us to the so-called hotel at Resht, where we found the accommodation to be of the very scantiest.

Resht is a squalid town of some forty-thousand inhabitants and is the capital of Ghilan, the most fertile province of Persia. It is celebrated for a sort of patchwork embroidery which is made there.

It was not until noon on the third day, Saturday April 13, that we started on our 230-mile drive to Teheran in a dirty and broken-down Victoria, drawn by four ponies harnessed abreast.

The road from Resht to Teheran was made by a Russian company which obtained from the Persian government a concession for it and for the posting-service which is, I should say, the worst in the world. The carriages are nearly all like the one allotted to us, and words fail to describe most of the horses, shamefully ill-treated, over-worked and starved, bodies covered with sores, and their knees often bare to the bone. I shall never forget their look of patient suffering. We frequently passed the remains, in various stages of decomposition, of the poor brutes that had been left to die on the road, it being nobody's business to remove them.

The scanty inhabitants of this country, who are poor to the verge of starvation, live in a few miserable villages situated in places where water is obtainable, and where a little soil can be scraped together. Their dwellings are little better than holes in the earth, with mud roofs often not more than one or two feet above the level of the ground.

One hundred-thirty miles from Resht is Kasvin, once a capital of Persia, but there is little left now to indicate its past glories. Between it and Teheran the road crosses a slightly undulating plain, the greater part of which is uncultivated owing to the difficulty of obtaining water for irrigation. It presents a most desert-like appearance, but where water can be procured it is capable of great productiveness, growing cereals, vines and fruit trees in abundance. Although a Mahommedan country, there is a considerable demand for good wine in Persia, the rich classes paying high prices for French and other imported wines.

For many miles before Teheran is reached the most prominent feature of the landscape is the mighty cone of Damavand, the crowning peak of the Elburz range, which runs like a great wall across northern Persia. This superb mountain is just under 20,000 feet in height, and its summit is covered in eternal snow.

As may be imagined from what I have already said, our journey was not accomplished without several unpleasant incidents. On more than one occasion our carriage broke down, causing considerable delay; and two or three times our horses became so exhausted in the middle of a stage that we had to wait until others could be obtained.

Once our way was barred in a narrow place by the freshly-dead body of a large camel left behind by one of the caravans. We met several of these caravans of generally fifty to sixty camels. They march in single file, each beast being fastened by a chain to the one in front of it. They are often exceedingly fine and strong animals with beautiful trappings of many-colored wool work and beads, and they carry enormous bales and cases of goods. Hanging at their sides are usually great booming bronze bells which sound very weird when one meets them at night in the mountain passes, and the ghost-like giant forms move slowly by.

Our horses much disliked the camels, and once our carriage was nearly upset over the precipice due to the horses swerving suddenly on meeting a caravan at night. I may mention that in parts, where the road is cut out of the side of the mountains, there is often a sheer precipice with nothing to prevent a carriage from falling over.

Our journey lasted three days, as we were obliged to stay part of the first night and all the second at *caravanserais*, as no horses were to be had. We traveled all through the third night, arriving at the Kasvin Gate of Teheran the next morning, Thursday April 16th.

The gateways are one of the most picturesque features of the place, being faced with the handsome-colored Persian tiles. Each gate is a different design, and they give a touch of Oriental brilliance, sadly lacking in the mud-brick house and walls of which the capital is principally composed.

Teheran is coeval with the present Qajar Dynasty, dating from the last decade of the 18th century, and contains therefore no buildings of historic interest and hardly any of architectural importance. The population is about 200,000, though no census is ever taken; the city covers a much larger area than the number of its inhabitants would seem to warrant, owing to the immense gardens surrounding the houses of the aristocracy and wealthy classes. Some of these gardens are very beautiful, and appear even more so from the fact of their cool shade being such a welcome contrast to the hot and dusty streets.

The Shah's town palace, with its courts, gardens, and lakes covers a great extent of ground, and still contains several objects of interest, though most of the treasures, collected by former sovereigns, have been dispersed during the present reign. There is the so-called "Peacock" Throne, said by some writers to be the one taken from the sack of Delhi by Nadir Shah, which however is believed to have been broken up after that monarch's assassination in 1747. The present throne was probably made during the reign of Fath Ali Shah, the second in succession of this dynasty, and the most magnificent of them all. Like most Eastern thrones, it is a sort of platform on legs, the occupant sitting on cushions. It is entirely encrusted with diamonds, sapphires, rubies, and emeralds, and there are jeweled birds standing on the sides. At the back, about level with the head of the sovereign when seated, is an immense star of diamonds.

Perhaps the most interesting thing of all is the alabaster throne which belonged to one of the former dynasties. It stands in a large hall hung with portraits of the Qajars, and is used by the Shah when he shows himself to his subjects at the Persian New Year. The drop-screen, which serves as an outer wall, is then drawn up, and the people file past their sovereign through the great courtyard facing the hall.

Another object of great value is a very large globe of the world, the towns, countries and seas being of rubies, emeralds, and diamonds respectively.

The British Legation occupies one of the best positions in the city and has a most charming wilderness-garden with great shady avenues. Besides the residence of the Minister, there are houses for the Secretaries, Military Attache, and the Medical Officer, all standing in their own little gardens within the grounds.

The minister when I was in Teheran is Sir Arthur Hardinge, formerly Consul-General in Zanzibar, one of the ablest representatives Great Britain has ever had at the Court of the Shah, where by his untiring energy, sound judgment and great tact in dealing with Orientals, he has already done much to restore the former prestige of this country, which had fallen to a rather low ebb when he reached his post about eighteen months ago.

The bazaars form a block of streets, roofed over by a succession of low domes, with small holes in the middle to let in the light and air. They are now mostly filled with common Russian, German, or Birmingham goods, though a few nice things may still, with trouble, be found among the accumulations of dust and rubbish.

The meager water supply is brought from the hills in the *kanats* or underground channels so often described by visitors to Persia. A few of the rich have their own private *kanats*; others only have the right to tap one for so many hours a day or week. *Kanat* rights are most jealously guarded and are a fertile source of quarrels and litigation. They form a most valuable property, one capable of irrigating a large garden being worth as much as L15,000.

The well-like holes, often very deep, made in excavating the *kanat* cover the whole country around the capital and are usually quite uncovered. There are many of them even in the streets of Teheran itself, and it is only in a few of the principal thoroughfares that they are covered over. Accidents are less frequent than one would imagine, but occasionally people or animals fall down the holes.

Teheran boasts a system of horse-tramways run by a foreign company. The latter had much difficulty at the start, owing to the number of the Seyids (descendants of Mahomet) who crowd the cars, and owing to the special privileges accorded them in Persia, of refusing to pay. These Seyids wear either a great turban or waistband, though it is more than probable that many don this distinguishing badge without proper right for the sake of the advantage. The Company eventually came to a compromise by which only certain Seyids were provided with free passes.

The Dervishes, a religious order of mendicants, are also a privileged class, and it is forbidden to disturb them wherever they choose to take up their abode. One day a child was run over by a tram and killed. As invariably happens in Persia when anyone is killed through the fault, or supposed fault of another, a host of relatives sprang up and made exorbitant claims against the Company, which the latter refused to pay. The claimants then hired a Dervish to pitch his tent across one of the principal points of the tramline, and the Company, knowing they would raise a storm among the fanatical populace if they ran over or ejected him, were obliged to pay the sum demanded.

The only attempt at a railway in Persia is the single, narrow gauge line about six miles in length running between the capital and Shah-Abdul Azim, and principally used for conveying the visitors to the mosque and shrine at the latter place.

Persia has allowed herself to be bound by a treaty which practically prevents her from making railways without the consent of Russia, who no doubt intends to make them herself, and use them for the furtherance of her political aims when she is ready.

While I was in Teheran the Vali-Ahd, or Crown Prince, arrived on a visit to his father. He is the eldest son of the Shah and is Governor of Tabriz, a post always held by the heir to the throne. Nearly all the princes, ministers, and officials went to receive him outside the city gates in a garden belonging to the Shah, where I also watched the reception. He arrived in a carriage with six horses, with coachman and footmen in gala liveries. He is very short and, unlike most of his family, exceedingly ugly, but is said to possess good qualities, and to be friendly disposed toward England, who supported his being chosen as Crown Prince, while Russia opposed his election, favouring the choice of one of his half-brothers.

After a number of presentations had been made and tea had been served in the garden, he was escorted in state to the Palace. As he passed through the gates to the strains of the Persian national hymn, a sheep was killed before him in the street as a mark of welcome.

The streets were lined with troops; and I may here remark that the ordinary Persian soldier must be seen to be believed. There is only one regiment, the Cossacks, worthy of the name of soldiers, and that is officered by Russians. The rest of the army cannot, I should think, be meant to be taken seriously, being composed of sort of pantomime soldiers, of all ages and sizes, dressed in the most ludicrous caricatures of uniforms of various European countries. They are hardly ever drilled, and never, I fancy, paid.

As the Vali-Ahd passed through the Grand Square on his way to the palace, I saw the officer commanding a regiment give the order for the salute. Nearly everyone did something different, and at last the officer, to despair, rushed along the ranks belaboring his men with the flat of his sword.

During my stay the anniversary occurred of the martyrdom of Hussan and Hussim, the children of Ali and Fatima and grandsons of Mahomet. As the Persians belong to the Shia sect of the Mahommedans, a great yearly ceremony is held to commemorate the above-mentioned event. Processions from different quarters of the city march to the *maidan* or square with flags and banners, and bearing litters with images of the martyred children, some stuck all over with arrows, and others representing the bodies being devoured by tigers.

I witnessed the ceremony from a terrace in the *maidan* which was lined with troops to preserve order, as it not infrequently happens that the fanatical element gets out of hand. Following each procession were about thirty or forty men, dressed in long white tunics who carried swords with which they gashed themselves on the head until they were literally drenched in blood. I saw several carried away fainting, having in their excitement cut too deep, and I afterwards heard that five or six had died of their wounds.

I drove one day to the site of the city of Rhages mentioned in the Book of Tobit and believed to be of immense antiquity. Among the ruins of the old fortifications I found some interesting fragments of ancient pottery and glazed tiles. Most of the inhabitants of Rhages were massacred when the hordes of Timur the Tartar, the "Wrath of God" as he was called, swept like a whirlwind over Persia and the surrounding countries, leaving death and desolation in their trail.

Near the ruins on the face of a rock was formerly a fine sculpture representing Darius and his court; but Fath Ali Shah, great-great-grandfather of the present Shah, had it obliterated and substituted one of himself surrounded by a number of his sons, of whom he had a regular army being, it is said, the possessor of about 1,200 wives.

Some fairly good shooting can be obtained in the vicinity of Teheran, woodcock and quail being plentiful at certain seasons; and further off, in the Elburz Mountains, mouflou and bears may be found. In the neighborhood of the Caspian an occasional tiger may still be met with. Good trout fishing may also be had at some distance from the capital.

There is quite a little English colony in Teheran, as besides the legation officials there are the staffs of the Indo-European Telegraph Company and the Imperial Bank of Persia, and the members of various business houses. I stayed at the "English" hotel which leaves much to be desired in the way of comfort until negotiations were concluded.

My negotiations for the concession were happily most successful, principally owing to the able manner in which General Kitabji Khan succeeded in winning over to our side some of the Ministers and other influential people, and also in large measure to the very valuable and timely support which I received from H.E. Sir Arthur Hardinge. Fortunately I was able to keep the subject of my journey unknown until near the end of my stay. I only took such steps openly in the matter as were absolutely necessary, ostensibly busying myself with the purchase of rugs, embroideries, etc etc.

It was not until the Grand Vizier had given a definite promise that the Concession should be granted that the secret was let out, and then the Russian Minister strenuously opposed the signing of the deed by the Shah, and would, I believe, have succeeded had it not been for the vigorous pretest of Sir Arthur against a breach of good faith.

The Teheran season lasts from about the end of September until about the middle or end of May, when it becomes very hot, and all who can do so go off to the hills, where the Shah and most of the Persian notabilities, and also the foreign ministers have summer residence.

Before my return home I spent a fortnight at the delightful summer quarters of the British Legation at Gulahek, which is about seven miles from Teheran and about 1,000 feet higher, being situated on the hills at the foot of the Elburz mountains. The Legation stands in an immense garden, very thickly wooded, with avenues in all directions. As at Teheran there are separate houses for the staff. The grounds are full of a great variety of birds, including quantities of nightingales, hoopoes, magpies, and the beautiful Persian jays and woodpeckers, also numbers of little ones not much bigger than sparrows.

In front of the Legation house is a large Indian tent, about eighty feet by forty feet with a stream running all round it and through a blue-tiled basin big enough for a swimming bath in the middle of it. Here we used to dine on hot nights.

We had a large dinner party one night to entertain a number of Persian grandees who seemed to thoroughly enjoy themselves. The Minister of Foreign Affairs who was one of the guests announced that the Shah had that afternoon (May 28) signed the deed of concession.

At the side of one of the avenues I noticed a Persian with his wife and child "camping out". On asking what they were doing there I was told they had taken refuge or *bast* as it is called.

It appears that in Persia anyone who has committed a crime or who has a grievance against the authorities can take *bast* in certain of the mosques and in some other places, including the gardens of the foreign legations, in order either to escape justice or to obtain justice, as the case may be. They cannot be arrested or turned out.

These people had some claim against the government which they wanted Sir Arthur to press for them, knowing that he would probably do so in order to get rid of them, as in addition to the annoyance of having them camping in his garden, he was practically obliged by custom to feed them while they remained.

Some time ago one of the present Shah's wives, who had long been trying to induce him to divorce her, attempted to poison him. The Shah is said to have been particularly fond of her and would neither punish nor divorce her; so one night she escaped from the Palace and took refuge in the Mosque of Kum where the Mollahs or preachers aided her in obtaining a divorce. She is now married to another husband.

She is the daughter of Mirza Paki Khan, formerly Grand Vizier to the late Shah, and the most remarkable man in modern Persian history. Of great ability and absolute integrity, he set himself the colossal task of reforming the abuses of a most corrupt system of government. During the three years he remained Grand Vizier he accomplished an immense deal, but his many enemies, who preferred the old state of things, successfully conspired against him and induced the Shah, whose mind they had poisoned with lying stories, first to banish, and finally to consent to the murder of the man to whom the country in general owed so large a debt of gratitude, and to whom Nasr-ed-din himself was in great measure indebted for his stability on the throne. And so the man who might have raised Persia once more to a state of prosperity, was "done to death" while in his bath, at his villa in the country.

The Shah is said to have been struck with remorse at what he had done, and had the two daughters of his murdered Vizier married to two of his own sons. The one who became the wife of the present Shah always hated her husband as being the son of her father's murderer.

While riding one day n the country with Sir Arthur we saw what at first appeared to me to be a regiment of cavalry approaching, but which proved to be the Shah returning from an afternoon drive. Preceded by about two hundred outriders and followed by some three hundred more, with Ministers and officials of the court riding beside the carriage, His Majesty was seated alone in a large landau, drawn by six horses with postilions in gorgeous liveries. In place of a front seat, a writing table was fitted into the carriage with silver candlesticks, a clock and other etcetera fixed in position.

We dismounted from our horses and with our grooms drew up at the side of the road, this being the etiquette of the country when meeting the Shah. The latter, on seeing us, stopped the carriage and conversed for some minutes with Sir Arthur in French, which he speaks with some difficulty.

A few days afterwards His Majesty honoured me with a private audience at his summer palace, to which I drove accompanied by General Kitabji Khan and Abbas Kuli Khan, chief dragoman of the British Legation and whom Sir Arthur kindly sent to act as interpreter, it being considered beneath the dignity of the Shah to speak any foreign language but his own when giving audience to foreigners.

On arrival at the palace about 11 a.m. we were told that the Shah would receive me in the garden. After waiting a little while in the anteroom, two chamberlains came to say His Majesty was ready and conducted us to the garden where we found him standing in a shady place with the Grand Vizier and the Minister of Foreign Affairs on his right and left. Numbers of other official and couriers stood in groups at a respectful distance.

When about twenty yards off we all stopped and bowed three times. We then went a little nearer and bowed again. The Shah then beckoned me to approach and came forward a few steps to meet me. The Grand Vizier introduced me as "the representative of Mr. D'Arcy", on which I bowed once more, keeping on my top hat all the time according to Persian etiquette. I was in evening dress. The Shah opened the conversation by asking after my health. I was told this was a special honour usually only accorded to persons of ambassadorial rank, and then asked several questions about the manner in which the operations would be commenced in starting the petroleum works. In conclusion I thanked him in Mr. D'Arcy's name for having granted the concession and also for having received me, and I said "I trust that the God whom we all alike serve may long preserve Your Majesty to reign over this ancient Empire." I then retired backwards.

Musaffir-ed-din Shah "King of Kings, Lord of the Firmament and Asylum of the Universe" was born in 1853 and succeeded his father in May 1896. Like most of the Qajars he is decidedly handsome, though somewhat melancholy-looking, and owing perhaps to ill health. He struck me as being both courteous and dignified. He is probably the most humane ruler that has ever sat on the throne of Persia, and it is said that he dislikes even to consent to the execution of criminals. He is fond of hunting and shooting, and is an exceedingly good shot.

It being the month of Moharrem, the Persian Lent, he and all his court were dressed in black, and he wore no ornaments except the "Lion and the Sun" composed of brilliant emeralds and rubies in his *kola* or Astrachan cap.

By far the most powerful subject of the Shah is the "Atabek-i-zam" or Grand Vizier. Amin-es-Sultan (the friend of the King) as he is called is about forty-five years of age. A genial smile and a general air of enjoying the good things of this life hide an indomitable will and the power of remarkable promptitude of action in emergency. Possessed of statesmanlike abilities he has already held the highest post under two Shahs.

He was with the late Shah when the monarch fell beneath the hand of the assassin, and to the great presence of mind which he showed on that occasion, together with his prompt and vigorous action, the present Shah largely owes his kingdom, as the following story will show.

Nasr-ed-din, accompanied by the Grand Vizier, had driven out to the Mosque at Shah-Abdul Azim, six miles from Teheran. They were kneeling at their prayer when a man suddenly approached the Shah and shot him with a pistol. The Grand Vizier sprang forward and, supporting the already dead body of his royal master, called to the attendants at the door to secure the murderer. This done, he said the Shah had been hit with the bullet and had fainted from the shock, but that the wound was not serious, and he had him quickly lifted into the carriage which was waiting before the mosque. Taking his seat beside the body and holding it in position, he ordered the postilions to gallop back to Teheran.

Arriving at the palace, he had the body carried up to a bedroom, then summoning the Shah's physician he caused a bulletin to be issued saying that an attempt had been made on the life of the Shah, which had happily failed, and that the royal patient was progressing as favourably as could be expected.

It was known that although the present Shah had been recognized by England and Russia as heir-apparent, one of his half-brothers would make an attempt to seize the throne at his father's death if he had an opportunity, and this is what the Grand Vizier wished to avoid. Taking care that none but those he could trust should have access to the room where the dead Shah lay, he went himself to the telegraph office and got into communication with the Crown

Prince, who was then residing at Tabriz where he was Governor, telling him what had happened and adding that, if he wished to save his kingdom, he must ride night and day to Teheran. In the meantime the Grand Vizier drew in, as quietly as possible, all the troops on whom he could rely, and posted them about the palace, and in parts of the city where disturbances were feared.

On the third day the Crown Prince arrived, having ridden as fast as relays of horses could carry him, and was at once escorted to the palace, when it was announced that Nasr-ed-din had succumbed to his wounds, and the Mussaffir-ed-din, his son, had ascended the throne of the Qajars.

If anything further were wanting to strengthen the bonds of friendship between the sovereign and his Minister, it will be remembered that it was the Grand Vizier who saved the Shah's life in Paris about two years ago by striking up the pistol which was being fired at him by an anarchist.

I paid two visits to the Grand Vizier during my stay at Teheran, on both of which occasions His Highness received me in the kindest manner, and expressed his good feeling toward Great Britain and her people.

He is said to be immensely rich and keeps up considerable state. Besides his palace in Teheran, he has a fine villa in the Italian style standing in a very large and well-kept garden on the outskirts of the town, and where he holds a public levee on fine afternoons when the court is at the capital.

The negotiations lasted for two months. I include a summary of related telegrams:

On March 23, 1901 I called on the British Legation to announce my arrival and to explain the purpose of his endeavours in securing a concession to explore for oil. For more than a month General Kitabji attempted to move the negotiations forward. The General offered to take the concession in his name, but I disapproved this arrangement.

On April 26 I was introduced to the Grand Vizier by Sir Arthur Hardinge, head of the British Legation. The Grand Vizier expressed to Sir Hardinge that he wished to maintain a balance between the Russian and English governments. The provinces of northern Persia under Russian influence were excluded from the concession.

Upon direction of Mr. D'Arcy, I offered to pay a ten percent net royalty on any oil production within the concession, and that the term be for sixty years. On May 20 the Grand Vizier stated that the Shah wanted L40,000 down and

L40,000 when a company was formed to explore for petroleum, and a sixteen percent net royalty payment on the value of any oil production. On May 14 Mr. D'Arcy agreed to "leave the business in the hands of Mr. Marriott, who is worthy of every confidence."

I agreed to the sixteen percent net royalty but included the proviso that the oil would be free of a five percent export duty, noting to Mr. D'Arcy that by being free of the five percent export duty, the gain equaled six percent of net royalty, though the Persian government don't see this.

I recommended that D'Arcy pay up to L20,000 down and L100,000 when the company to explore for oil was formed. On May 21, I agreed to give L5,000 upon signing. On May 23, without authority from Mr. D'Arcy, offered an additional L5,000 down. The Grand Vizier found the additional L5,000 "most useful".

On May 26, 1901 Mr. D'Arcy telegraphed that L10,000 pounds would be credited to the Imperial Bank of Persia and that, in addition to the concession, I should buy blue pottery salt cellars from Kum and embroidery from Resht.

The following day I wired that the deal was agreed to, but feared the Russians were trying to de-rail the negotiation. It was later discovered that the Czar telegraphed the Shah and tried to persuade him not to sign, but the next day Sir Arthur Hardinge met with the Grand Vizier and following their meeting, the Shah signed the document, which was written in French and Persian, on May 28, 1901.

I left Teheran on June 8th. My return journey to Resht was even worse than the one from there, the carriages having apparently become more dilapidated and the horses more broken down during the months I had been in the country. The heat was very trying and to make matters worse I was taken ill on the road.

The steamer by which I was to have sailed from Enzeli could not embark her passengers owing to the rough weather, and had to return to Baku. I was therefore obliged to wait some days at Resht until fine weather arrived. From Baku I traveled by the railway across southern Russia and Poland to Berlin, and thence home, arriving in London on June 23rd, exactly three calendar months after my departure.

Despite the disagreeables of the journey, I shall always look back on my short stay as a most interesting experience, and shall ever remember with gratitude the great kindness and hospitality I received from the many friends I made there.

The future of Persia, owing to the proximity of that country to our Indian Empire, should be a matter of deep interest to England. Russia has of late years greatly extended her influence in the country – more especially in the north – and it is difficult to see how she can be prevented from some day gaining possession of the Caspian provinces, which she already looks upon as almost her own. It rests with England to take measures to prevent these encroachments from being a menace to our Empire. Fortunately our present representative in Teheran is fully alive to this and has done much to check Russian advances.

If the oil scheme of Mr. D'Arcy succeeds, as I believe it will do with tact and good management, it should have far-reaching aspects, both commercially and politically, for Great Britain, and cannot fail to largely increase her influence in Persia

Alfred L. Marriott

About the author:

Sam L. Pfiester was born and raised in Ft. Stockton, Texas. He graduated from the University of Texas in 1967, joined the U.S. Navy in 1968 and spent two tours of duty in Vietnam. His second tour, he was the senior advisor to a Vietnamese river and coastal patrol group, and wrote *The Perfect War* about his experience. Since 1971 he has worked in the oil exploration business. In 2012 he wrote *The Golden Lane, Faja de Oro*, a historical novel about the Tampico Oil Boom of 1910-1914. He and his wife Rebecca have three children, and reside in Georgetown, Texas.

Made in the USA
San Bernardino, CA
14 February 2015